I0550145

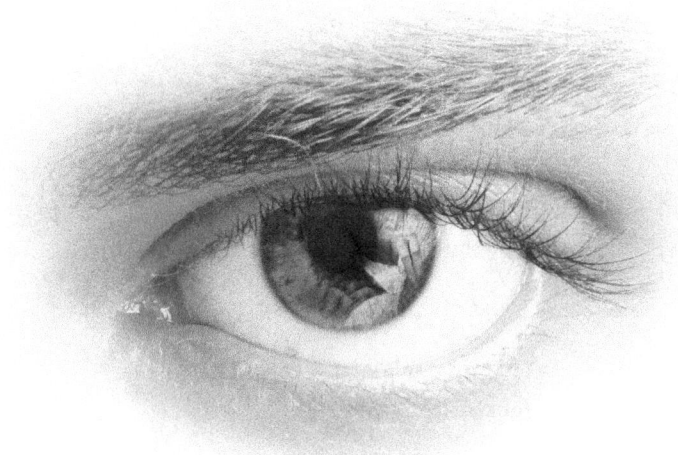

LOOKING?

TECHNOLOGY'S IMPACT ON MODERN RELATIONSHIPS

Dog Tag Books, Inc.
San Francisco

Copyright © 2015 by MD Johnson
All rights reserved

Published in United States by Dog Tag Books, Inc.
San Francisco

ISBN 978-0-578-15664-4
eBook ISBN 978-1-4951-3958-1

Printed in United States of America

Cover Design by Rachmad Agus
Graphics by Zoran Maric

FIRST EDITION

This is a work of fiction. Names, characters, businesses, places, events
and incidents are either the products of the author's imagination or
used in a fictitious manner. Any resemblance to actual persons, living
or dead, or actual events is purely coincidental.

This book is dedicated to
the friends I've made and the friends I've lost.

Rick, Lexi, Brian,
and especially Andy.
Miss you, my handsome man.

Special thanks to
PJ Ferguson
Brent Heinz

INTRODUCTION

This book is about sex. It contains graphic descriptions of gay sex and intimacy. You've been warned, so don't act shocked or come complaining when you get hit with the sexual content scattered around these pages. We're all grown ups here so if talking about sex makes you uncomfortable, or you feel it's "unprofessional" then for the love of Pete put down this book and go grab *Good Housekeeping*! Frankly, we don't have much to talk about anyway.

In my defense, I really didn't have much choice, given my topic. When I sat down to write this book a decision had to be made about how delicately to dance around the topics of group sex, three-ways, fuck buddies and open relationships. After considering what I wanted to say, I settled on being painfully blunt and descriptive, since these topics don't lend themselves to polite conversation and tender treatment anyway. The fairest way to present this information was to honestly and graphically lay it out there without any filter, and especially without any shame.

At the same time, there needed to be a discussion of these topics from an analytical perspective, without boring readers with volumes of studies and data. To treat the topic fairly and completely, examples of the changes in relationship structures needed to be interwoven with data demonstrating my points and supporting my conclusions.

The format of *Looking?*, therefore, is an alternating storyline of relationship/sex adventures and data driven discussions. While this approach may be jarring to readers, I've tried to do my best to keep the stories relevant and on point, and the analytic discussions as entertaining as possible without giving up credibility.

The name of the book might be confusing to some. "Looking?" is a common phrase in online hookup apps or dating sites used to signify that the conversation has reached a point where it's time to put up or shut up. You've talked about the weather, your day and where you live; now you wanna know if the person is "looking" to hookup, i.e. have sex, so you ask the question, "Looking?"

Looking? is a work of fiction in that the people and events contained in these pages are fantasy. There is no Tony, or Robbie in the real world, sadly, and while my experience certainly helped shape some of these stories, these relationships never existed. I can't say my life is boring, far from it, but I only wish I had some of the relationships that are invented on these pages.

It was a bleak and snowy day in Denver when I opened my computer, sad and hurt, and began typing out the first part of this book. For me writing is cathartic, and that day I needed to process the end of an important relationship in my life. The idea for the book had been rolling around in my head for months and I knew I was close to committing to this project, but little did I know when I started typing away that cold morning where my sadness would take me. In a way, I suppose that relationship is responsible for this book, but don't expect me say thank you. I've still got enough sadness pent up to write another.

Regardless of its genesis, this book contains my beliefs and opinions about where modern relationships are heading. For some time now, I've been living my own life within the framework of the pyramid structure and love it. There are things I miss, momentarily, and I've been rejected more times than I can count when I say, "I'm not looking to date anyone right now." Life is better on this side of history, though, at least for me. Every time one of these rejections occurs I feel like I've slipped the noose, or dodged a bullet. Men who come looking for a boyfriend, a sugar daddy or a therapist can keep on walking. I don't need another project.

Modern relationships aren't for everyone. I'm not making the argument that everyone should bail on their marriage or dump their partner and join a commune. To each his own. But the option of a modern relationship should emerge from the shadows to be understood as a legitimate structure gaining predominance every day. These modern relationships should be respected rather than judged as promiscuous and immoral.

If this book does nothing else, I hope it makes the reader think about the influence technology is having on the shape of modern relationships. The power of this force is difficult to overstate, yet equally difficult to appreciate. We're willing to admit technology has changed almost every other fundamental aspect of society, but are willfully blind to the influence it's having on our relationships. My goal is by the end of *Looking?* you concede that technology is impacting our relationships at least in some small way. I think that's a good place to start.

MD Johnson
Denver, Colorado 2015

TABLE OF CONTENTS

Part I

AWAKENING

Chapter 1
A MODERN FAMILY

"I think I'm gonna go to New York Pride in a couple weeks with Sean, Kip, and Mark," Tony said as he looked away and pulled up his black Calvin Klein underwear. He was always shy about his body after sex, rushing to cover up, almost ashamed of the act of ejaculating. Tony was probably one of the most handsome men in the entire country, and also my best friend. "Some really good friends invited me to come stay with them."

By "really good friends," I knew Tony meant some especially persistent Facebook followers who also had rippling abs. Tony had thousands of followers, or "friends," on Facebook. A constant production of shirtless selfies fed the alligators, and the list of followers grew daily. Tony didn't have "really good friends" as much as he had desperate, insecure circuit queens in need of validation by an "A"—lister.

It was how Tony dropped the news about New York that sent a chill down my spine. The tone of his voice, the deflected glance, and the timing all told me he waited until the last minute to spring it on me.

Always in a hurry to leave after sex, he pulled up his gym shorts and stretched into the two-sizes-too-small tank top with a cryptic "Obey" splashed across the chest. With his broad chest, big shoulders, and thick arms, it's hard to begrudge all the men across the country wanting to get him naked. He's a sight to see, except for one small thing no amount of working out was going to make any bigger. Tony was always going to be a bottom.

Sex with Tony was a strange thing; selfish and focused on his own needs I wasn't so much a partner as a prop. With his needs met, he was ready to bolt. Tony was also specific about the things he liked, like getting his ass rimmed and giving blow jobs with his head off the side of the bed. He also had a spot on the inside of his leg that would make him cum without touching himself. If I went through his checklist, one sweet spot after the other, he was happy.

I was his first in many ways. I was the first guy he had sex with, the first guy he let cum in his mouth, the first guy he had unprotected sex with, and the first person to get off inside him. I was the first guy he dated after he came out, and the first man he said, "I love you" to. I know, I know. Big mistake. Don't worry, it didn't last long.

Even after he cheated on me in epic fashion (more on that later) we managed to stay best friends. One night, after a particularly bad fight, Tony broke down crying, telling me he needed me in his life and I was all he had and he didn't know what he would do without me. This was after we'd broken up and while he was dating another guy, mind you.

Two years after we'd broken up, Tony and I started hooking up again. It was angry, stolen sex at first, but eventually it became more, even though Tony never fully committed to it; the whole time he was cruising around, hooking up with others, sometimes telling me about it, sometimes hiding it. It wasn't cheating, since we weren't dating, but we both knew being with others would cause drama. I always found out. Or I think I did.

"New York, huh?" I said, rolling over and grabbing my own shorts. Felt like a conversation I should be clothed for. "That sounds fun. What brought that on?"

"Those guys invited me to go and said I can use a buddy pass." One of the circuit queens worked for an airline. "And I need to spend some time with Sean. He's starting to give me shit for not hanging out," he said, fixing his sandy blond hair in the bathroom mirror. Sean was perhaps the only other living, breathing, friend Tony had other than me. They shared a passion for music, playing guitar, and smoking pot. Tony avoided my eyes the whole time he tried to sell this pretense, focusing on getting every hair just perfect instead.

See, what was actually going on was that Tony and I started getting close during the last few months, and he liked the sex. There were nights when he wouldn't let me stop. Three or four hours of sex and more sex. I remember having a rash on my nose because he wouldn't let me stop eating his ass.

As the months wore on in our renewed sexual relationship, Tony got more comfortable with us as a couple. We were usually together all day long, and at night he'd stay at my place later and later. We were sliding into a boyfriend relationship without talking about it. Most people assumed we were dating even though we both emphatically denied it, and both of us kept hooking up with others.

Tony desperately wanted a boyfriend. He told me once that his sole purpose in life was to find the right man. Seriously, he was made to be someone's partner. His few relationships all rolled out the same way. He'd latch onto someone, anyone actually, as long as they were attractive and good kissers, and he'd become whatever they wanted; a San Francisco leather boy one time, a perfectly smooth Miami beach boy another, a beer pong alcoholic for yet a third, always morphing into whatever he perceived his partner to desire, just to maintain a relationship.

He didn't want to be my boyfriend, though. I doubt it could've worked in the long run, but I was always confused at why he wouldn't date me. That boundary was absolute, and there was no second guessing it. Maybe I smelled bad, or he didn't like my hairstyle. Regardless, I never found out the truth.

So here he was, enjoying my companionship, support, connection, and sex, but knowing it was a dead end. He was getting lonely; and now NYC.

Looking back at that conversation, I knew it was over right then and there, as soon as the words hit the floor. I knew he was desperate to find the next boyfriend to latch onto and morph to satisfy. He'd gotten a taste of what regular sex and a close, supportive relationship were like with me, and he wanted it full-time and in the open but with someone else. I was right; we never had sex again. From that point forward, our relationship deteriorated for six months before I finally cut it off completely.

Tony went to NYC and had a dance floor "spark" with a beach boy from Mobile, AL. A few trips back and forth and two months later, Tony quit his job in Seattle, picked up everything he owned, and left the city he'd lived in his whole life for the love of his life, his soulmate, and moved to Mobile. He's since developed a Southern accent (after six months), become a huge 'Bama football fan (in the six years we'd known each other, he always despised football), and like his beach boy, drinks scotch; a lot of it.

They even have the same haircut.

Chapter 2
A DAY IN THE LIFE

San Francisco wasn't what I was expecting. I imagined sophisticated, opera-going older people, wearing expensive overcoats, sampling new and delicate cuisine, all while valet parking their Teslas. I pictured the gay-side of the city as small, local bars with an older, overweight leather crowd, everybody wearing a pink ribbon and their cars all having HRC bumper stickers on the back. In actuality, not everyone has an HRC sticker.

The city I found exceeded all my expectations. I've been lucky enough to travel the world and see some of the most exciting places on the planet. Since my first trip to Madrid, at age fourteen, I've been traveling as often as time and money permit. While I haven't been everywhere, and there are magnificent cities that I still need to see, San Francisco is one of the most amazing places I've been. Its beauty, its character and yes, even its weather make this place unique in all the world, but by far my favorite thing about this city is its people.

Especially if you're gay, this city has to be on your bucket list. You need to make the hajj once in your lifetime to see the streets of the Castro where countless activists and progressive thinkers made their home. Visitors miss out if they skip a trip to Delores Park, either quietly in the morning as the sun comes up over the city or in the heat of the afternoon at the gay beach. No one should miss the sexy bar-backs at 440 and Midnight Sun, or shy away from the SF Eagle, arguably the home of leather fetish.

For the gay world, San Francisco has led our culture for decades, at least since the '70s. We may look to LA for the pretty boys, NYC for muscle men, Miami for dance parties, but, at the end of the day, San Francisco holds court. None of these other cities can claim to have a rainbow flag at its heart the way this city of just about one million people does.

There's no place in the world where sex is so casual as San Francisco. It's so easy to get laid in this city you almost have to try not to. Men cruise you without shame at every level of society here, from the board room to the bathroom. There's no boundary nor limit in the pursuit of a hookup.

It was here, in San Francisco, that I first began to doubt the survivability of the one-to-one, monogamous relationship.

It was here that I first began piecing together my experiences as a divorce lawyer, and as a gay man traveling the world, to see relationships in a more modern light. The changes in San Francisco relationships were so stark that I started asking myself, why?

My law firm decided to open an office in San Francisco. As managing partner, it was my job to get into the city and figure it out and start identifying places and people, to immerse myself in everything San Francisco. I needed to learn the layout of the city, its neighborhoods, its character, how people moved through the city, where they lived, what the word on the street was about certain locations, etc. It was my job to evaluate the potential market there. We're a divorce law firm, and relationship demographics are essential to gauging our likely success.

This means while I was scoping out the BART and Muni, Hayes Valley and Noe Valley, Pacific Heights and Berkeley, I was also looking at census demographics, marriage studies, social activities and cultural centers, and frankly, online interactions (more on that later). If you're a divorce law firm moving into town, you need to make sure there are some married people around, and that potential clients have assets to fight over; otherwise, they don't need you.

While I compiled my data and compared it to other cities, including my home, Seattle, I noticed a distinct demographic difference in San Francisco. Personally, the city hadn't been at the top of my list of places to open a new office, but after seeing the numbers, I decided to check it out.

Tony came with me on my first exploratory trip to the city. We planned to check out the people, enjoy some food, and maybe hit some of San Francisco's nightlife together. He and I weren't dating at the time, so it was all about seeing what the city had to offer.

Tony is great for hitting the gym and for going out clubbing, but he's worthless when it comes to anything deeper than a bird bath. On the first morning of my campaign to tackle the city, I left him in bed at the hotel and told him to catch up with me around lunchtime if he wanted to see some of the city. A vague mumble of "text me" came from the lump under the covers.

My iPhone charged, running shoes on, and logged into Grindr, I began my physical, and metaphysical, exploration of San Fransisco. A whole new city, completely unknown, was about to unfold for me. No idea what I may stumble across, nor what adventure awaited me around the next corner, I hit the pavement.

The most energizing part of exploring a city this way is remembering of how resourceful I am. We forget how little we need in our daily lives, as everything is given to us by the drive-thru lady and our valet dry cleaners. So many people are afraid of the unknown on the streets of an unfamiliar city. They fear the people, the traffic; they may even be afraid of finding food. These most basic of fears arise from deep within our primordial selves, but at the same time, so do the coping mechanisms that enabled our survival as a species. Most people fear this challenge; I get excited by it.

I left the Marriott in the financial district and headed toward Embarcadero Center. It was early on a Saturday morning, and downtown was deserted except for the homeless people sleeping in the doorways, on bus benches, and under trees. During my exploration of San Francisco, one of the first things I learned concerned the plight of the transient population here. Too many people called the streets of this magnificent modern city of opportunity home.

Homelessness is a serious issue for San Francisco, and the city is constantly trying to accommodate the ever-growing number of people forced to turn to it's streets for survival. To clear their streets, other cities like Las Vegas would buy their mentally ill and homeless bus tickets to San Francisco. This was the Vegas strategy for managing homeless residents, right up until they were sued in 2013. "Classy" and "Las Vegas" continue to be polar opposites.

At Embarcadero, I grabbed a coffee and walked out onto the pier as far into the Bay as I could. The Rocky Mountains were my home growing up, and I'll always be a mountain man at heart, but the ocean holds a deep fascination for me. I stood there a long time, just breathing in the sea air and watching the gulls fly around the end of the dock.

From the pier, I followed the water up to Coit Tower and Telegraph Hill where I got my first adult look at the Golden Gate bridge. That's when I realized it doesn't, in fact, go to Alcatraz.

Coit Tower is the biggest penis in all of San Francisco. It demonstrates the "length" men will go to prove their virility as a potential mate. Another of these giant penises was constructed in Kansas City, but I can't remember the name of it right now. No surprise that the giant penis in Kansas City is a gay pickup site.

Another amazing display of penis envy is the capitol domes spread all around the world. Have you ever stopped to look at these things? Someone once told me this form of structure has been around since the dawn of civilization and always for the same reason--to demonstrate the hyped-up masculinity of the people building it. Sit down and look at these structures and you can't help but be struck by how much they resemble flaccid, circumcised penises. Look at the amazing proliferation of these domes throughout the world--India, China, England and pretty much every capitol in every state of the Union. Did you know there's a law that no state's capitol dome can be bigger than the dome in Washington DC? Texas didn't care--theirs is seven feet taller--and the designers of San Francisco City Hall didn't think the law applied to them, either; it's eleven feet, seven inches taller.

From Coit Tower, I started my walk down into Fort Mason. Along the way I stopped in shops and stores, sometimes just to check them out, sometimes because there was a hot guy, sometimes just to take a break and have a cup of coffee on a bench out front. Meandering is a great way to see a city; just wandering wherever you want to go.

I could've read a book, or looked on Google maps, or rented a car, but I'm glad I used my feet and saw things first-hand. I saw the city from street-level, the same way someone who lives here would.

At Fort Mason, I wandered through the farmer's market and grabbed some local food, fish tacos and cheese fries, and found a spot under a tree near the trail. Let's see what was going on in the world of Grindr. Athletic, active men were all around the Fort Mason pier area, running, biking, and just sitting out in the park. I wondered if that translated into a good looking gay crowd cruising for a hookup. It did.

As soon as I logged in, the chirping sound was nearly continuous. "Hey." "You new?" "Looking?" Indeed I was, but not for long. I started conversing in three word sentences with about five different shirtless, bathroom mirror selfies. Time flies when you're "looking," but after ten minutes, "MascFit" and I were ten pics deep into a cyber-fuck.

"Host?"

"Can't. Visiting."

"Me Neither. Damn."

"Grrr"

"Ok with public?"

"ummm yeah maybe."

"Empty baseball dugout by my place."

This is a baseball city, right? "Is it safe?"

"Mostly"

I did say I was on an adventure, right? Here it was, setting aside judgment about sex in public; how hot is that? Fucking in a baseball dugout in the middle of the day with a hot, athletic, married guy whom I only knew as "MascFit"?

"Where?"

I got to the baseball field where MascFit told me to meet him, took off my shirt, and sat in the bleachers, soaking up sun, trying to look for all the world like I was taking a break from a long run or just coming from the gym. Sure enough, the place was as empty as a graveyard.

I easily spotted the dugout, but it wasn't at all what I was expecting. In my head, I pictured a covered, sunken area, open only to the field. This was just a stairwell built straight into the ground, about shoulder deep, uncovered and wide open to the bleachers. My anxiety level definitely became elevated.

Soon, I saw this dark-haired, muscle guy, 6'4, about 25 years old, wearing gray gym shorts, a loose white tank top and a backwards red baseball cap walking across the field from the community center. My anxiety began to dissipate. His pictures didn't do him justice.

MascFit is married, to a woman. I didn't ask if he had kids, but after further research about the city, given the area we were in, it's a pretty sure bet he was a family guy. I suppose, given the nature of our hookup and the anonymity of our arrangement, it was best to keep things simple. He seemed fine with that. He also seemed completely unashamed of the whole thing. Most married guys will never send a face pic, but MascFit had no problem with it. Could be because I was from out of town. Could be his wife was okay with it. I didn't ask.

He saw me, gave me the nod, and headed toward the dugout. I didn't want to stand up and head there at the same time, just in case someone was around. I gave him the nod back, leaned forward, and waited until he was down in the dugout area before I stood, stretched, and started making my way down the bleachers, casually checking along the way to see if anyone was watching. There was no one even close, so I moved down the stairs, and into the dugout, where MascFit was leaning against the wall. He looked exactly like a coach watching his best batter head out to the plate.

I walked up behind him, slowly put my hands around his waist, and leaned in to kiss his neck. His hard, muscular body responded by pushing back into me and leaning his head against my shoulder. I slowly slid his shorts down. He was naked underneath.

Obviously, it was quick and not safe, but my God it was hot. I sent married guy home to his wife with a big smile, and continued my adventure across this city of unexpected exceptionalism.

At the Palace of Fine Arts, I texted Tony to see if he was ready to meet up. Just out of the shower, he's grab an Uber and meet me; perfect. I'd have about thirty minutes of lying in the grass in this beautiful place that I never knew existed until I stumbled on it, just because it was the next thing down the coast.

If you think I told Tony about MascFit guy, you've got the wrong idea about our relationship. I needed a stress-free weekend, without argument. If I told Tony about the baseball dugout, the fun part of the weekend was over. Fucking Mascfit in a baseball dugout was a fantasy come true, and Tony would be ridiculously jealous and angry at me, even if he'd never admit it. I eventually told him about it, but weeks later and even then he still stormed out of a workout, allegedly because I hadn't told him about it.

Instead, I bored him with details of geography and the neighborhood economics till his eyes glazed over. It didn't take long. Both of us were pretty blown away by the Palace of Fine Arts. I suppose some people say it's just a cheesy, overdone eyesore in the middle of some expensive real estate, but you have to wonder why the damn real estate is so expensive but for the Palace. It's stunning, quiet, and a peaceful place to just sit under the yew tree, if you know what I mean.

Tony and I continued the walk, taking Divisadero over the giant hill of Pacific Heights, through Haight-Ashbury and down into the Castro. It was physically exhausting but worth every step.

I'd never been in the Castro before. My only other two trips to San Francisco were brief and limited to family interactions in Berkeley and sightseeing downtown one afternoon, so walking into the Castro was an eye-opening experience, indeed.

I immediately knew I was home. From the giant rainbow flag at the corner of Market and Castro, to the line in front of the Castro Theater for some obscure indie flick, to the bears hanging out the window at Club 440, this was where I belonged. Tony was busy posting selfies; a guaranteed 1,000 likes, at least. I knew he was itching to take his shirt off and get another 1,000, but there were too many people around.

In many ways, the gay world orbits San Francisco, and San Francisco orbits the Castro. It was here so many things began. The American sexual revolution, the original Age of Aquarius, got started right around the corner at Dolores Park and in the Mission in the 1960s. The organized battle for civic rights for gays and lesbians may have been ignited by the 1969 Stonewall riots in NYC, but that torch was undeniably passed to this four or five block neighborhood during the AIDS epidemic of the '80s and '90s. Gay marriage battles crystalized here with San Francisco Mayor Gavin Newsom. This little street is at the epicenter of our gay history.

I discovered it's also a prime example of a transformation in the structure of intimate relationships.

Chapter 3
THE PYRAMID

We think of marriage and relationships as immutable, incapable of evolution or change. We've convinced ourselves that marriage is, and will always be a static institution, a bastion of consistency in a world of change. In fact, nothing could be further from the truth. Like every social invention, cultural adaptation, and survival strategy, the structure of relationships, including marriage, has evolved over time in response to ever changing environments. Today, relationship structures are continuing this unbroken history of evolving, now at a phenomenal rate in response to the external pressures of our modern technological society.

The traditional relationship structure is linear; it's a line between two points, two partners, and isn't open to any other connections. A vow of monogamy operates to prevent sexual relationships with anyone outside of this linear structure. Friendships are kept at a distance to prevent a "back-up" situation. A linear couple builds a wall and mote around their preverbal castle, to defend it against all invaders.

Things are changing, though. I see it in my law practice and I see it in my community. My travels around the world, especially San Franscico opened my eyes to a fundamental evolution in our relationships. Everywhere I look I find exceptions to the traditional linear structure. In fact, I rarely find a relationship that fits the traditional paradigm anymore; the exception is now the rule.

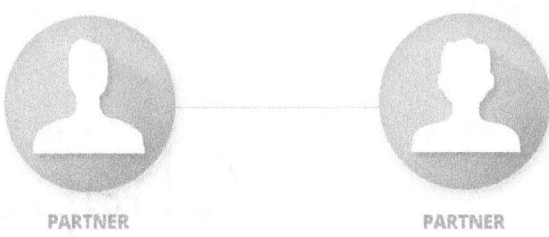

PARTNER　　　　　　　　PARTNER

Figure 1 - Traditional Linear Relationships

Right under our noses, society is evolving a new paradigm and defying the traditional linear structure. Our relationship needs are pushing us into something new. Society is demanding more than the old linear structure can give.

What does the new relationship paradigm look like? Based on my travels, research, and twenty years as a divorce lawyer, the developing modern structure of relationships is made up of layers of connections, not just a single linear one. In contrast, the modern structure is open to other relationships of varying intensity. This layered structure:

- Provides freedom of choice
- Allows for independence
- Is flexible
- Creates expectations consistent with today's lifestyles

Instead of a linear relationship structure, my experience leads me to the conclusion that the most prominent structure of modern relationships is a pyramid.

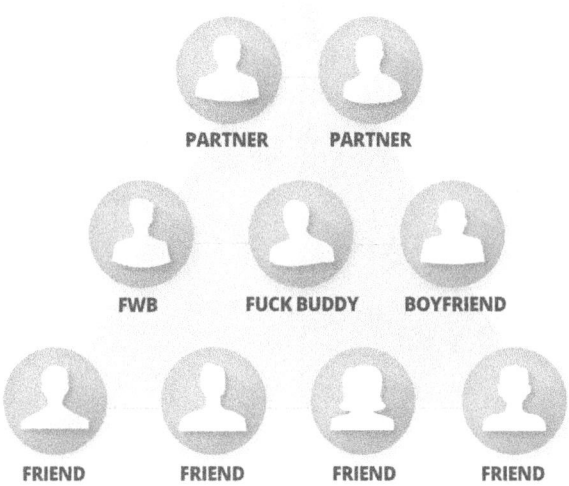

Figure 2 - Pyramid Structure

In a pyramid structure, there's one primary, or pinnacle, partnership at the top, with an indeterminate lifespan. This pinnacle relationship is intended to last as far into the future as a couple can see. It may last a lifetime, or it may not, but there are no plans to change it. The pinnacle relationship is the one a partner "comes home to."

The next layer down from the pinnacle contains the other intimate relationships a partner may enter. For example, that layer may include friends with benefits, fuck buddies, and second boyfriends. This layer may also contain relationships based on romantic love.

At the base of the pyramid, in a place of underestimated importance, are the close friendships of each partner. These friendship may've been sexual at one point, but aren't now.

Our lives are changing fast. The way we do everything is being impacted by technology and the modern age. Our relationships are no different. They're evolving just like everything else around us, changing to fit the modern world of technology and new personal expectations. While traditional linear relationships are a long way from sharing the fate of the dinosaurs, there's no questions they're heading that direction.

Chapter 4

DATING ADELE

One afternoon, about six months after Tony and I broke up, we were at the gym together. It was legs-day, and that's a rare event for Tony. Legs aren't one of the "beach muscle" groups, and I usually had to trick him into training them at all. Even during a leg work out, Tony tried everything to slow it down, drag it out, or end it early.

It didn't surprise me he was busy with Grindr between sets. He was single, for the moment, but that wouldn't last long. I'm not sure what drove me crazier, when he was single and hunting around for the next "ex," or when he was with the newest, "most incredible man." Either way, it was a stressful existence.

That night, we were doing a set of deadlifts in the corner of the gym. Tony was wearing a shirt I bought years ago in London. I managed to keep it for ten years before he appropriated it as his own because it showed off his arms. Bouncing around to whatever playlist he was listening to, the shirt was doing its job. Secretly, I enjoyed Tony's music, but could never let him know that. With his nearly perfect body and handsome face, the last thing he needed was me to tell him how much I liked his music.

"Oh man! I'm in love! Check out this guy!" he said as he pulled out his earphones, swung his baseball cap backward, and pushed his iPhone toward me. He never gave me his phone to hold anymore following the night we broke up.

It was a headless, shirtless Grindr profile pic of a nicely defined guy with dark body hair. No doubt it was a hot pic, but Tony's introduction of a headless, shirtless Grindr selfie as someone he was "in love" with in the middle of a leg workout was too much irony all at once. I laughed out loud and handed the phone back to him, shaking my head.

"What the fuck is that all about?" he said with a flash of anger. "Fine, I won't show you guys anymore," and the phone disappeared back into his pocket. An angry pose in the mirror to be sure his hat was working in its new backwards position and he moved to do his next set of lunges.

A little surprised at his reaction to my near non-reaction, I shot back, "Well, what'd you expect me to say? You don't even know what the guy's face looks like, what he's interested in other than 'looking for now,' or anything else about him and you're 'in love,'" I said, still smiling. "How can I take you seriously with that shit?"

I could tell from his body language he was mad.

"Fuck, dude. I was just saying he's hot, and you go judging me." He shoved his earphones back in and turned to do another set of deadlifts. He was fuming.

I was judging him a little. It was hard not to, but still, I shouldn't have laughed out loud. Tony just caught me by surprise, and I let my first reaction go unchecked. A few sets of lunges and I prepared my ego for the inevitable apology.

"Look, I'm sorry, Tony. I shouldn't have laughed. The guy has a nice body. Looks like he works out a lot." I offered up, and meant it. I shouldn't have reacted that way.

"You always judge me with shit like that. You're on Grindr so why are you judging me for it?" He was working up steam now. My apology just gave him license to start dumping on me for whatever fight was still unresolved and kicking around his head.

"Well, yeah, I'm on there sometimes. I'm not saying I don't use Grindr! But I don't shove some headless pic at you and tell you I'm in love!" I shot back. "It's a fucking hookup site not match.

com. Go hookup with him! I don't give a fuck!" I said, but of course I did, and he knew it.

"I'm going to. We're meeting at Pony tonight for drinks," he said defiantly. The truth came out. His act of showing me the pic and his exclamation about how hot the guy was, was just that, an act. It was his roundabout way of telling me he had a date tonight.

"Great. You've got a date with the headless horseman. Gonna make a blow job a special challenge," I shot back. "Good luck with that." Now it was my turn to express some anger. Of course, I was still jealous. My feelings hadn't healed yet and the way he sprung this news on me, by acting like he just discovered this guy while we're were working out, was deceptive. Tony's deception was a trigger, thanks to the way the intimate side of our relationship ended.

The rest of the workout was tense, angry, and nothing resolved. We walked out together and gave each other a hug. This wasn't one of our apocalyptic fights where we refused a nightly hug, and we headed home. I was angry at the way he told me about his date and jealous that he was going to be with someone else tonight. He was apparently mad at me for laughing at his new man's picture. To this day, he still thinks I hated this guy because I laughed at his picture the first time I saw it; little does he know.

Tony's pattern repeated. He met the guy at the Pony, and they hit it off but didn't have sex that first night. Tony needed to lay the groundwork for an emotional connection first, fearful of rejection over his size. Instead, they had a special night of laying on the roof of the building next door after the bar closed. They watched the stars, held hands and quietly talked about music, family, and dreams. It was very romantic I'm sure.

We were off to the races. Gianni didn't live in Seattle, but rather Vancouver, and was only in town for a volleyball tournament. They went to dinner the next night and spent the night together at Tony's place, but the next morning Gianni had to head back up to Canada. Tony drove him to the airport, and they said their goodbyes. Tony cried on the way back from SeaTac.

That was mid-April, and by the beginning of May they were going back and forth every weekend. Tony declared he was in love. I tried to keep my opinions to myself, but inside, I found it humorous and frustrating. It was silly they'd fallen in love so quick, and he was already talking about moving to Vancouver; Tony's new favorite city in the whole world.

During our workouts, he was texting non-stop and if the phone rang, he'd disappear for twenty minutes to say "I miss you!" 150 times. We couldn't hangout at night as often because Tony needed to go home and Skype with Gianni. Gianni was everywhere; he even changed his phone screen to a sweet picture of the guy, head included this time.

Tony never introduced me to Gianni. He claimed that I was against their relationship because I laughed at his picture. Tony's other friends were invited over for BBQs and cocktails and nights out clubbing with this new "most incredible man," but I never got an invite. Facebook had lots of cute pictures of them together with Tony's other Seattle friends, but never me. How could I not resent this treatment, treatment I only received because I laughed at his picture?

I was cut off. We still spent all day together at the gym and eating and even hanging out at night sometimes, but all things "Gianni" were off limits. I started hating the guy, and I still hadn't even met him.

By mid-May, Tony was celebrating their two-month anniversary; the timeline math for every single boyfriend was completely manufactured. His need for validation truly knew no bounds.

I was pretty bitter at the situation. Tony and Gianni were the celebrity couple of Facebook with daily "totes adorbs" pictures posted. Every where we went, Tony made me listen to Adele since that was their music. I wanted to shout at him, "You know every song she sings is about breakups, don't you, dumbass? Don't you listen to the words?" But no, I kept all that inside and listened to

Adele cry the scars of love remind her that they almost had it all. The scars of her love made me wanna puke.

As you might imagine, Tony's fiction came crashing down one day. It was the third weekend in May, and Gianni was in town. I needed to be away from my forced banishment, so I headed down to Oregon. Being out of town gave me at least a pretext for the insult of not being invited to anything; plus, I couldn't handle the anxiety that came with being kicked to the curb whenever this guy came to town. I needed some space, and the great expanse of Mt. Hood seemed almost adequate.

I was hiking Huckleberry Mountain in the Mt. Hood area when I got the text. "Gianni broke up with me. What the fuck is wrong with me?"

I stopped and sat down. I was up pretty high on the trail by that point, but the break felt good.

"What happened?"

"I took him to the airport. Dropped him off. We said I love you and I cried. I think it freaked him out. After I dropped him off he texted me that it got too intense. He said we should just be friends. I'm devastated."

I knew he was. As much as I hated the way Tony treated me over the past month, and as much as I disliked this Gianni guy for cutting me out of my best friend's life, I felt his pain. I knew Tony's heart was broken, and he was feeling alone and crushed.

"I can be there in a few hours. Want me to come over?"

"Yeah. I need company."

"Ok. Be there soon, bubba. I'm sorry this is happening."

After the way this shit-head treated me all month long, and despite being the one friend completely cut out of his life with Gianni, I was the only friend he texted. I was the only friend to come stay with him. And for the next two weeks, I did my best to drag Tony to the gym, to dinners, and to hangout with friends.

Slowly, Tony got past the intense pain of Gianni, and it settled into a general sadness that lasted months.

Chapter 5
WHERE GAYS LEAD, STRAIGHTS FOLLOW

As far back as I can remember, hiding my sister's easy bake oven in my room at six, and at twelve staring at Spiderman's crotch in comic books hoping to see something, page after page, I knew I was different. Don't roll your eyes; I'm not going to relive my trials and tribulations as a young, gay kid. Odds are you've already heard more than a few coming out stories and don't need one more to qualify as "evolved".

The reason I bring it up is because my story, and the lessons I've learned from relationships, come from the context of the gay world. This perspective is important for a couple of different reasons. First, my world doesn't have the same rules and paradigms as the straight world. Second, the shifts I see in my world are also gaining steam in the straight world.

Historically, us gays live outside the social contract; we've already broken some of the most important, sacred rules and are, by heavenly decree, condemned to hell. We pretty much don't give a fuck about the rest of the rules. Doesn't get much worse than being sentenced to death for "lying with another man" and being condemned to the eternal flames of hell. If you have nothing, you have nothing to lose.

There's a freedom that comes with living outside the traditional straight-world social contract and paradigm. We're allowed to express and explore things that are off limits for straight people. We venture into relationship structures, fetish, and the kinky side of sex more easily than the boys and girls on the straight side of the tracks. We're creative, innovative, and prone to thinking outside the box; mainly because that's where we live our lives.

Over the past twenty-five years of being out, especially the last five years, what I see is the straight world catching up. I see the distinctions between my gay world and the straight world disappearing or becoming irrelevant, not because the gays are adopting a more traditional paradigm; far from it, but because the straight world is coming out of its own closet and venturing into our *ad hoc* paradigm.

I have mixed feelings about this progress. On the one hand, it's awesome to see the acceptance and, in fact, the "non-issue" status of someone's sexuality. With today's twenty-somethings, announcing they're gay has become a curiosity for about the first twenty minutes of an introduction, then it's back to snowboarding, mixing music, or playing beer pong. Who cares? "Gay" clubs are disappearing, unless they're tied to a fetish, or a particular subculture. All the hot clubs are simply gay and straight.

It's gratifying to see victory approach and to see us treated as equals, but it's also sad to see the loss of our separate identity, culture, and history. Those same twenty-somethings who are subjected to a few minutes of curiosity have no idea the battles earlier generations fought and the humiliation we endured during our own coming out. They never sat with AIDS patients, whose families turned them away due to the stigma, and who left them alone in the world to die, as these men drew up their last will and testament leaving everything they had to a boyfriend, a partner, or the cause. Do these beer-pong playing twenty-somethings know what they owe these nameless men?

The straight world follows, or lags behind, the gay world in many ways, but it's quickly catching up. It's always been this way with art, theater, fashion, and sex. While I'll be talking about the evolution of relationships in the context of the gay world, I firmly believe the straight world is only a few steps behind and will eventually follow our path.

As I tell my stories about relationship structures and my experiences with them, they're certainly all about the gay world and the changes I see occurring in that community, but based on the failure I observe of the institution of traditional marriage, the adoption of so many gay social structures by the straight world, I believe the changes I see in my community point the way for the straight world.

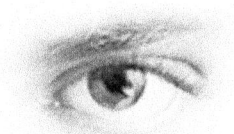

Part II
FAILURES OF A PARADIGM

Chapter 6
THE FANTASY OF
TRADITIONAL MARRIAGE

For the last twenty years, I've been a practicing divorce lawyer. By now, I've probably divorced four thousand spouses, and seen thousands of marriages fail, some for pretty run-of-the-mill reasons and some for extraordinary reasons. For the longest time, I kept my nose to the grindstone, worked my files, made my arguments in court, counseled my clients to do the right thing, and tried to get them to make smart, long-term choices, all the while believing in the underlying paradigm that created these failed relationships. I believed in marriage, monogamy, and the vows spouses made to each other at the altar.

As an activist in the gay and lesbian community, I went to war to bring gay marriage to my state and protect our families with incremental, statutory successes. Our community deserved the right to be married, if they choose to, and I fought to give them the same rights to stand at an altar, or before a judge, and make the exact same vows.

While handling these thousands of divorce cases, I began to see patterns emerge in relationships and adjusted my practice to be responsive to those patterns. For example, I learned the divorce process is substantially similar to the grieving process, with spouses going through the same steps, though almost always at different paces. Sometimes, a spouse would come into my office already having gone through the entire process, just wanting it to be "done".

Other times, I'd get the spouse who was forced into a divorce and had barely begun the grieving process, but always, it was the same; these people needed to grieve the loss of something paramount to them. I adjusted my approach to these clients to match up with the stages I sensed they were in and did what I could to push them through the grieving process to the next stage in life.

Another pattern I saw emerging in my practice was that people in these failed marriages went into their relationships with completely unrealistic expectations; expectations that couldn't long be met in today's modern world. They expected their lives to be mirror images of their parents' lives, they expected they would never want to be with anyone else, they expected their spouse would always be honest, and they never expected to fall out of love.

Almost all of the cases I handled were the same in this regard. The failure of the marriage stemmed from unreasonable expectations, a fantasy or fiction about what should happen for the rest of their lives. There was always a fictional script they were supposed to follow. It usually didn't take long for the spouses in these failed relationships to realize that the honeymoon phase wasn't going to last forever and that the script didn't fit their real lives, but it almost always took too long for them to decide it was time to move on.

For these starry-eyed couples, the fantasy of married life gave way to reality of the daily grind, and for some, they preferred the fantasy and looked elsewhere to try and find it again. For others, they developed an annoyance, then a distaste, then a dislike, and finally a hatred for their spouse who failed to live up to the promise of Cinderella that the utopian spouse fantasized about during the courtship and honeymoon. Marriage became a war, and war ends in a variety of ways, not just divorce. Sometimes, there's just decade after decade of cease fire.

Attending weddings is a strange experience for me, first because I'm gay, and for the longest time, I couldn't have one of my own, but weddings are also strange for me because I became jaded about the entire institution shortly after starting to practice in the field of family law.

Sitting in the audience, all dressed up, I knew there was a 60% chance this marriage, so beautiful, promising and touching it gave the crowd collective chills, would end in divorce, and do so relatively quickly. I looked at the pomp and circumstance of the wedding and wondered, why're they doing all this? Who're they trying to convince? Their individuality, the specialness of their relationship, was being boxed in by the expectations of family and friends.

The vows! Knowing the likely fate of this marriage, and having watched so many couples descend into bitter wars over the expectations set in those vows, I couldn't help but cringe as they stared deep into each other eyes and repeated the same vows as their parents, grandparents, and most of the people in the room.

I began to question the wisdom of marriage at all.

So, one day in San Francisco, after being smacked in the face by reality versus fiction myself, I decided to lift my head off the grindstone and look around at what was going on in the world of relationships. I started to think critically about why the marriage rate was now the lowest in the history of United States, and why the divorce rate was likewise higher than at any time in our history. Those are pretty exceptional statements, if you stop to think about it.

I decided to use my experience as a divorce lawyer, anecdotal though it might be, do some research, and think about my own relationships. My goal was to step outside the assumptions in my head from years and years of life's intractable trajectory toward marriage and family, to see if I could identify the driving force behind these changes.

My conclusion is that the institution of marriage as it's traditionally defined, is a failure in the opportunistic, modern world of technology. Fewer people are entering traditional marriages, most are waiting longer, and those that do chose this structure are fleeing in record numbers after the shortest time ever recorded. What I see is the unconscious development of a new relationship structure arising in connection with technology that's meeting the expectations of the generation we would expect to see getting married.

That structure is a modern relationship.

Chapter 7

DID THAT REALLY JUST HAPPEN?

The hottest guy in San Francisco stood me up that night. Robbie and I planned on having dinner and hanging out and talking about books, trips and our friends in common, but it didn't work out. Dark hair, dark eyes, scruffy face, and a muscular but lean body, Robbie was just too handsome to resist. Add to the mix that he liked leather and had a dark-side, and I knew I was his for life if he'd only have me.

My flight was late, and Robbie ran out of time to meet up before work. Instead, I met up with a group of friends at a local gay sports bar called High Tops. I'd never been there before and was looking forward to yet another new San Francisco experience. This group of friends is too much fun to pass up. It's one of the consistent features of people in San Francisco; they're more laid back, casual, and yes, happier, than most; always with smiles on their faces! I know it's a generalization, but it's held true every visit.

Everywhere I looked that night, it was couples, not a single, single man in sight, it seemed, and certainly not within my group. Maybe it was my mind set at that moment, but what's a single guy to do in a bar full of couples? Apparently, quite a bit.

I got hit on by couples, parts of couples, by multiple couples, and even by my coupled friends. By no means was I a virgin to a three-way with a couple, or even two couples; okay, not even four or five couples. But what was unique that night was that there didn't seem to be a couple in the room that wasn't looking for action with others. Apparently, all the couples were open in one way or the other. It's not that way in Seattle.

"Seattle! My parents just moved up there for my dad's job," said a nice looking blond guy, about 6'2 wearing an orange Giants jersey, #48, after he sagely pointed out, "You're not from here are you?"

"Yeah! Been there my whole life. It's a nice place. You should come visit," I replied, with just a hint that I might be interested. He was hot and athletic, but he was also a little drunk.

"Oh yeah? You gonna show me around?" he said, sliding up a little closer. "I've always heard it's a great place to go out. Everybody up there look like you?"

I laughed nervously. Blunt compliments like that aways made me uncomfortable. They come off canned, forced, or wholly manufactured. This one was no different. I changed the subject.

"Sandoval is turning out to be worth the money," I said, referencing his jersey.

"Wha . . . oh! Yeah, he's knocking it outta the park this year. My husband and I have tickets, but there're so many games!" Husband! Okay, well now I had to figure out if this was a "discrete" cruising, or if the partner was going to magically appear out of the restroom in a minute.

"Where's your guy tonight?" I asked.

"He stayed home. Long week." #48 grabbed a fresh drink from the bartender with a nod. The bartender looked at me with a thumbs up and a questioning look. I waved him off with my own thumbs up.

Turned out, #48 was looking for someone to take home to his husband of five years for a group. #48 didn't even look like he was thirty. They loved to play with other guys, and there was no problem with it all, he told me. Pushing pretty hard, I finally caved and gave him my number, then he staggered off. Nice guy, but I doubt he'd remember my name in the morning any more than I can remember his right now.

Next came James and his partner Patrick. James was former Colt porn star and is built like a tank. Patrick is smaller, younger, and Asian. I learned from them that San Fransisco is home to a booming porn industry, with Hot House, Lucas, and Kink.com headquartered there. Nice guys, and I still stay in touch with James, but no chemistry.

A parade of couples ensued that either hit on me or expressed their openness during our conversations. Sometimes it was just one partner, sometimes both. Regardless, they were open sexually and open in their willingness to talk about it.

High Tops was a lot of fun that night, and I enjoyed spending time with my San Francisco friends and making new friends along the way. I'm not a big drinker, so I sipped my way through a couple cocktails before it came time for the next stop; Jorge and Tom's house for a smaller cocktail party.

Their home was beautiful and would be stunning in any other city but was jaw dropping in San Francisco, where property values have exploded with the tech boom. A perfectly manicured lawn to match a perfectly modern, hi-tech interior. Also, a perfect setting to ask questions about the modern relationships in the city I'd observed at High Tops.

"So many couples at the bar tonight! Where do the single guys go?" I asked Jorge while he mixed me a pink vodka-something drink.

"Ha! I suppose they're over at the Eagle or maybe Steamworks or some place. Most of the couples act like single men, though. You should have no problem hooking up with one, or both of a couple," responded Jorge, looking me over with a sly smile; handsome, but not my type.

"I certainly got hit on enough tonight by couples," I said, taking the pink vodka drink, now with a fruit accouterment. "I felt a little uncomfortable! Hooking up with a couple is tough. One always seems more into it than the other, plus, you have to deal with all the jealousy issues."

Jorge paused and looked puzzled for a second. "Well, the couples I know wouldn't be jealous. It's just part of it. Sometimes a guy is into you and sometimes they're into your husband. I've gotten up in the middle of a three-way and made a peanut butter sandwich because it just wasn't for me," he said, moving on to mixing another pink drink for himself. "It's just sex. My husband is coming home to me at the end of the night. I get kind of turned on by the thought of him being with another guy anyway. Sometimes the best sex we have is after one of us just hooked up with someone on the side."

Jorge leaned over the drink he was making and lowered his voice even though there was no one remotely near by to overhear. "This is gonna sound sleazy, but I love the taste of another man's cum on him, or in him. Fuck!" He leaned back and rolled his eyes with the "too hot to handle" look.

I laughed and shook my head. We headed back into the other room with a twenty foot ceiling and a wall of glass looking out onto their amazing garden. Fifteen or so people stood around the room talking, industrial sounding dance music playing in the background. The house was littered with beautiful pieces of modern art that I could only dream of collecting.

The night was getting late, and by then I was at four drinks, enough to make me a little more forward than I normally am, and that's saying something. I'd been talking with two super hot guys, a couple I knew from Seattle, Scott and Greg, and it was clear we were going home together. The invite was seamless, natural, non-threatening, and with no debate. I responded the same way.

At their place, they offered me another drink, and we started making out. Clothes were off shortly, and we were at it. The sex was good, but I noticed that the two of them seemed to be using me to satisfy separate desires. It was like things they didn't want to, or couldn't do, for each other. Both seemed satisfied at the end, but I didn't cum. Hugs and promises to see each other later and I was in an Uber back to my bed and breakfast. It was 3:00 a.m.

At that moment, my night pivoted, and my San Francisco experience shot off in a new direction. Once I got back to my place, I undressed and quickly crawled into bed, deciding to check Scruff real quick before bed. Scruff puts a little green dot on your profile picture to indicate you're online. Robbie must have seen me online and sent me a message, remember him? He's the hottest guy in all of San Francisco.

"Are you up?"

Despite the fact that I'm drawn to Robbie in more ways than one, our relationship was just beginning and was built on a few areas of common interests. It wasn't sexual and hadn't wandered there yet, so to be chatting with him on Scruff at 3:00 a.m. was quixotic. Hell yes I wanted to take it to a more intimate level, but it felt like the Grand Canyon between here and there.

A few tentative messages later, assessing interest, and he was on his way over. I was nervous. I like him. No, I mean I really like him. There was no presumption we were going to hook up, just hang out, but I could sense his interest.

I met him at the front gate of the bed and breakfast. San Francisco was cold dark and quiet that morning. Handsome beyond words, he walked up with a dark jacket on and a backpack slung over one shoulder. It'd been over a year since I last saw Robbie and here he was, handsome, strong, with dark, knowing eyes.

Robbie walked up to the gate and looked shyly at me for a split second. We moved together; no words, just a hug--a hug that kept going. Feeling him pressed against me, pulling me in closer, I reached around to the back of his head and lifted his lips to mine.

A mix of emotions flooded over me; desire, disbelief, excitement and fear. I could feel a spark with this man, whose arms wrapped around me close and tight.

Four hours later, the only thing said between us was my whisper to his ear, as I kneeled naked between his legs, "Can I fuck you?"

I walked him home around 8:00 a.m. After dropping him off with a long kiss at his front door, the walk back to my bed and breakfast through Delores Park was one I'll never forget. The early morning sun hanging low over the city, I could feel the crisp, cool air coming off the ocean a few miles away.

I was now in a shit-ton of trouble. Robbie is Tony's ex-boyfriend.

Chapter 8
MONOGAMY IS THE PROBLEM

The old rules of the traditional linear relationship worked for a different age, but in the modern age of technology, near income parity between the sexes, dwindling interest in raising children, marriages occurring later in life, the old paradigm creates unworkable expectations.

The bullet that ends a marriage is fired at the altar. Most of the time, it's the unreasonable expectations that kill it shortly after the honeymoon phase ends. Most people enter relationships for the wrong reasons. Pressure from friends and family is the biggest driver, but there's also the insecurity of being alone and the need to feel "completed" by someone else. Finally, a paring makes the pursuit of sex easier.

Almost simultaneous with the creation of a traditional relationship, "rules" descend on the couple; monogamy, gender roles, finances, texting, phone calls, etc. Couples draw these rules from society without thinking about whether the structure works for them. It's a difficult self-evaluation and discussion to have with your partner about what may work for your relationship, rather than defaulting to the paradigm you see all around you, but I believe wholesale adoption of someone else's paradigm dooms more relationships than survive it.

Based on the relationships I observed during my travels, and my own experience with partners, I came to a powerful conclusion; the expectation of monogamy is suffocating relationships of all types. It's an unreasonable, unworkable expectation that couples adopt just because they think they have to; we've been raised to think that monogamy is the only way relationships work.

Tragedy strikes when a spouse discovers his partner is cheating, and his expectations get shattered. The infidelity and broken promise of monogamy can mean the immediate end of a marriage. Sometimes, the couple works it out with a whole lot of arguing and crying, and enters into a new commitment and pledge of fidelity. Maybe those new pledges work but in my experience, they mostly doesn't. Either way, the covenant entered at the altar is forever broken.

The cheating spouse owns his choices and bears responsibility for breaking his vow, but I have to wonder if this was a marriage that should have happened at all; should this couple have entered a monogamous relationship in the first place? Did they kill off this marriage before it began with a vow of monogamy purporting to last "till death do us part?"

A monogamous marriage isn't a requirement anymore for a successful relationship. Two partners can live together and cooperate in basic needs like food, clothes, and shelter, and create a business sort of relationship giving the individuals in the partnership a competitive advantage. This cooperation in basic needs doesn't necessarily go hand in hand with sex, however. In other words, a couple can still work together to gain a competitive advantage and not have sex, or not be exclusive.

Where does the idea of monogamy come from? This sexually committed pairing of one animal to another, like every other behavior in the animal kingdom, may have its roots as an evolutionary advantage, or it may be a cultural adaptation deemed beneficial to success within a society. Research indicates that it developed as the latter; monogamy is a cultural adaptation, not a hard-wired genetic evolution.

Of the approximately four thousand mammal species on Earth, only a few dozen form lifelong, monogamous relationships. Even these pairings of animals aren't always sexually exclusive.

Many monogamous mammals form pairs to mate and raise offspring, but also regularly engage in sexual activities with partners other than their selected mate.

Even in modern human cultures, only 43 of 238 societies across the world are monogamous, according to professor Roger Rubin, at University of Maryland, and author of *Alternative Family Lifestyles Revisited*, or *Whatever Happened to Swingers, Group Marriages and Communes?* In fact, monogamy is one of the several different mating systems found in the animal world. A pair of animals may be socially monogamous, but that doesn't necessarily make them sexually or genetically monogamous.

Social monogamy, where a couple lives together and provides for each other's basic needs such as food, clothes, and also has sex with one another appears to have evolved as a mating strategy. Since social monogamy exists in a diversity of species, it suggests that monogamy isn't inherited from a common ancestor, but instead developed independently.

"It is debatable whether humans should be classified as monogamous. Because all the African apes are polygamous and group-living, it is likely that the common ancestor of hominids was also polygamous," says Timothy Clutton-Brock, a leading zoologist at the University of Cambridge. "One possibility is that the shift to monogamy in humans may be the result in the change of dietary patterns that reduce female density. While another is that slow development of juveniles required extended care by both sexes. However, reliance by humans on cultural adaptations means that it is difficult to extrapolate from ecological relationships in other animals."

Cultural adaptation is the evolutionary process by which an individual modifies his personal habits and customs to fit in to a particular culture. It can also refer to gradual changes within a culture or society that occur as people from different backgrounds participate in the culture and share their perspectives and practices. Cultural adaptions are the expectations we set upon ourselves, as a society, not genetic foundations for our species.

Today, the cultural adaption of monogamous paring is unraveling marriages and these marriages are failing in record numbers.

Studies prove that the cultural adaptation of monogamy in marriage is collapsing; of all married people, about 10–15% of women and 20–25% of men regularly engage in extramarital sex. Today, in United States, 63% of men and 70% of women say it's always wrong to cheat on a spouse. Paradoxically, 60% of men and 50% of women reported having extra-marital affairs at some point in their relationship. A study of gay relationships in San Francisco found that the majority of gay male couples aren't monogamous.

There are two important distinctions between these two data sets, one for straight marriages and other gay relationships. First, at the time of this last study, gays and lesbians didn't have a legal right to get married in California, so, for the vast majority of the sample, there weren't any marriage vows to break. More important, though, the researcher didn't ask if the lack of monogamy was also a lack of fidelity, meaning there was no break down in the data of how many of these relationships were open, and monogamy was not an expectation.

If monogamy is a cultural adaptation as research indicates, not an evolutionary survival characteristic, what cultural purpose did it serve with its initial adoption? Shockingly, the modern cultural adaption of monogamy through marriage appears to be directly related to a single piece of farm equipment, the plow, and consolidation of family wealth from agriculture.

In her groundbreaking work on the role of women in economic development, published in 1970, Ester Boserup argued that the sexual division of labour in plow-based agricultural societies gave rise to the functional requirements that led to the adoption of monogamy as a cultural adaption. In plow agriculture, farming is largely men's work and is associated with private property. Marriage tends to be monogamous to keep the property within the nuclear family. Close family members are the preferred marriage partners to keep property within the group.

A survey by Carol Ember at Yale University of other cross-cultural samples confirms that the absence of a plow was the only predictor of polygamy, although other factors such as high male mortality in warfare and pathogen stress had some impact.

Socially imposed monogamy existed in cultures prior to the creation of the plow, however. Also, cultures with the plow often included alternative relationship structures in addition to monogamy.

For example, in elite French society monogamy was outwardly shown, but concubines were common. Since the time of the Renaissance, the French rule was, "First and foremost, they must remain hidden at all times and never be visible enough to embarrass the spouse. Second, you never do it with someone in your own 'back yard'--neighbors, friends, work colleagues etc.--where the risk of exposure is greatest," according to Catherine Hakim, former professor of sociology at the London School of Economics.

At various times in human history, monogamy also served functions of the state and was encouraged, even legally prescribed, for a range of purposes. For example, Augustus Caesar tried to encourage marriage and reproduction to force the aristocracy to divide its wealth and power among multiple heirs. In response, the aristocrats kept their outwardly monogamous structure and the number of legitimate children to a minimum, ensuring their legacy, but all the while the aristocrats had several sex partners on the side.

Throughout world history, monogamous systems have not been not common, and instances of strict social monogamy were rarer. In a recent study of 348 better-known societies, 20% are defined as monogamous, whereas another 20% displayed limited polygyny, where a man has more than one wife and fully 60% more frequent polygyny. Polygyny appears to have been the dominant sexual mating mechanism for millions of years.

According to ancient history professor Walter Scheidel at Stanford University, in the ancient Greco-Roman world, societally imposed, universal monogamy was firmly established as the only legitimate marriage system. Polygamy was considered a barbarian custom or a mark of tyranny, and monogamy was regarded as quintessentially "Greek". However, monogamy co-existed with concubinage even for married men. As far as we can tell, Greeks were supposed to draw the line at cohabitation, which was considered inappropriate. At the same time, married men's sexual relationships with their slave women or prostitutes was free of social and legal sanction. Despite the imposition of monogamy, elite polygyny was prevalent in ancient Greek culture.

Is monogamy a more advanced relationship structure or a relic of some evolutionary need that's no longer relevant in today's culture? Research indicates that human <u>nature</u> is adapted to a one husband, many wives structure (polygynous). Most ancestral men aspired to polygyny, and some ancestral women preferred to be the co-wife of an impressive man than the sole wife of a second-rate one.

Human mating behavior was naturally selected in a world in which striving for polygyny was often reproductively advantageous. That's why people living in modern societies often seem inclined toward polygyny, even in cultures that have attempted to abolish it.

Societally imposed monogamy though traditional marriage, as a mating mechanism is failing the couples entering relationships, including marriages. The advantage conveyed by the cultural adaptation of monogamy no longer exists and, in fact, runs contrary to the pressures of the modern technology age. Accordingly, marriages based on this outdated adaptation aren't so much a fulfillment of love's young dream as they're disasters waiting to happen.

My conclusion is that monogamy is a relic and that modern relationships no longer include an imposition, or expectation, of monogamy. Modern pyramid relationships often start out open and stay open. A couple may decide they don't want to be sexual with anyone else right now, or maybe never, but the option of sex outside the primary relationship is always available.

Chapter 9

MOST INCREDIBLE MAN #4 . . . OR SO

It was May, a couple years after Tony and I met. Tony and I were at a microbrewery downtown for a going away party for a friend from the gym; a strange place for a going away party for a person obsessed with eating healthy, but the change of scenery was nice. The bar was loud and crowded and its patrons were enjoying the microbrewery's specialties in great quantities.

Our friend, Chad, just went through a bad breakup with a woman he'd been dating for several years. He was in pretty bad shape and needed a fresh start, so much that he was packing all his stuff and moving to San Diego. No job, no place to live, and not much money, he planned to rely on the kindness of friends for a new beginning.

"Hope Chad is okay. He and Lauren were as good as married," I said, seated on a stool at a barrel-turned-cocktail table, a wheat beer with an orange in it in front of me. "Man, he sure took it hard. Do you know what happened?"

"Never told me. Just said he was moving outta town next weekend," replied Tony across the barrel from me, as he tried intently to peel the label off his microbrew bottle. "I guess Garrett was pretty mad at him for sticking him with the lease." Garrett was Chad's roommate and also our friend. "I'd be pretty upset too, but I guess Chad needs this."

"Yeah, he and Lauren were together since high school, I think. He always thought they were gonna get married," I said. "But picking up and moving justing like that? Seems kinda drastic. He's leaving a job where he makes almost six figures, and he's gonna sleep on a couch. Almost like he wants to punish himself."

Tony squirmed a little, looking up from his half-torn label. "Well, I don't think there's anything wrong with wanting a fresh start. He's only twenty-five and has plenty of time. Hope he finds a nice girl out there and settles down with her." He turned his attention back to the label, eyebrows wedged together.

Yes, because that's the only way to be happy, I thought. Find the next person to build your life around because God knows, you can't do it for yourself, but I couldn't say that. It was a little too close to home for Tony, and a fight would ensue.

"So I met this guy from San Francisco on Facebook a couple weeks ago. We've been talking every day. Seems like a good guy. I'm thinking about going out there and meeting him for a weekend," Tony said, without looking up from his label as if he was telling me the weather.

I hated it when he dropped this type of shit on me in the middle of something else, but I guess there's never a good time or place to do it. A wave of anxiety was inevitable when he started a new flash-in-the-pan relationship.

"Right on. San Francisco's a great place. Haven't been out there in years," I said calmly. "When you thinking of going?"

He said he was planning on flying out to see this guy in two weeks on the weekend of my birthday which ticked me off since we'd been talking about hanging out and doing something fun.

Tony assured me, as he told me about his flight plans, we'd make the most of the weekend before, and, true to his word, we did. We went out and got drunk with some friends, then he passed out in my arms in the car ride home. We woke up the next morning at my place with his head on my chest.

Tony headed out to San Fransisco anyway, to meet his new Facebook crush, some guy who found him on there and managed to get through the hundreds of other messages Tony receives to get his attention. This lucky Facebook friend won the lottery and managed to convince Tony to jump on a plane and come down for the weekend.

When he came back on Monday, I knew it was going to be the same old leftovers, just reheated. He was into this guy and "got chills" when he saw his texts and heard his voice. They started Skyping, and our workouts began getting interrupted with texts and phone calls, same shit, different Prince Charming. A new shirtless pic popped up on the background screen of Tony's phone, no Adele this time, thankfully.

This was the fourth one of these "sparks" I had to endure in a year and my patience was running thin. This time I didn't try hard to hide my opinion. I let Tony know how I felt about the depth of his relationships, and this one in particular. It was an odd pairing, and I started to feel he was seriously disconnected this time.

Before I start discussing the nature of Tony's relationship with his newest "most incredible man," I want to say that a job is a job, and we all just make mud bricks; you, me, everyone. No job is more important or prestigious than any other; just mud bricks. Most jobs serve the function of getting us the resources we need to live and hopefully enjoy some of the nicer things the world has to offer along the way. Whether you're a teacher, an EMT, a lawyer, a bartender, a shopkeeper, or a tech CEO, get over yourself. Next life, you could be a slug.

This new guy worked in the porn industry as a video editor. He was also heavily into the San Francisco leather scene. The weekend after Tony went to visit him, he headed to Chicago for the International Mister Leather festival to compete for the title. The circles in which he moved were of a particular flavor.

It wasn't Tony's flavor; it was mine. Tony thought leather was a joke and too weird, too kinky. Prior to this guy, he refused to even try on a harness and could hardly even wear a jock strap without feeling uncomfortable. Tony was a traditionalist. He was looking for monogamy and marriage with Prince Charming, not Captain Nasty Pig.

Tony was all about circuit music, big dance clubs and the LA boys, not the rougher, more adult scene in San Francisco. Here he was, though, talking about how San Francisco was a place he could see himself living after just two weeks and only one trip.

I knew what was coming my way next; exclusion and isolation. I was never gonna meet this guy, and my time with my best friend would dwindle down to the required functionality for a friendship to continue to exist and still be called one.

For all intents and purposes, I was exactly correct. It got so bad that at one point, all communication was cut off between Tony and me and I just wanted him to move to San Francisco as quickly as possible. It took weeks before we could talk to each other again.

Maybe I'm just someone who doesn't like change, but I resent the fact these guys, this guy, in particular could come into my life and turn everything on its head and there was nothing I could do about it. It was frustrating that no matter what I did, it was the wrong thing. It was humiliating to be Tony's best friend, but never be invited to do anything with him and his new boyfriend. No, I didn't like this guy, but I didn't like him because he took away my job as best friend, and he didn't even know he was doing it! Tony did a complete job of being sure that this new guy didn't even know my name.

I was always hurt and confused by Tony's exclusion of me so completely from his life when these new guys came along. He didn't like it when I got upset about being excluded, but why do it in the first place? Since I made the mistake of laughing at Gianni's Grindr pic that day at the gym, I was behind the eight ball, never to be let out again. That's the only thing I can think of.

No doubt my frustration and anxiety got the best of me, and sometimes I lashed out at Tony. Once, I even turned my anger directly toward this new guy. My behavior with regard to him was mean and unnecessary, and I'd take it back if I could. I caused a lot of hurt with my personal attack on someone I didn't even know, and there was no excuse for it.

This, like all his other relationships, was doomed by reality sooner or later. The new "most incredible man" who caused Tony to get the "chills" whenever he got a text realized that they were too different and their situations made a relationship impossible. I think there were other things at work here, but it's all in the past, mostly.

His new guy came to Seattle for a final visit and told Tony it wasn't going to work out, that he didn't trust himself so far away, and that they were different people. I think the guy was genuine, and I respect him for it. I know it was hard saying goodbye.

Tony was devastated. His world came crashing down around him. This was the guy who "taught me the meaning of the word love." He was ready to move to San Francisco for him and already morphed his life to make this guy want him more. Now he was alone.

Once again, I got the text, "Are you happy? We broke up." He was driving back from SeaTac after dropping him off. I wasn't happy.

No one else got a text. No one else got a call. I went over to his house and spent the night. I spent weeks helping him try to piece his life back together, hardly letting him out of my sight for the first few days; not too difficult since he wouldn't move off the couch. Tony couldn't understand why it didn't work out. Not a good idea for me to point out the obvious, that they were different people and this guy was right to call it off, but I figured there'd be a better time for that teachable moment.

It took a long time for Tony to get to the point where he could talk about the real reason for the failure of his relationship with Robbie.

Chapter 10
COURTSHIP AND DATING

Whether you like it or not, the mechanisms for meeting people, getting to know them, and going on "dates" has forever changed in the modern world of technology and instant communication. Limitless availability of possible partners, voluntary online disclosure of personal information, and a dwindling window of free time are combining to end dating in the traditional sense. The prerequisite act of dinner and a movie has given way to "host or travel?"

Is this a bad thing? More and more people are saying "no".

In answering this question, we have to challenge society's prejudice toward online dating and hookup sites. These services have expanded their presence into the mainstream of American culture, but there's still a stigma associated with their use, as if they're the last resort of the desperate and undesirable. If you enter this discussion about modern dating with the opinion that online dating and hookup sites are base and vacuous, I hope you'll keep in mind the trajectory of statistics showing where our culture is heading, as well as the user demographics of people looking for online connections. You can bet Homecoming King and Queen probably have Tinder profiles.

Once upon a time, Dick asked Jane, a secretary in his office, out to dinner. She agreed, and they scheduled a time for Dick to pickup Jane at her house at 6:30 p.m. Friday night. Dick made reservations at a nice restaurant and reserved a table for two on the water.

Dick arrived promptly at 6:30 p.m., met Jane's parents, and they headed off to a nice, two hour dinner. They talked about their interests, families, goals, religion, and sipped their way through just one bottle of wine.

Dick returned Jane to her home before 10:00 p.m. Over the next few weeks they went on several similar dates. They learned more and more about each other, and started to assess whether there's a long-term future here. After a few months of dating, the couple became engaged. Shortly after, they had a nice big wedding.

Most people over forty would recognize this scenario as the dating expectations laid out for them while growing up in middle America. Few of us actually engaged in this antiquated puppet dance, but this was what our parents beat into our heads about meeting the "right" person. By the time I was dating, it was a much-abbreviated version of this dance that included sex early on, but not always right away, to my chagrin. We still had to do dinners and buy roses for the girls, but the end game, i.e. marriage, wasn't so obvious. Yes, we were looking for the right person to marry, but other forms of relationship options were appearing, such as living together indefinitely.

Things have now changed drastically. Most fundamentally, the objective is no longer to get married. For most people, the objective is to find someone to have sex with, hopefully on a regular basis. That's not to say a large segment of the singles crowd isn't out there looking for love; they're just motivated by sex. Sexual attraction is the precursor to love for this crowd, not the other way around.

As for using a hookup app or website to find a potential mate, any stigma has largely evaporated, since this is the first generation of kids to come of age on the Internet. They get jobs and apartments and plane tickets online, why not dates?

According to a Pew Research Center survey, 59% of Internet users feel online dating is a good way to meet people, an increase of 15% since 2005 alone. Only 21% said it's for the desperate. The number of users who feel online dating creates a better match than traditional dating went from 47% to 53%.

Tech companies aren't sitting on the sidelines of this burgeoning industry either. Match.com, which represents nearly one-third of what's a $2.1 billion market, saw growth of 7.1% in 2013. Use is quickly expanding onto phones, too, with dating companies focusing resources on the development of mobile versions of their products. Grindr and Scruff don't even have desktop versions. The Pew study shows that 39% of online dating now happens through mobile apps.

The trends of the past year have done more to lift the stigma than anything in the previous nineteen. Things have now reached a tipping point, according to Pew research, where approximately 60% of Americans know of someone who has used online dating services or apps, and 29% know someone who's now in a long-term relationship thanks to finding a mate though one of these services. It's now socially acceptable to pass your phone around to friends at a club or party and share potential mates. The conversation has come out of the closet and onto the dance floor, so to speak.

To keep things clean, Apple's app store sets requirements that no pornographic images can be shown in the primary functioning of any mobile app sold on its App Store. Users with profiles are free to have private pictures of virtually any type, but the pictures of public profiles have to be "G" rated.

In a push-back against superficiality, an app called Twine Campus available for iOS users blurs each user's profile image so that the basis for selecting someone isn't as narcissistic as other online options. One has to wonder what the point of having a profile picture at all is, then. In any case, Twine Canvas is an effort to reduce the perceived shallowness of social dating apps.

Of course, outside of mobile apps, everything is free game, and sexting becomes normative. Sexting is the act of sending sexually explicit messages or photos electronically, primarily using mobile phones. People sext to show off, to entice someone, to show interest in someone, or to prove commitment. With this option, no app, and therefore no editorializing, is needed, and people are free to share whatever they want.

Nearly 70% of teen boys and girls who sext do so with their girlfriend or boyfriend, and 61% of these sexting teens have sent nude images. Outside of the boyfriend/girlfriend scenario, 15% of teens who have sent or posted nude images of themselves sent these messages to people they've never met in person, but instead met on the Internet. In general, 24% of high-school age teens (ages fourteen to seventeen) and 33% of college-age students (ages eighteen to twenty-four) have been involved in a form of nude sexting. Problems arise when relationships end and someone is left in possession of highly compromising material.

Dating and courting in the modern world of technology looks nothing like the dating and courting of Dick and Jane. It doesn't remotely resemble the structures we were raised with. Society is creating its own structure on-the-fly, almost instantaneously, as technology develops new options for communicating. Society is in reactive mode to the creative power of technology. This reactive mode has ended dating in the traditional sense.

Chapter 11
ABE AND ROBBIE

My experience with couples in San Fransisco opened my eyes to new relationship structures. Certainly, the paradigm I saw at work in the city wasn't uniform nor perfect, but everywhere I looked, couples were open and looking for additions to their relationship and for greater satisfaction in their sex lives.

It was arms day at one of the Castro gyms. The gyms in Castro are an interesting experience. First, space is limited because real estate is so expensive that everything is packed in tightly; second, it's almost all gay men at these local gyms. Since these gyms are in the heart of the Castro, guys feel at liberty to cruise hard pretty much all the time.

Before going to a gym in San Francisco for the first time, I asked some friends if I should go to one in the Castro or go across town to the Fitness SF in SOMA. They said the Castro gym was fine, that it was nice and clean, and the people were friendly. Not nervousness about being cruised, I just asked because I was hoping to get a good workout without distraction.

Relying on their assurance, I headed to the Castro gym and got in about an hour of cardio and a half-hour of arms. By the time I was done, brunch with some friends was across the street in ten minutes, so I rushed around and headed for the shower. To my surprise, the "shower" was a small communal room with about ten shower heads and no dividers nor curtains. The picture in your head is probably pretty accurate. Too late for a plan "B", I was standing there sweaty, stinky and nothing on but a towel. My shower audience turned in unison. That was my first, and last, experience showering at that gym. I still go there to work out, but now I leave time for a shower at home.

While rushing to get dressed, I ran into a lawyer friend of mine from Seattle, Jason. Jason had since moved to SF to be with his husband and work for a big firm here. It was great to see him again and he invited me to join him and his husband that night at Midnight Sun for cocktails. No plans for anything else, I jumped at the chance to hang out.

Midnight Sun is a nice, trendy cocktail bar one block off of the Castro. It's been around forever, but has a comfortable modern feel to it. It's one of the places I like best for meeting new people, so having a couple of friends to hang out with and be my wingmen sounded like a great night.

We met around 9:00 p.m. and started catching up on people and events. Jason, a tall, lanky red head with a receding hairline works as a corporate lawyer at a large international firm handling intellectual property claims. Jason and his husband Chris travel quite a bit, so we had a lot of catching up to do. Trips and gay geography ("you know Tom and Fred", "How was Parrot's lounge?", "what happened to the Black Party?") kept us busy for awhile. Around us, the bar filled up with a decent crowd.

Jason and Chris introduced me to a bunch of new people that night. They live right up the street, toward Noe Valley, and are neighborhood staples, so pretty much everyone who walked in, they knew personally or at least by sight. Most of the people walking in were couples or groups, but not always. Some poor single guy would wander in alone occasionally. I felt their pain as they looked around for a friendly face or a place to stand and not look too desperate. I love traveling alone, but the first few minutes in a bar by myself can be uncomfortable.

"So you been finding any guys out here this trip?" Chris asked me. Chris was about 35, shorter, horn-rimmed glasses, with a Middle Eastern heritage. He and Jason met about six years ago while Jason was living in Seattle. Back then, they were both into the leather scene, traveling a lot, but mostly keeping to themselves. Jason was the one I was closest with; I didn't get the chance to know Chris outside the context of that relationship. Here in San Francisco, Chris worked for a tech startup in their finance department.

"A few here and there," I said with a sideways smile, a sip of my vodka and something tasteless, but no calories. I always feel bad discussing my sex life with people, afraid of their judgment. I like sex, and I like meeting new people. Not to sound full of it, but it's pretty easy for me to find attractive men to spend time with. Problem is, when I'm talking about my sex life I'm afraid if I just come out and say, "Yeah, man! Yesterday, I met up with a massage therapist, a personal trainer, and this guy who said he was a VP of Amex," judgment comes down with a loud boom, so I played coy. "Nothing too crazy."

"Aww come on, Dave!" Chris laughed. "I know you've got guys all over you out here. We don't have many people with your look. I bet they zero in for the kill." It's true. I'm big, muscular and fit, and I get told all the time, "you're not from here, are you?"

"Ha ha! Yeah, I don't get that. You guys have great gyms, and they're always crowded, and people are always active in this city. I don't know why I stand out here, but it sure seems like I do."

"It's the food and the cocktails," he said as he pulled the olive out of his drink and chomped on it. "There's such great food here, and I think people do a lot of dinners together or go out in groups. We hardly eat at home, just the two of us."

Abe, the bar-back, swung by and grabbed my butt. Abe and I had been talking on Grindr for a couple days, and it was only a matter of time before we were naked and crawling all over each other. Tall, dark, Middle Eastern, with a thick beard and a lot of tattoos, Abe's body was lean and muscular. He was wearing a completely unbuttoned, short sleeved lumberjack shirt, showing off his broad chest and defined abs. He recognized me when I walked in and gave me a sly smile and nod.

"Man, I'd get so fat if I ate out here all the time. I can't cook, so my meals are always pretty simple. The lady at Chipotle sends me Christmas cards," I said.

"A gay man who can't cook," he said around the olive. "Now that's something you don't see every day. Jason is more the cook than me, but he works late a lot. You lawyers can't seem to relax and enjoy life." He rolled his brown eyes and looked away. "I probably go over to Mickey's house a couple times a week for dinner anyway. Now, he can cook!"

"Who's Mickey?" I asked.

"My boyfriend," he said as he reached over to get Abe's attention to hand him a couple empty glasses from our table.

"Wha . . . boyfriend? But you and Jason . . ." I said with some surprise. Threesomes, or thruples, are nothing new to me, but I didn't want to offend Chris by jumping straight to that conclusion. Feigned shock and surprise seemed a more polite tactic. That way, he could also brag a bit. He took the bait.

"Oh, I've been seeing Mickey for about six months now. We have rules, but it's pretty casual. He's so fucking hot, 24, from Florida. Works doing some kind of marketing at Twitter," Chris said, relishing my big eyes and open mouth, drink stopped mid-way up. "It's no big deal. Jason had a guy on the side for a few months, too, while I was in Hong Kong."

"How's that work? Is this guy that hot? Doesn't Jason get a bit jealous?" I asked. I knew what was coming next, and here it was.

Chris fished around in his pocket and produced his phone. A few seconds later I was looking at a bathroom selfie of an attractive, blond kid, about six feet tall, wearing a baseball cap, a smile, and nothing else; well-endowed, too.

"Jesus, Chris," I laughed. "Very nice. I'm pretty sure I'd be jealous if my husband were sleeping with that guy!" I was even jealous Chris was sleeping with that guy, but you shouldn't appear to be hitting on someone else's trick, so I left that part out.

"Yeah, he's a sweetie," Chris said as he took his phone back and gave Mickey a long stare. "Mmmm. So damn hot!" he said wistfully. The phone disappeared back into his pocket.

"Why do you date him if Jason is here in town, though?"

Chris glanced at me over his glasses, then grabbed his drink. "Well, it's just sex, mostly, but I do call him my boyfriend. I have a husband and a boyfriend!" he said and spread his arms wide, almost to invite a comment from the crowd, daring the world to pass judgment. "Jason works late and sometimes doesn't want to go out and do the same things I do. He doesn't like movies, and he hates the beach. I still get to do those with Mickey. Jason and Mickey get along great, and sometimes, we all three hookup, and it's awesome. I love Jason, and I'll be with him until I die, but that doesn't mean I don't wanna be with other people, either emotionally or sexually."

"How does Mickey feel about it? Have you talked to him about how he fits into your relationship?" I've seen a third person in one of these three-way relationships get jealous of the "primary" relationship and try and break them up so he can have his favorite. It's also something like a "second class" citizenship in that, you only get what the other two are willing to give.

"Mickey doesn't want a full-on relationship," Chris said emphatically. "He's career-oriented and has goals and wants to move up in his company. It works out well for him because there aren't a whole lot of demands on him, and he's got plenty of free time. He goes out and hooks up on his own, too, but I think he enjoys what we have more than random hookups. It's stable, safe, doesn't take a whole lot of work," Chris laughed.

"So you're easy," I concluded wryly.

"Like Sunday morning," he said without missing a beat.

We moved on to other topics. The night was winding down and the crowd at Midnight Sun thinning; time to make a choice. Go home alone or find someone. It was 1:00 a.m.

A few hard eye-fucks with Abe and I knew he'd be down for meeting, but I also knew that wouldn't be until he got off work around 3:00 a.m. or so. Not wanting to stay up that late, I figured I'd save him for another day.

Something didn't feel right that night, though, and there wasn't an urge to be on the hunt. It was just two nights ago Robbie and I shared a quiet, early morning together, and frankly, it was hard to imagine anything more desirable than that right now.

I said my goodnights and made my way out of the bar and onto 18th Street. My rental house was to the right, near Dolores Park, but instead I turned left and headed toward Castro. I learned early on that San Francisco weather is completely unpredictable and it's a mistake to assume you're prepared for what may come; you're not. That night, it was chilly and foggy despite being the middle of summer. I was already in the habit of wearing layers, or bringing a jacket, even in the summer time. Throwing on my black leather jacket I headed for the warmth of Castro, nowhere particular in mind.

Ambling down the sidewalk, I passed a homeless kid who asked for a buck. Fishing out $5, I stood there and talked with him for a few minutes about the old guitar slung over his left shoulder. We joked about the broken string and what songs he was stuck playing without it. He had a broad smile on the boyish face buried beneath his beard and long hair, and his eyes were bright and intelligent. He said thanks for the help and made a friendly goodnight. His name was Ben.

A little farther and I turned right onto Castro and headed toward the theater. It was late and cold, but there were still crowds of people moving along the sidewalk, mostly gay men, but there were plenty of others.

Just meandering with nowhere in particular to go is good for the soul. My mind is open to the world around me when I'm not focused on getting anywhere in particular. I'm where I want to be already. On Castro that night I felt very present.

As much as I regret eating pizza the next day, it's the most incredible late night food on the planet. In the cuisine capitol of San Francisco, I knew I should be hunting down some exotic fusion of sushi and Ethiopian food, but there's nothing so satisfying as pizza by the slice at 2:00 a.m. When I walked by the welcoming glow of "Pie Hole," a pizza by the slice joint, the battle was lost before it was begun. My feet took over, and I slid up to the counter and ordered two slices.

The dark haired, twenty-something woman who took my order was one of the kids struggling to express their individuality in this town filled with people doing the same. Everything's been done! It's no big deal to be pierced or tatted, or to show some tit. You won't get a second look. "M'tama," her homemade name tag advised me, was pushing the piercings and tattoos just about as hard as she could; teardrops printed on her face, ears with huge gauge piercings, and jet black hair spiked in a random fashion, all in an effort to establish herself as someone different, someone special in this sea of special someones.

Her enthusiasm for selling slices of pizza was admirable, though, as she greeted me with a loud, gum chomping, "Well, hello there! What can I cut up for you, handsome?" she asked, pushing up her horn-rimmed glasses.

They've got a narrow bar with stools along the wall where you can sit and eat your pizza. Grabbing an empty spot, I pulled out my phone and began inhaling the gooey mess of bread, sauce and near-liquid cheese. Grindr was jumping with activity, after all, this is the middle of the Castro at desperation hour. No surprise it took five pages of scrolling through profiles before guys ">250 ft" away began to appear.

I switched over to Scruff real quick, then I saw it, a message from Robbie about two hours ago. Mid-bite of pizza I gasped and started choking. "M'tama" interrupted her loud conversation with the cook to glance at me to be sure I was okay. All good, her spiky hair turned back. Eyes watering, I hoped there wasn't pizza coming out of my nose.

My entire body was tense and tingly. Before opening his message, I experienced divergent feelings of excitement and fear. Was he going to say it was a mistake, and we should never have hooked up? Or maybe he'd say he had to tell Tony. Or was he gonna tell me it was amazing and special? The fear of the unknown rushed through my body, triggering sensation everywhere. I could feel myself getting aroused.

"Hey. What are you doing tonight?"

I'll take it. My fear melted into excitement, and I immediately started typing back, but realized I should think though my response first. Best thing was to finish this pizza, now mostly having slid off the bread and onto my paper plate in a pile of something vaguely edible, carefully think about what to say, then respond.

I settled on "Just met friends at the Sun. Eating pizza on Castro now. What are you up to?" The message was keeping to the same topic, neither desperate nor disinterested, ending with a question so that he'd be invited to write something back, something that would better direct the conversation where he wanted it to go. The real problem was his message was two hours old, and unless he was working late that night Robbie was probably already in bed.

After sending my Scruff note, I put my phone away, cleared my mess, and returned to wandering Castro.

Chapter 12
THE SPARK!

Love at first sight! A "spark"! Fireworks! The imagery overflows with Hollywood enthusiasm. Two lonely people find each other across the expanse of the entire universe, and the world stops to witness the birth of their undying love. The audience, all the rest of us mere mortals, stands in awe as the lovers' eyes lock, hearts quicken and they become unable to speak even simple sentences. We witness the touch of the divine.

I've had "sparks" before, and I've certainly heard breathless friends claim this type of firework. Clients also tell stories of how they first met the love of their life and "knew" this was the "one". They gave up promising careers, educational advancement, friends, and sometimes even relocated. Of course, if they've come to my office, things didn't turn out so well. Personally, these "sparks" never turned out well for me either.

I can think of one couple at the moment whose relationship began with a spark on the dance floor of a circuit party. As far as I know, they're still in cosmic bliss, with magic rainbows coming out of their assholes. So maybe I'm wrong, and these sparks are true touches of the divine, based on this one, fabulous relationship, but I doubt it.

My experience with sparks is that they feel amazing, almost overpowering. More than anything, though, a spark gives the mind an opportunity to create someone it's desperate to find, rather than someone actually found.

One summer night in Rome, at a popular venue called the Gay Village, I was waiting for two friends to show not knowing they'd both missed their flights. Not aware yet that I was on my own for the night, a tall, blond, athletic man-in-the-green-shirt walked by. He was so muscular and handsome, I stopped in my tracks. At first, he just walked by and smiled and I was left staring at the hole the crowd where he'd disappeared but, a few minutes later, he reappeared behind me and slid his arm over my shoulder.

"Why are you on your phone?" he asked. I'd been texting my friends to see where they were, plus, since I didn't speak Italian I was trying to look busy so no one would come talk to me.

Nonsensical babble rolled out of my mouth, something about "important texts" and "need a drink" and "lost friends," but he didn't notice, just stared into my eyes. Spark! We danced, laughed, drank, and made out for most of the rest of the night. At one point, he disappeared after going to the WC and I felt my heart drop thinking he'd left me. After walking around looking and not finding him, I started making my way out of the party, hands in my pockets and head down. Just before I reached the exit, he came up and put his arm around me again. "Where do you think you're going without me?"

The taxi cab back to my place was one of the most memorable experiences ever. The driver was gay-friendly, loved the Gay Village, and was a fan of trance dance music. We rode in the back of his taxi as he blasted trance and flew through the windy streets of Rome at 4:00 a.m. It's one hell of a way to see that city.

There was a definite spark with Rick, man-in-the-green-shirt, that night in Rome. We spent much of the next two weeks in Europe together and he eventually moved in with me back in Seattle. It was truly a magical time.

Sparks are beautiful while they last, but often extinguish fast, unless something deeper gets ignited. A transition from one beautiful night to romantic love or, if you're lucky, true love is tricky, isn't it? It's hard to keep your head on straight and avoid the pitfalls of creating a fantasy in this amazing new person; that is, if you want to at all.

Chapter 13
MARRIAGE IS LIKE VHS

My High Tops experience, drinks at Jorge's beautiful home, and three-way with Greg and Scott, added to the perception, already rolling around in my head from my law practice that the world of relationships is changing. At that time, I had generalized feeling that the old linear structure was failing, based on my observations as a divorce attorney and travels as a gay man, but I hadn't yet given any thought as to why or what comes next. Looking back at that night, the events were examples of what's changing in the world of relationships in San Francisco and other major cities across the country. No formal research or data at that point to back up my feelings, just my personal observations that things are different in the city.

First, couples are much more eager to refer to their partners as "husband". They do so without skipping a beat or special emphasis just to make sure I heard it right. Admittedly, this could be because gay marriage is newly legal in California, but I wonder if it comes from something deeper.

Second, being open came naturally to all these couples. Not one was monogamous. Maybe they had someone on the side already, like Chris and Jason, or maybe they were just looking for someone that night, like Greg and Scott, but the couples were actively looking for sex with others. There wasn't any judgment from the people I met, and there wasn't any shame on the part of the couples.

This triggering night made me step back and look at all the data I had in front of me from years as a divorce lawyer, from years of being in relationships myself, and from my time as a single gay man traveling the world. I finally started to think critically about my observations of failing relationships and the nature of a new structure of relationships I saw replacing them.

Traditional constructs of a marriage function on "autopilot". These are the steps you're supposed to take, and this is the order in which you take them. People sleepwalk into marriage, a paint-by-numbers coupling of soulmates. Sadly, stepping back and looking at your artwork, you see it's just like a million other tacky Elvis paintings.

Historically, there was pressure to pair up so as to be deemed successful in life. Having a partner, the right partner, fulfilled the expectations our family and peers set for us. A strong expectation to couple into a "productive" partnership, with gender defined responsibilities was built into our culture. This inherited construct of a productive partnership was hammered home by Hollywood, and TV studios and romance novels. They all scream at us, "this is how it should be!" The truth is, these Disney fantasies fail in the modern world.

Today, thanks to our technology-driven society, a partnership is less relevant to our productivity. No place is this more evident that the fast paced, progressive, hi-tech world of San Francisco. In this city, so dominated by the incredibly fast changes in technology, till death do us part, 2.5 children and a white picket fence is about as relevant as an episode of *Leave It to Beaver*.

I've heard thousands of stories of failed lifetime commitments, individuals who thought they'd found their soulmate, where someone's hopes and dreams, even their very purpose in life, has collapsed and I often wonder who knows more about marriage than I do. I know there are certainly people out there who do, but it's rarified air. There just aren't too many people who deal with marriages as much as me. All these autopsies of marriages have taught me a lot about "in sickness and in health" and "till death do us part."

Based on these autopsies, I can say that the traditional concept of marriage, as an institution, is failing in the modern world of technology. We no longer need to marry for a meal ticket, for a legitimate or fun sex life (the opposite may be true), to secure social standing, to convince people we're not gay, to certify paternity, or even to raise children. You might think this means cohabitation is a better bet; it's not. Many cohabitation arrangements operate like marriages and are just as challenging for the same reasons.

Monogamous marriage had a chance to survive but has, so far, utterly failed to morph from the original cultural adaptation as a "productive" arrangement, designed to protect the family name, property, or other interests, into an expression of love and fidelity compatible with our modern expectations. The death certificate for the institution of marriage is filled out and ready for signature. Who's got a pen?

What's the difference between a mystic and a prognosticator? One's always right, and the other is always wrong. Predicting where relationship structures will "end up" in this ever-changing environment of technology is a fool's errand, as the course is not set, but there's one thing that's certain; change is inevitable.

Everything in existence changes, and the structure of our relationships is no different. With the rise of the modern technology, the time has come to hold the institution of marriage up for inspection and consider whether it can function in the modern world. We need to analyze why traditional marriages fail more often than they succeed and why there's an epidemic of extramarital affairs.

High Tops triggered an epiphany for me. It was time to look up from the grindstone, question my assumptions about the immutability of monogamous marriage, and try and answer these questions.

Chapter 14
NEVER MARRIEDS AND OTHERS

Marriage has been failing spouses for a long time, but the opinions about its value are changing quickly with a near majority of people believing that the institution is a relic of the past.

While a new Pew Research survey finds that 53% of all never-married adults say they would like to marry eventually, this share is down significantly from 2010, when 61% of never-married adults said they would like to marry someday. Roughly one-third of today's never-married adults say they're not sure if they'd like to get married while 13% say they don't want to.

The relationship between education and marital status has also changed over time as more people finish college and pursue further degrees. In 1960, men of various education levels were about equally likely to have never been married. Today, there's considerable disparity in the shares of never-married men along educational lines. Men with a high school education or less are much more likely than men with advanced degrees to be married (25% vs. 14%). Today men with advanced degrees have goals in life beyond finding the perfect partner and are focusing their energies on their education and careers, rather than looking for Prince Charming or Cinderella.

This change in priorities is accelerating as young people are turning away from marriage in record numbers. According to Pew Research projections based on census data, when today's young adults reach their mid-40s to mid-50s, a record high share of this population (25%) is likely to have never been married.

People are recognizing that the existing structure is failing modern times. When asked, about four in ten Americans, regardless of age, agreed "marriage is becoming obsolete," according to a 2010 Pew survey. In a similar poll of voters conducted by Time in 1978, only 28% felt that way. This degree of shift in something so fundamental to society must be driven by some major change in expectations of this generation. Nothing happens in a vacuum.

As the only institution viewing these changes as a moral failing, churches themselves see the writing on the wall. "The findings do not represent trivial facts, but rather a massive moral reorientation of our culture," Heath Lambert, assistant professor of biblical counseling at Southern Baptist Theological Seminary in Louisville, Kentucky, said. "Couples that delay marriage will not also delay intimate relationships and sexual gratification. That means that this study portends increased rates of sex outside marriage, cohabitation, illegitimacy, and pornography usage."

I would agree with Professor Lambert about sex outside marriage and cohabitation, would wonder what century he lives in when he refers to another human being as "illegitimate," and don't give a damn about increased pornography usage. His conclusion that there's a massive moral reorientation underway, though, is bang on.

Predictably, San Francisco demographics point the way for our future. In that city, 82% of adults between 25 and 34 have never been married, the largest share among big U.S. cities. The city also has the lowest percentage of children of any major city in the country. Only 13.4% of the city's residents are under the age of eighteen. The number of kids in San Francisco has gradually declined since the 1960s, when they made up a full quarter of the population.

More and more people are rejecting marriage, or delaying it indefinitely. This trajectory, if it continues, means the end of traditional marriage except as a subcultural relic within a couple generations.

Chapter 15
WARMTH OF MOONLIGHT

Castro, even at 2:00 a.m., is a bustling place of diverse activity;
bears, twinks, drag queens, homeless people, and even parents
with baby strollers cutting paths up and down the newly
completed "walk of fame" that is the Castro sidewalk.

I often wish I could pull up a park bench and people-watch the
parade of lives meandering up and down that street; naked guy,
with nothing on but a sock, the "real" Pope signing autographs
and handing out blessings for a dollar, mysterious chicken guy
whose appearances are as common as Big Foot, and so many more,
one-in-the-world characters. It's the best entertainment money
can buy.

That night I was too preoccupied to enjoy it, however. Every
two minutes I was grabbing my phone to see if Robbie messaged
me back on Scruff. I don't know why we didn't communicate by
iMessage; we had each other's numbers. Maybe Scruff allowed just
that extra distance to make things more comfortable, safer, with
not so much pressure. The feeling of being "present" on Castro
had given way to thoughts of what might be, tonight, tomorrow,
for the rest of my life.

Bars started closing and the street filled up with people spilling
out from places like 440 and Q. A drag queen in a combination
of cabaret and dungeon master gear stopped square in my path.
"Oh damn, honey! You're fine! Where's your man? Why are you
alone?" she demanded. She wore a black corset, black fishnet

gloves with matching pantyhose and steep high-heels. A black leather collar, with metal spikes, wrapped around her throat and her hair was done up classic Grace Jones-style.

"I don't know!" I laughed, shrugged, hands lifted. "I've been trying all night and no one wants me!" I made to sniff my arm pits. "I even went without deodorant, too!"

"I don't believe that for a second, sweetie." She looked me up and down, turned to the side, licked her pointer finger and slid it between her man-breasts. "You just say the word and momma is all yours. You can take her home and make her do whatever feels good." It was only a half joke, I knew, but respectful.

I laughed, gave her a high five, and made my way past. "Don't lose my number, precious!" she shouted as I walked off, more for the audience than for me. I smiled, and grabbed for my phone.

A message from Robbie.

"Just finishing work. Out in 30. Want to hang?"

Does a fucking bear shit in the fucking woods?

"Yeah. I can meet you on Castro when you're done if you want," I typed back. Send. Robbie worked nights as a bar-back at one the clubs on the Castro to pick up extra cash.

Instant response, "Sure. See you in 30."

It was a long fucking thirty minutes, and I wasn't living in the present; Buddha would not approve. This guy had no patience! I couldn't tell you anything interesting about the crowd, the place, the weather. My mind was completely focused on meeting Robbie and what I should say or how I should act. Time marched slowly, but finally, 2:30 a.m. rolled around, and I started loitering around the front of Robbie's bar. Not wanting to appear too eager or seem desperate, I ended up walking around the middle of Castro Street like a stray puppy looking for handouts. I even gave the Pope a buck for good luck. Desperate indeed.

Out the front door he came, backpack slung over his shoulder, jacket on, looking so handsome I couldn't believe he was interested in me at all; 29 years old, dark with a short beard, athletic, a quick, infectious laugh and a quirky interest in science fiction books and comics. He was such a great catch; it boggled the mind he was single.

He quickly spotted me, and a smile spread across his face. I stood up from the fire hydrant I was leaning against and walked up to him, tentatively opening my arms for a hug.

Again, what started as a hello hug descended into something intensely passionate as our bodies pressed against each other, and he buried his head into my chest. I wrapped my arms around him all the way and pulled him in close. My hand pressed against the small of his back. Not waiting for anything else, I bent my head down to his, and our lips met.

I'm not sure how long we stood there like that, but there was no rush to stop nor any embarrassment of an audience. I didn't care, and I don't think he did either. Our bodies only separated when the kiss came to its own natural end.

I reached down and grabbed his hand. Robbie turned and nodded for me to follow him toward 18th Street, guiding me with a soft tug.

We held hands for a few blocks down 18th Street and headed in the direction of Dolores Park. At some point, I let go and put my arm around him. It was cold, and I wanted to keep us both warm, plus I needed to feel his body pressed against mine. We spoke softly about his night and my night and my trip and the construction at Dolores Park. Ben, with the missing guitar string, was asleep in a stairwell, I saw, his arm wrapped tightly around his guitar. I hoped he was warm enough. Robbie and I walked that way, through the foggy, cold San Francisco night until we came to his place.

It was my first time inside Robbie's place. The long narrow apartment was clean, organized, and warm. Like so many people on the peninsula, Robbie needed a couple roommates just to be able to afford to live in the city. There was a homey feel to the apartment, an easy comfort. His room was messy, the bed unmade, but it felt like a place I could spend days laying around, quietly talking and cuddling.

Everything was slow and gentle; everything. His body felt so good under me, then on top of me, and we came at the same time. No rushing to disengage, clean up nor get dressed. I stayed in him, and he laid down on my chest. We held each other like that for what seemed hours.

We did talk between sex that night. A little late, we had the discussion about HIV status, but it was good. Robbie rarely had sex without a condom, so he was concerned. I felt guilty because I knew he preferred to use a condom, and once again, we'd gone without. I let him know I was negative and tested, and was taking PrEP (more on this later). When I said this last part, I could see him physically relax a little. "But still . . ." he said, yet appearing much less worried.

We had sex three times that night. There was nothing wild and crazy about it. It was slow and gentle the entire time. I knew he liked wild and kinky, and so do I; that's one reason I always felt Tony and Robbie were such a mismatch, but every time I was with Robbie, we both seemed to guide sex to the slow and gentle, versus the wild.

We slept, Robbie in my arms, for a few hours before I felt I needed to go. Since Robbie worked late some nights, his body was used to sleeping past noon. My body's clock is set to wake at 6:00 a.m. every morning. We said a quiet, simple goodbye as he lay curled up in bed, and I asked if I could see him again before leaving for Seattle. Looking up at me with those dark brown eyes and scruffy face, he whispered back, "I'd love that." Robbie grabbed my head and pulled me in for one last, long kiss, then I dressed and quietly left his apartment.

My route back to my condo once again took me through Dolores Park. I grabbed a cup of coffee and climbed to the top of the park to sit in the grass and watch the sun rise over this city that was feeling more and more like home.

Part III
PRINCE CHARMING'S CRUMBLING CASTLE

Chapter 16
ROMANTIC LOVE

The bell tolls for traditional relationships, and you can hear it in the demographics. Attitudes are shifting faster than experts can write papers. Facebook and Match.com are giving us data that we never dreamed of before. Between those sites and the observational evidence from cities like San Francisco, the obituary is all but written.

How fast are these changes in relationships playing out? There's no doubt that the cultural normative of relationships is changing, and though it might not be changing as fast as Moore's Law, a premise that's held true since 1970 that computing power doubles every two years, it's nonetheless directly linked. The difference is, a "drag" factor, i.e. those partners stuck in a relationship have to wait for the bitter end before they have a chance to start over and explore a modern one.

The changes happen fast for new relationships, but take time to see in existing ones. A Sleeping Beauty romance isn't constantly reinventing itself, and society isn't starting from zero. Almost 60% of people are currently in relationships. In the case of traditional marriages, a spouse may stay in that dying, outdated structure for up to seven years, on average, fighting against the inevitable truth of its collapse.

It's impossible to gather statistics on the remaining 40% of "surviving" traditional marriages and their degree of happiness. It's equally impossible to believe a large share of those aren't marriages that are horrific and on the verge of failing all the time. Of the 40% of marriages that manage to survive, how many contain spouses too scared, too desperate, or too stuck to pull the plug? We may never know, but my bet is most.

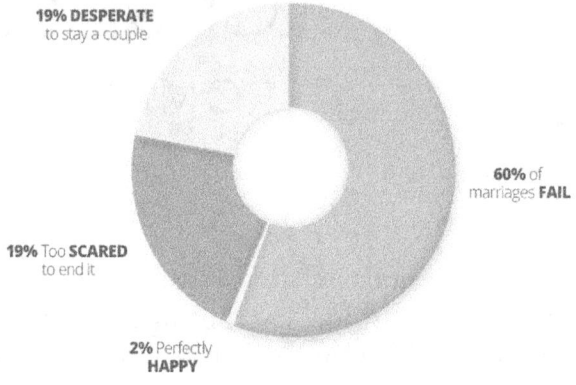

Figure 3 - How the other 40% lives

"But I'm happy!" and "my wife loves me!" you say. Who am I to disagree? No doubt there are marriages where both partners are equally, deliriously happy. I guess as a divorce lawyer, I don't see that crowd. Honestly, as a living breathing human, I don't see that crowd. I hear they exist, but as with Big Foot, I'm slightly skeptical they walk among us.

Much of what people may mourn in the death of traditional relationships is the unabashed fantasy. What they called "love" and "romance" was a farce, generated from fictional characters in a Disney movie programmed into their heads by societal expectations; but that fiction provided so much comfort! We felt the world was right in the realm of Disney, where all married couples are blissfully happy, in narrow black ties and blue checkerboard aprons. This is the castle Prince Charming built.

Prince Charming's beautiful castle, standing on a distant hazy hill, is a decrepit ruin when you get up close. What was once a bastion of strength and virility, and legitimately so, is now a pile of moss-covered rubble left to generations future for $2 tours. It's no longer occupied, alive, nor relevant.

This isn't to say traditional relationships didn't work for their time, they did. It was a necessary step, just like the budding modern structure is today, just as any step on the evolutionary path is necessary, no more right or wrong than another step along the path forward. The love affair in *Breakfast at Tiffany's* was exactly what the couples in that period in our history needed, and just as it's being replaced today, so too did it replace the paradigm before.

There will continue to be a "drag factor" between the existing, traditional relationships and the modern relationship structure replacing it, no matter how quickly things change. The traditional relationship structure will continue to exist as long as those relationships remain intact.

A question persists, does the modern structure now developing mean the end of love and romance? With sex so easy and relationships opening up, are love and romance being replaced by hedonism and promiscuity?

The short answer is, "No". Love and romance are alive and flourishing in the modern relationship. The difference is, couples who are in a romantic love stage of a modern relationship have fewer expectations of each other. I believe in adult love, especially within the modern relationship structure, and I believe people's feelings can be real, deep, and meaningful. It's romantic love that's evolving.

Like the "spark," much of what we call romantic love is manufactured and temporary. It comes from pure Disney fantasy. This fictional romantic love is a relic of the traditional relationship and comes from unreasonable expectations we place on potential partners. We paint the subject of our romantic love with our own colors, but sooner or later, their true colors shine through.

Reason and rational thought give way to emotional decision-making when you're in the grasp of romantic love. Brain science tells us romantic love is an irresistible drive like thirst. It's an illogical, irrational craving for a specific person. Without the guidance of rational, logical thought, it's easy to "lose control" in the early stages of a relationship.

My English literature professor once posed the question, was Romeo and Juliet ironic comedy? Was Shakespeare, in fact, making fun of romanticism by telling such a ridiculously over the top story of love at first sight that eventually destroyed everyone around it?

As in Romeo and Juliet, romantic love's external presentation can be ridiculous and sometimes even dangerous. From couples wearing each other's clothes (gay world, obviously), a sudden conversion to a football fan, or returning to a physical abuser; we observers can only stand on the side and shake our heads, relegated to waiting for a chance to help the deluded friend come back to the rational world. Being blinded by the obvious is the best indication of romantic love.

What constitutes romantic love? How is it distinguished from infatuation? One definition says romantic love is the addition of drama to a relationship of deep and strong love. Another defines it as "when the chemicals in your brain kick in and you feel an emotional high, exhilaration, passion, and elation when you and your lover are together." Or, as a Facebook friend of mine said when I asked him:

> When you love someone, you give everything
> without thinking twice, deny the truth, believe
> in lies, do crazy things that you can't explain
> and you cry over things that hurt you but still
> stay and say "I'm great!"

Most of the time, the intensity of romantic love tends to last somewhere from six months to two years before turning into adult attachment if it survives at all. This holds true within the modern relationship as well.

In her book, *Love and Limerence,* Dorothy Tennov tries to answer the question of what distinguishes romantic love from mature love. She differentiated between "love" that's a sincere concern and caring emotion (true love) and "love" that's fiery, euphoric, and ephemeral (romantic). In the process of her research, she discovered there's something irrational and complex about the romantic kind of love.

Tennov coined the phrase "limerence" for romantic love so she could discuss it separate from true "love". You see this phrase in much of the research on the topic of romantic love, still. She defined true love as an emotion, a feeling from the inside which is acted upon by the lover, while "limerence" is a transitional state a person enters.

She interviewed hundreds of people for her research and put together a list of identifying characteristics of romantic love:

- Intrusive thoughts about the object of passionate desire
- Acute longing for reciprocation
- Mood becomes dependent on the other's actions
- Inability to react limerent toward more than one person at the same time
- Unsettling shyness and fear of rejection when in the presence of the other
- Intensification through adversity
- Acute sensitivity to any act or condition that could be interpreted as favorable
- An aching of the "heart"
- Buoyancy or a feeling of "walking on air"
- An intensity of feeling that leaves other concerns in the background
- A remarkable ability to emphasize the positive traits of the other, while rendering the other's negative traits as "endearing"

A lover in the throes of romantic love needs to be with his or her lover all the time and will overlook faults, conflict, alcoholism, and abuse. A lover in romantic love feels like he's in the middle of the most unique, rapturous experience in the world and his partner is "the most incredible man" he's ever met.

Over time, though, the illusion frays and the true nature of their fantastical new boyfriend fades. The romantic love phase of their relationship is declining/wearing off and a nagging sense of disillusionment sets in.

At this stage, a couple becomes more critical of each other and easily irritated by things that didn't bother them before. Prince Charming has less patience with Cinderella's demands for attention and time and may be indifferent to her feelings. Cinderella is tired of Prince Charming putting his dishes into the sink, throwing his clothes onto the floor, and drinking too much.

The collapse of romantic love is nicely scripted out by our culture; the initial "spark," the honeymoon phase, the ensuing anxiety and self-consciousness, intense distraction and euphoria, capped off by a devastating disillusionment.

The tragedy of our cultural understanding of romantic love is that it makes us place unreasonable expectations on our romantic partners because we believe that they have "the responsibility for making our lives whole . . . making our lives meaningful, intense, and ecstatic," says Tennov. This burden is simply too much for a partner, and over time, wears him into anger and frustration; too much pressure on a relationship and something's gonna give.

Research shows that when we're in the state of romantic love, we're consumed by a fantasy we've created consistent with the expectations laid upon us by society. Our romantic partners are idealized, God-like versions, disconnected from the reality of who they are, giving us a sense of euphoria. We've finally found our perfect soulmate!

The fundamental problem with romantic love is that it can never result in a truly human relationship as long as it continues to exist in the world of fantasy. It can't become anything else until reality is accepted and the fiction crumbles. Until then, we're only in love with a fantastical creation, not a real person on the other side of the string of spaghetti.

Prince Charming's tale of romantic love is just as illusory as his beautiful castle on the hazy hill. While romantic love continues within the structure of the pyramid, the fictional aspirations of Prince Charming's story line aren't the same for modern relationships. Romance and love endure and always will. Today, however, they're becoming detached from marriage and monogamy.

After twenty years as a divorce lawyer, my answer to the English Literature professor's question is "yes," even if Shakespeare didn't intend on Romeo and Juliet being a comedy for the wise, it certainly turned out that way.

Chapter 17
ESCAPING TONY AND MEETING RICH

The morning after Tony cheated on me with my friend Mark, I was in pretty bad shape. I opened myself up to Tony and fell hard for him and when he rolled over in the morning and said, "I love you," even my toes tingled. Despite the fact that he cheapened the phrase, "the most incredible man I've ever met," by saying the exact same thing to Mark, it was forever etched into my head. I ridiculously still believed him. How naive of me to think that phrase was special when Tony was willing to say it to pretty much any beach boy who stumbled into his crosshairs, but there it is. Stupid me, I believed him.

That morning, while still debating whether to ever speak with him again, I drove out to SeaTac with the intention of catching a flight to LA. I'd texted an LA friend, Zoran, and told him what happened with Tony. Zoran demanded I get on the next flight and come forget about that "fucking ass-wipe". Zoran met Tony at the gym one day during a visit and was taken aback by how handsome he was. It's the same impression most people have when they first meet Tony. But for Zoran it evaporated within a few minutes of talking with him. Zoran, a talented screen writer, had only one word when we got back to my place, "vapid". I had to look it up.

I sat in front of the United ticket counter for hours as one flight to LA after another ticked off the departures screen. I knew if I got on a flight, I'd never speak with Tony again, and we'd be done. There was certainly something attractive about that idea, but I also knew if I left it unresolved, I'd hate him. It'd be impossible to see him in the gym or around town without grinding my teeth and wishing him harm.

My parents' divorce was horrific. It destroyed everything in its path, including the kids. When my dad got fired for fucking his secretary in his office, my family went from having almost everything we could want to living in a discount basement apartment hoping we had enough baloney left for dinner. We had nothing. Homelessness was just a few dollars away every month.

I watched my mother's hatred consume her. At first, it was just hatred for my dad, but as she aged that toxic emotion, tapped to give her security and a place in the world, was turned to others. It became her go-to response whenever she felt wronged. I don't blame my mother for having this human response; times were different, and the expectations she had for marriage were the foundation of everything in her life, but I knew I couldn't live that way myself. I didn't want to feel hatred for anyone.

I never got on that flight, and I never did fly down to visit Zoran for a recovery weekend. Instead, I picked up my bag, went back to my car, and headed home. Later that afternoon, I finally responded to Tony's incessant texts and said, yeah, I'd meet him.

Living without hatred is one thing, but living happily is another. As the days turned into a week, then two, I was still distraught at being left behind, emasculated by Tony's deception. He was done with Mark, as I said earlier, the very next weekend, but he moved on to someone else promptly after. That one lasted another week, before yet another "most incredible man I've ever met" reared up. It was more than I could take. I had to leave town and escape this revolving door of substitutes, so I booked a last minute, solo trip to Puerto Vallarta for New Years Eve.

There are moments when life pivots. You're on one course and suddenly, something happens to shoot you off in another. Puerto Vallarta was that moment for me. I went out to SeaTac for my flight, defeated, timid, and unsure of myself. I came back a week later a new man. Life pivoted in a wonderful way, and at just the right moment.

It started when I boarded the plane and saw this big, handsome man I'd seen around Seattle sitting in first class. We made eye contact as I walked back toward the coach seats, and he smiled at me, checking me out. I smiled back and headed for my seat. He was one of those hot outdoors guys who never gave me the time of day, so I was a little surprised by his attention. I couldn't recall his name right then, but learned later it was Rich.

Maybe eight years had passed since I was last in Puerto Vallarta, and can't recall why I picked it as my escape, except that I knew it was a gay destination. On the last trip, my experience was limited to a gated community and a private beach, so this trip, Puerto Vallarta might as well have been a completely new destination. I was meeting no one there and don't recall hearing of anyone I knew going. As far as I knew, I was the only one of my friends down there for New Year's Eve. Perfect.

Since it was a last minute trip, I had to take what I could get. All the favorite gay, or gay-friendly, hotels were booked solid. The only place available was a nice gay-owned hotel, outside of Old Town a bit.

The place was nice, clean, and quiet. In fact, it was perfect. In hindsight, I couldn't have planned it any better. The hotel catered to an older gay crowd, and was removed from the center of Old Town, so I had my escape from the craziness when I needed it. My room was a large, homey suite that opened onto an outdoor courtyard with a pool surrounded by a garden. There was also a small pool on the roof. The bed was huge and comfortable, and the shower was a room all to itself with a domed ceiling.

I'm a beach person. I can sit on a quiet beach for the rest of my life and be perfectly content. Sign me up, man. So the first order of business, after dumping my things off at my new Puerto Vallarta home, was to head to the beach. I threw on my headphones, packed my backpack, stripped off my shirt, and headed out onto the streets of Puerto Vallarta looking for a place called "Blue Chairs".

Every gay man who's been to Puerto Vallarta knows about Blue Chairs. Ask them what it is, though and you'll probably get different answers. Some will say it's a bar on the beach, others a hotel. Some will say it's a bar on top of the hotel and still others will tell you it's the palapas in front of a hotel, where all the chairs are blue!

On this trip, I had no idea which was correct, but I vaguely understood that it was a place on the beach with blue chairs where all the gay men hung out. Sounded like a perfect combination of my favorite things. Since it had to be on the water somewhere, I walked out of my hotel and followed the streets down the hill to the beach. I'd figure it out from there.

Lucky for me, I turned left at the ocean and headed south down the beach, which coincidentally happened to be the correct direction for Blue Chairs. It felt amazing to be walking in the sun, on a beach, with all this activity going on, in a new and foreign place.

CeeLo Green was singing along in my headphones, empathizing with my feelings about being dumped; "you're driving 'round town with the girl I love and I'm like fuck you and fuck her too." Yeah, maybe not the most positive message, but it made me feel more in control of my life at that particular moment. I'd move on to Adele in a bit, and she could sing to me about rolling in the deep.

Some people cringe at the idea of traveling alone. These people must be extroverts, drawing energy from groups or perceive security in numbers. Not me; I'm totally recharged by traveling alone, using my life skills to negotiate a new place and discover what it's all about. I don't fear for my safety. It's not because I'm a big guy and can "take care of myself." I simply feel that fate will direct me, and if it's my time to go, then so be it. Until then, life's an amazing adventure, and it awaits in the narrow winding streets of places like Puerto Vallarta.

It turns out Blue Chairs isn't where all the gay men hangout. That's the green chairs next to the blue chairs. I learned later on that the bar running the real Blue Chairs started charging to sit there, so people moved over to the green chairs next door where they don't. Sure enough, that's where all the men were too.

By the time I got down to the beach it was already after 5:00 p.m., but I found a place under a palapa, and made myself at home. Stripping down to a speedo, pulling off my shirt, I put this triathlon-trained, muscled physique to work. I now had the attention of the men in my neck of the beach.

Quickest way to meet men? Open up Grindr. I did. It was, and I did.

First, I met up with Isaac from NYC, a dark haired, fit 23-year-old staying nearby, then I grabbed some dinner on the plaza, alone, and pulled out Grindr again. This time, it was Sam from LA who was here with his boyfriend. We had to make sure the boyfriend was preoccupied before we headed up to his room. Afterwards, I didn't feel like trudging all the way back to my hotel, so I decided to check out the bar on top of the Blue Chairs hotel, which, I discovered, really did exist.

Turns out it's a strip club some nights, with some athletic local men walking around in nearly nothing. There was a big crowd with plenty of attractive guys, including Rich, from my flight earlier in the day. We made eye contact and he smiled, so I made my way over to where he was sitting and introduced myself.

"I know who you are," he said. "You almost got my cats killed today."

"What?"

"Yeah. Don, the guy who's watching my house while I'm down here has a crush on you. I texted him this morning and told him you were on my flight. He said if I slept with you he was gonna kill my cats!" He started laughing.

"Oh shit!" I laughed back. I was a little embarrassed that I didn't know this guy Don. I immediately pictured some crazy troll-looking man standing there petting these cats, mumbling "my precious!"

The threat didn't phase Rich; that, or he didn't care about his cats anyway. We stayed at his place that night.

Chapter 18
WHY MONOGAMOUS RELATIONSHIPS ARE FAILING

Nothing happens in a vacuum. With the failure rate of traditional marriages continuing to climb and monogamy becoming less of a vow and more of an option, we're forced to ask "why?"

Some theories point to the economy. Some argue Millennials don't feel the same societal pressure to marry. Still others suggest that the younger generations simply don't need marriage anymore, instead choosing to cohabitate.

Adults are also marrying later in life, and the shares of adults cohabiting and raising children outside of marriage have increased significantly. The median age at first marriage is now 27 for women and 29 for men, up from 20 for women and 23 for men in 1960. Additionally, 24% of never-married young adults ages 25 to 34 are living with a partner.

These powerful statistics don't answer the "why" question; they just continue to demonstrate the magnitude of the cultural shift. I believe that to answer the "why" question we need to look at three things that provide strength to a traditional relationship, compare those same factors in a modern relationship, identify the differences, then look for causation.

Watching thousands of traditional relationships fail, teaching several courses on managing conflict during a divorce, and mediating these relationships to an agreeable, but rarely amicable, conclusion, led me to the conclusion that relationships survive only when all three of the following conditions exist:

- Absence of alternative partners
- Satisfaction of expectations
- Emotional investment

If a relationship lacks one or more of these three things, then I expect to see one of the spouses walking into my office sooner rather than later. Without these three elements a relationship lacks the ability to survive long-term.

To get to the bottom of the "why" question, we first need to compare these three factors in the traditional relationship against the same factors in a modern relationship.

AVAILABLE ALTERNATIVES

Chapter 19

AVAILABLE ALTERNATIVES AND BACKUP PLANS

The greater the availability of alternative partners, the more likely the relationship is to fail. Put your partner in the middle of the Castro on a Friday night, and you might be in trouble; dinner at the Steak 'n Shake in Gainsville and I'd bet you're pretty safe, except from heart disease.

If a person exists in an environment of constant temptation, where alternative partners are always presenting themselves, it's not surprising that some cave. As the fantasy of romantic love fades and reality settles in, the disillusioned partner's needs can be met through easily available alternatives.

This is exactly what social media sites like Facebook, promise, not constant temptation so much as a constant, casual reminder that alternatives exist. Even the Steak 'n Shake in Gainsville becomes a threat when the iPhone is whipped out and Facebook opened. "Can't find a better man," the Pearl Jam song goes, but with social media, she always can, even in a swamp.

A recent study by researchers at the University of Indiana found that Facebook users in relationships frequently use the social media site to keep in touch with "backups"; exes or friends they could potentially connect with romantically, should their current relationships go south. These researchers found that the practice is widespread among both genders, but that men have "backups" at roughly twice the rate of women. On average, over half of respondents who are already in relationships said they were having romantic or sexual conversations with at least two other people besides their current partner. So prevalent is the use of social media to find alternative partners, sex researchers have recently begun to treat "remote infidelity," aka emotional cheating, via social media, as a valid topic of research.

A not-so-scientific survey of 1,000 married women conducted by the *Daily Mail* found that 50% have a "fall-back partner" should their current marriage take a turn for the worse. In fact, 10% of participants said their backup guy had previously confessed his love, and 20% claimed the guy would "drop everything" to be with her, if she asked.

So who exactly is Plan "B"? Who are these men and women acting as "backups"? The most common backup husbands tend to be old friends with romantic intentions, ex-boyfriends, ex-husbands, colleagues, or someone from the gym. Backups tend to be close already, instead of random contacts from your friends list on Facebook, but the rapidly growing trend is that more and more of these relationships are developing from purely social media contacts.

People who use social media and cellphones have much larger personal networks than people who don't. A person can have thousands of friends on Facebook, following them on a daily basis, picking and choosing which to chat with, comment on their photos, or simply "like" something they post. These simple "touches" foster relationships that would otherwise die between exes, former lovers, or "near-misses."

Also, this vast reservoir of alternatives provides greater opportunity to develop a new, perhaps fantastical relationship with someone interesting, in addition to sustaining pre-existing relationships. These new relationships can be highly fantasized due to the limited information available on the prospect and the inherent distance of chat as communication; fantasy is easy when reality is in a galaxy far, far away.

Even though a recent study, published in the journal *Proceedings of the National Academy of Sciences*, says that 35% of married couples now report meeting their spouse online, Facebook is also blamed for causing 20% of breakups in the United States and 33% in the United Kingdom; and that's only one source of social media. The availability of an alternative or backup, is a primary factor in the eventual end of a traditional marriage or relationship.

"Digital cheating" is a modern twist to the oldest story. The difference is, the availability of alternatives is pervasive, thanks to technology. Where before your pool of alternative partners was limited to arm's reach, like the people at the bar, now availability is virtually limitless. Before online social media, like Facebook, Tinder, and Scruff, allowed us to find friends, special friends, tricks, and husbands with a few strokes on a keyboard, an elaborate courting process required us to dress up, wear some nice cologne, buy the guy at the bar a drink and practice clever pickups lines. Our pool of possible lovers was limited to those sitting to our left or our right.

Now though we can mass-flirt by posting a shirtless selfie of ourselves playing with the dog just to prove we actually have personality and not be so obviously narcissistic. This shirtless selfie substitutes for the former cruising go-to, "Can I buy you a drink?" Since these practiced selfies hit thousands of potential candidates, they're much more efficient at giving you alternatives to choose from.

Social media is breaking down monogamy and traditional relationships by giving people so many choices and so much power to flirt. Everywhere you look, there's a hotter, younger, more sexual alternative. How's a man supposed to concentrate on his boyfriend, Prince Charming, when he could upgrade to Tarzan at any minute?

Then again, maybe Prince Charming needs his whiskey-drinking, football-watching ass dumped. Maybe a woman wants more from life than the Steak 'n Shake in the middle of a swamp.

Maybe having alternatives offered up by Facebook and other social media sites and having a Plan "B" can actually be a good thing for a partner trapped in a fiction, a fantasy, or held prisoner in bleak and abusive relationship.

Is there an upside to having a Plan "B" in the modern relationship?

Chapter 20
PUERTO VALLARTA - LANCE & GREG

Rich and I were sexually incompatible, but that week, we were perfectly compatible to take over the aptly named Romantic Zone of Puerto Vallarta. By 3:00 p.m. the next day, we had a new group of friends from all over hanging out with us on the beach; Chris from Chicago, a disarmingly handsome dermatologist with a quick and biting sense of humor, Octavio who owned one of the local restaurants with his partner, Greg and Lance, a couple from San Francisco, who were both total sex pigs intent on hooking up with as many guys as they could, Alán from Montreal and Ivan from DC, two circuit queens who just started dating a month ago after meeting at Miami White Party, and finally Eric who was US citizen living in PV helping run some of the clubs.

Each person took a different path in joining our group that day, but we were fast friends. I ran into Eric at the gym in Seattle just last week, and I've stayed in touch with each of the others over the years. Rich and I have gone back to Puerto Vallarta together twice so far.

That week, we took Puerto Vallarta by storm. We got the best spots on the beach, had the stage at the dance clubs, danced in the shower at Wet, the gay strip club, and laughed ourselves silly at the Blue Chairs happy hour on top of the hotel.

Everything was easy and nothing forced. Somebody would suggest something, like going to Fuego for some food and drinks after the beach, and most everybody would say, "Sure!" Going out clubbing, someone would suggest a time and a place and everyone would be up for it. We all danced together, in the same area on the dance floor, but it was never a closed group, and people were constantly coming and going and doing their own thing.

I was hanging out with Lance from San Francisco one afternoon under our palapa on the beach. Lance worked for Steve Jobs' charitable foundation, giving away the billionaire's money to worthy causes. Jobs was private about the causes he supported, so Lance couldn't give me any details, but what a great profession! Imagine the difference this guy was making!

Lance was about 38, tall and muscular, but lean, with more of a runner's build. Handsome in the way I picture a volleyball player; smooth, strong, preppy. Greg was dark, scruffy, stocky, 32, and tall. I found him to be sexy both in looks and mannerisms. They lived in an area called SOMA, "close to the gay bars" but at that time I had no idea what any of that meant. The city was a complete mystery to me. For example, I didn't know San Francisco is situated on a peninsula, and I'm embarrassed to say, thought it was an island. It's not.

Lance and Greg met five years ago on Facebook, while Greg was dating someone else. Both lived in San Francisco at the time and had friends in common, but had never met in person. Getting to know each other was a sticky situation when they first met because Greg's partner at the time was abusive and violent. The guy was controlling and prone to random outbursts. Lance told me Greg got hit with a pan one time because he put the dishes in the wrong place in the cabinets.

Over the span of a few months, their online chat turned to friendship, turned to interest, and finally touched on intimacy. They managed to start seeing each other, tenuously at first, without hooking up, in secret, stolen moments throughout the day, and never at night. Greg was desperate to get away, but he had no family in San Francisco, and his abusive partner made sure he didn't have any close friends to turn to. In desperate moments, Greg thought about suicide but told Lance he was just too scared to go through with it. He was still only 27 years old.

Lance is a smart man. He opened himself up to Greg and made himself available to help as a friend. He didn't tell Greg he had to get out. He didn't judge Greg by asking "why do you let him do this to you?" Lance just listened, supported, and made himself available 24/7 no matter what.

One morning at about 3:00 a.m. Greg showed up banging on Lance's door, crying. The abuser had just beaten him. Bleeding from a cut on his head, his eye was so swollen that only a sliver of red around a pupil was visible. He could barely talk and collapsed onto Greg's floor crying uncontrollably.

Apparently they'd gone to a fancy dinner for date night, dressed in tuxedos, with champagne and roses. During dinner, the abuser thought Greg was overly attentive to the waiter. He played along, biding his time to 'get even' with Greg for what he'd done. It wasn't until they walked through the front door that he made Greg pay.

As soon as the front door closed, there was a flurry of punches. Greg was shoved to the ground and beaten with a closed fist, then a book, and finally a tennis racquet. It only came to an end when the abuser fell down the stairs while swinging the racquet so wildly it unbalanced him. Tumbling down the stairs, the abuser injured his ankle and couldn't stand back up. Even though Greg was a bloody mess, he took his chance to dodge past the abuser who was lying at the foot of the stairs, fled the house, and drove away.

Lance wanted to call the police and take Greg to the hospital, but Greg didn't want either one and begged Lance not to involve the police. Conceding for the time being, Lance asked if he could have a doctor friend come over and check Greg out, just to be sure there were no major injuries. Greg agreed. Lance contacted his doctor friend, Russ, at 4:00 a.m. and said he needed help right away, only briefly explaining the facts. Russ was there in fifteen minutes.

Russ cleaned Greg up and bandaged the cuts on his head and face. He gave Greg some pills to help him relax. Lance didn't want to leave him out of his sight, so Greg was laid down on the living room couch. It was now 7:00 a.m.

At this point, you might want Lance to jump into his car and beat the holy hell out the abuser. You might want Lance to disregard Greg's desire to keep the police out of it and call them on his own. You might want Russ to insist on a visit to the hospital. I don't disagree with you one bit and, at least about beating the fuck out this abuser, I don't think you could've talked me out of it.

Lance is smarter than I, though. He talked with Russ about the injuries, and they took pictures while Greg slept. Russ made extensive notes. Lance called another friend, Andrew, whom he knew worked at the Riley Center, a well known San Francisco program for survivors of domestic violence. Keep in mind what Lance does for a living, and who he works for. Andrew was there within the hour.

Andrew, Russ, and Lance sat in the kitchen, while Greg slept on the couch, and they talked about what they could do. It sounds callous to say they "came up with a plan," but, between these three smart, caring minds, they decided on a strategy to help Greg, and it worked.

Hours later, when Greg woke up, he was feeling better, but terribly sore all over. He couldn't move off the couch. Lance and Russ made an excuse of going to the store to get some food and more medical supplies, and they left Andrew to do his job.

Andrew is an expert, Lance told me, as he teared up on the beach that day. This is what Andrew does day in and day out; such delicate, caring, and supportive work.

After a couple hours, Andrew texted Lance and said he and Russ could come back. The police were on their way over.

The next call Lance made was to Steve Jobs' personal lawyer.

The police officers entered a protection order on the spot. The abuser was arrested an hour later. Greg was able to make it to the hospital later that day. Lance kept Greg surrounded by supporters for a solid week.

The next week, Greg, Lance and three police officers conducted a "civil assist," and Greg got all his things out of the house. He never went back, and he never saw the abuser again.

The nature of humanity is described by our flaws, but the expression of humanity stands in our compassion.

Chapter 21
HEDGING YOUR BETS

There are many reasons for keeping an available alternative in the "green room," so to speak, waiting for his or her chance to get onto the main stage. People have a Plan "B" for one of four reasons:

- Unsure of their partner's commitment
- Believe partner may not be faithful
- Enjoy flirting
- Lack of a feeling of value

If a partner or spouse has cause to doubt the commitment of his partner, he may be inclined to seek out the security of another, perhaps more committed, lover and hedge their bets against the loss of the primary relationship. A Plan "B" provides security in the event his fears are realized, and the other partner breaks up with him. This way, a partner can minimize the potential heartache if he gets dumped. A supply of Plan "B" prospects eliminates the need of total commitment to the 'one'.

Similarly, if one partner feels the other is inclined to be unfaithful, he may likewise want to insulate himself from the shame and embarrassment of being told that someone else is better. The reassurance he gets from his Plan "B" partner that he's amazing, handsome, and desired, may help him realize he can do better too.

Conversely, he may feel his partner is getting all the fun, and he don't want to be left out. Studies show men are more likely to cheat on their partner, and at the same time expect their partner to be faithful. "I know he's cheating on me already, so why not do it too?"

Men and women both love to flirt. Flirting can make you feel sexy and wanted. The compliments and attention can do wonders for your ego. Maybe your partner is neglecting you or not affirming you in ways that make you feel special. If you start chatting with the amazingly sweet guy in Chicago, you're bound to feel better. Even if it's not a sexual relationship, the partner would at least appreciate the fact that someone admires or wants to flirt with him.

Both spouses need to feel valued in a relationship, but sometimes that doesn't happen. Sometimes a backup lover is more romantic than the partner, and sometimes the backup lover is more charming, caring, romantic, and persuasive as well, and this makes the partner feel valued and desired.

Plan "B" partners aren't merely short-term sex partners. A Plan "B" partnership isn't an affair. This backup relationship is in a separate category and is viable as a serious partner in his or her own right. An affair is an attempt to fill a need missing from the primary relationship. Plan "B", on the other hand, has the capacity of a full-on replacement of the primary relationship. Unlike marriages, where one may take a lover to fulfill sexual needs the spouse cannot or will not provide, a backup lover arises from fear of rejection and a desire to have something ready to replace the failing primary relationship.

Typically, there's a big distinction between the romantic love a partner may have for a Plan "B" lover, and the deep feelings of love and trust someone may feel for his partner. Both are forms of love, but are associated with different brain responses and hormones. Plan "B" relationships start as romantic love relationships, fleeting and based in fantasy.

It's possible for a person who's truly and deeply 'in love' with his partner to find himself falling in romantic love with someone else.

Chapter 22
ALÁN & IVAN

New Year's Eve is a huge night out in Puerto Vallarta. Fireworks, parades, dancing in the streets; this place knows how to throw a big party. What's normally a relatively sleepy little vacation spot turns the speakers up full blast for the week of New Year's Eve.

The big night rolled around, and my group of new friends decided to meet at La Noche for drinks at 10:00 p.m., then make our way to Mañana for the rest of the night. La Noche is a trendy cocktail bar in Old Town, usually too small for all the people wanting to get in.

The bar was crowded, as men of every variety piled in for cocktails. Some would later head out dancing, others would head to the pier to watch fireworks, and still others would find a hot guy to take home and spend the night with. Since it was their biggest night of the year, the staff was busy trying to push as many drinks across the bar as possible, and the dancers were busy working the crowd for tips.

Our group of ten arrived in pieces and parts, and we staked out a spot by the front door near a couch. I had my eye on the couch, currently occupied by a loud and obnoxious group of Jersey Shore gays I'd spotted on the beach earlier. My bet was they wouldn't last long at La Noche and were destined for other, more glitzy venues.

I ended up crammed into a little space near the front window with Alán and Ivan, the two circuit queens who just met in Miami a month ago. Alán is 29, dark, trimmed beard, about 6' ft, with a moderately nice build, but softer. He's more into softball, watching hockey, and drinking scotch than he is about getting into the gym. Alán worked in pharmaceutical sales. For months before, he was planning on coming down to Mexico with a group from Montreal. When he and Ivan had their "spark" last month on the dance floor of White Party, Ivan was a quick add.

Ivan is 27, sandy blond and scruffy, shorter, about 5'7, with a football player's build and ridiculously handsome. When muscular and handsome Ivan walked around the beach in his white speedo, the crowd parted, mostly because of his abs, but also because of the nice budge in his speedos. He worked as an administrative assistant at a vet clinic in DC. Needless to say, Alán was picking up the tab for this trip.

Octavio, the Puerto Vallarta local in our group, told me Alán and Ivan ended up together in Miami when their two groups of friends converged on the dance floor at White Party. Ivan spotted Alán across the dance floor and was instantly in love. Romeo and Juliet spent the rest of the party holding hands and strolling around the beach, only stopping to cuddle for a few hours. No sex that night, but Alán drove Ivan to the airport for his flight early the next morning, and they decided they'd try to see each other in the next couple weeks. Alán had chocolate-covered strawberries delivered to the vet clinic the very next day.

Romantic love at first sight; they were ridiculously swept away by each other. In Puerto Vallarta, they were always holding hands on the beach or sitting in one chair together, other times cuddled up on a blanket. It was odd they wanted to spend time with our group at all, but they were fully engaged and even flirting with others. I felt a like a prop for Ivan's Facebook wall, though, with a constant feed of highly orchestrated "candids".

We weren't the only audience for their storybook romance, as I quickly discovered when my phone started lighting up every few minutes. Ivan's iPhone was busy snapping euphoric selfies for his five thousand Facebook friends, and every time I was tagged in one of the group photos from the beach, my phone vibrated every ten seconds with comments and likes. "OMG!", "I'll be the meat in that sandwich," "You guys are totes adorbs," and at least twenty friend requests from strangers.

Standing in La Noche with them while they held hands, sneaking kisses now and then, wasn't just uncomfortable; it was annoying as fuck. I felt like a third, and not in a good way.

That night, Alán was wearing black jeans, boots, and a gray t-shirt with a cool looking logo for "Club Athletique Mansfield" splashed across it. It was nice and tight, and he looked good. Ivan was wearing tight Diesel jeans, a tight, plain white muscle shirt, and a US flag-turned-bandana wrapped around his head. There was no guessing about what Ivan had under his shirt, and I could see his religion through his jeans.

"You guys like your place?" I asked. They were staying at a condo in Old Town with Alán's friends from Montreal.

"Yeah, it's nice. Great location. It's close to the bars and the good restaurants. I like that we don't have to walk too far for anything," said Alán with his French accent. "It has its own pool, hot tub, security, and a chef."

"Damn! Sounds amazing. How'd you guys find it?" I asked.

"VRBO. One of the other guys arranged for it. I gave him money when he asked, then it was done!"

"Did you guys hear that music on the beach today?" said Ivan, turning away from the crowd to face Alán and me. "I mean what the fuck was that? That DJ sucked. I wish he'd played more industrial stuff, you know, after-hours music. That's what everybody wants to hear."

I thought the music was pretty good at Blue Chairs, given it was just a beach DJ, and there wasn't a dance floor in sight, but I figured I'd be agreeable.

"Yeah, it was crazy." Just a bone. "I bet there's better music tonight at Mañana. I guess they brought in a DJ from Mexico City who's supposed to be pretty good. What kind of music do you like, Alán?" I said, trying to play the middle by bringing Alán back into the conversation.

"Umm, well, I pretty much listen to everything, Adele, Rihanna, Eminem, Journey, you know, stuff like that." He was struggling to even come up with those names. "Pretty much whatever they play at the clubs." His French Canadian accent made him so much sexier.

I'm not a big clubber and couldn't be mistaken for a circuit queen, but I'm not sure I'd ever heard Journey played at a gay dance club. Yeah, a safe bet there.

"You go out dancing much in Montreal?" I asked, knowing the answer. "I've got a friend who bartends at one of the dance clubs there and he says it's a great scene."

"Sometimes, but not often," Alán said, as he put his arm around Ivan and pulled him close. "Montreal doesn't have a good nightlife I think. You?"

"Me? No, I'm not a clubber at all. I'll go out to the neighborhood bars sometimes, but mostly to watch football or hockey." I made an educated guess at Alán's real interest and apparently nailed it.

"You like hockey?" he said and removed his arm from around Ivan. "I've had Canadiens tickets since I was 21!" the French accent becoming more pronounced.

"Yeah, man! How can I live in Seattle and not be a fan? I've followed the Canucks since before I could walk. Grew up with names like Kirk McLean and Pavel Burel. I'm hoping one day Seattle is gonna get its own team. There's been talk for years now."

"Hmm. The league is so damn tight with the expansions. I was surprised when . . ." he started. I never got to find out what surprised Alán.

"I always heard the clubs down here were bigger," interrupted Ivan. "Everybody always talks about how fun it is, but everything is so small. Is Mañana the same size as this place, do you know?" It wasn't malicious, like he was trying to cut off our conversation; he just wasn't paying attention to what we were talking about, or, I suppose, to the fact that Alán and I were talking at all.

"I was there last night before I met you guys at Wet, and yeah, it's huge. It's got a big open area in the middle with this pool right next to the dance floor," I said, curious that Ivan didn't even notice he'd interrupted us. "Kind of a stupid place to put a pool, but it's unique!"

Done with me, Ivan turned to check out the crowd again, looking pensive. I figured I should try and bring him into a conversation.

"You always lived in DC?" I asked him.

"Huh? No, I was born in Connecticut but lived most of my life in Cincinnati, until I came out to my girlfriend and she kicked me out," he offered up. Now it was my turn to take the bait.

"What? You dated a girl? How'd that happen? What'd you do when she kicked you out?" I said with a look of shock and disbelief. Just give me my Oscar now.

"Yeah, we were together two years. I just sat her down one day and said, look I'm gay. She threw things, tore up all our pictures, then told me to get out. I stayed with my dad for a few weeks, but I didn't have a job then, so he only let me stay for a bit. I had a gay friend I met on Grindr, who lived in DC, and when he heard what happened he offered to let me stay with him." Yeah, I bet he did.

"Damn, man! That's a lot of change all at once. How'd you hold up? Most people have a hard enough time just coming out; forget about trying to find a new place to live." That was only partially true. Coming out usually precipitated a wide range of major changes in a person's life, but this was Ivan's story.

"Hard as fuck. I never lived anywhere else, so it was pretty scary to try and find a place. The guy in DC put me up for a few months and helped me get a job," he said. I wondered what a couple months was. I also wondered what his Grindr buddy was more interested in; sex, friendship, or something more. I thought I'd tease that out.

"Where did you guys live in DC? I've been there a few times and loved the city. What's your buddy's name?" i.e. What's the lifetime of a Grindr buddy's patience?

He looked away with a flash of irritation and adjusted the ridiculous US-flag-turned-bandana. "Yeah, I don't live with him anymore. We don't talk. I'm in Georgetown with a friend from work now. He's actually my boss."

There's the pattern. Ivan needs someone to take care of him. First his girlfriend, then his dad, then his Grindr buddy, and now his boss. Batter up, Alán.

"Fuck, man. Nice to have friends, huh?" I said with all seriousness. Ivan went back to checking out the crowd, bouncing to the background music.

"How old were you when you came out?" I asked, turning to Alán.

"Oh, I came out while I was studying for my masters, so 22. It was pretty uneventful. My parents were totally okay, and my sister was excited!" he laughed. "She said she'd always known. I began dating right after I came out, but there wasn't so much time with trying to get through school. The guy I dated didn't want to wait around, so . . ." He spread his hands. "Coming out in Montreal is different I think because . . ." I never got to hear why Montreal was different.

"Hey! Let's take a picture!" Ivan blurted out. "Come on. Dave, you stand next to me . . . wait, let's get the bar in the background. Hey, do you mind?" Ivan positioned Alán and me and interrupted the couple behind us, handing them his phone. "Thanks so much! Okay, I'm in the middle. Take a couple more just to be sure."

Phone back in his hand, Ivan set about the work of picking the best pic and posting it to Instagram. I was beginning to think this was a full-time job, by the way. He took great pictures, no doubt; Ivan always looked amazing. I braced myself for a new onslaught of friend requests and comments; "Take off that shirt!", "This picture is porn," "How come you haven't called me?"

Alán reached over to Ivan and gave him a starry-eyed kiss, and Ivan looked at him like he was about to cry.

I just wanted to puke.

"You guys look incredible together!" I said dryly, choking on each forced word.

Ivan disengaged with a huge smile, and said, "I know right? All my friends say the same thing!"

Okay Ivan, you win. I left to get a drink and made sure to walk around to the other side of our group on the way back.

Greg was sitting on the couch near the front when an attractive, young Mexican dancer wearing just a thong walked over to play with our group for a bit. He flirted around and made a few tips, but he seemed to like Greg. Appearing to move on to the next group, the stripper walked behind the couch, where Greg was sitting. Without Greg seeing, he pulled out his dick and balls and placed them on Greg's shoulder. Mid-sentence, Greg turned to see what was touching him and screamed like a sorority girl, jumping up and bolting across the couch.

I fell out of my chair laughing so hard. Greg's partner, Lance, sprayed his drink and started choking. Alán turned away and bent over double, and the crowd around us turned to see what all the commotion was about.

Greg only managed, "Oh my God!" for a few minutes, hand over his eyes, face red. His shock turned to embarrassment, then to laughter. The dancer laughed hysterically and was busy telling the other dancers in Spanish what had happened.

Ivan stood with a general smile but looked to have missed the whole joke, or maybe he was unnerved because the attention wasn't on him; just a guess.

Leave it to Ivan to tell us all it's time to ditch La Noche and head to Mañana. He was ready to go dancing and so, apparently, were we. Finishing off our drinks, we asked for our checks. Laughing about Greg's girlie scream at the sight of a fat, uncut dick, we made our way the two short blocks to Mañana.

Crowded! Sweaty! Loud! Shirtless hot men! Our group immediately headed for the center spot on the dance floor and made space. Shirts off and tucked away, music and lights doing their thing, we spent hours dancing and finding adventure on and off the dance floor. There were some seriously hot men spread around the crowd.

If there's one thing Ivan does well, it's dance, and he was getting plenty of attention. At first, he ignored the swarm of men as he and Alán continued their lusty stare off, bumping and grinding, but about five group pictures in, Ivan started looking around, and the crowd moved in for the kill.

I only partially watched, since I was busy with a tall, dark-haired guy, about 25, from Vancouver, wearing a Blue Jays baseball cap. He didn't talk much, but that was probably for the best. We snuck off to a dark corner at one point and made out pretty intensely. He was bigger than I, which frankly is rare, and I could tell he wanted to bottom. Sign me up.

Back on the dance floor, Ivan was moving around independently of Alán. He was quite a dancer, doing gyrations that left no doubt about how much time he spent at circuit parties. A few drinks, some music that he obviously approved of, and it was time to get on the box, so he did.

At gay dance clubs, sometimes there're boxes that act like one-man stages, scattered around the dance floor. Maybe there's just one, maybe more. Sometimes boxes are reserved for dancers/strippers and sometimes they're open to anyone. At Mañana that night, they were open to anyone. Ivan grabbed one and made it his stage. Alán was left to the side.

At first, Alán just danced with our group, looking mildly entertained, but I could see the anxiety building. I would have been pissed if the guy I was dating jumped onto a box and left me behind, so this whole thing was giving me anxiety, too. On top of that, Ivan was drawing the attention of the hottest guys at the club who were now in proximity to his box, giving him plenty of attention. No surprise that Ivan was loving the attention of these beautiful men. Honestly, though, who wouldn't? Ivan could pass as the hottest stripper in town.

It doesn't take a genius to predict what happened next. Rather than wait around for the uncomfortable shattering of a fantasy that was about to happen, I grabbed my Canadian and headed up to the deck above the dance floor overlooking the city. We made out, groping each other, getting hard and nearly breaking a few laws. Before it got that far, we decided to go to my place. He had roommates and was sleeping on the couch.

Heading back downstairs, I kept my eye open for someone from my group to let them know I was taking off. As luck would have it, I found Alán heading out of the club at the same time.

"Hey, bud! Where you going?" I said, pretty much knowing the answer.

"Just tired, man. I'm gonna head down to the beach for a bit before bed," he said, avoiding my eyes, trying to sound upbeat.

"Everything okay? Where's Ivan?" I asked, taking a quick look around, ignoring the obvious fact that Alán intended to leave without Ivan.

"Yeah. Everything's good. He's dancing with those guys from Austin." The Jersey Shore gays. He looked away, no doubt left about where this was going. "He can enjoy his night with the muscle guys," he said with a tinge of anger. Like I said earlier, Alán wasn't the most fit of guys. He played sports, but didn't work out regularly.

"Hang on just a second, Alán."

I glanced at my Canadian, who was starting to look impatient. Damn it. I was gonna have to send him on his way and hang out with Alán. I couldn't just leave Alán in this state, to walk along the beach alone at 5:00 a.m. I pulled Canadian aside and told him we couldn't hookup right now because I needed to take care of my friend. He seemed to get it but was obviously disappointed. We swapped numbers and made a vague promise to meet up later in the day. Canadian turned to go back to the dance floor.

"So what's going on, man?" I said to get Alán to start talking about whatever he felt like. We left the club, walked out into the street, and headed toward the beach.

"Just feeling pretty stupid right now," Alán mumbled back. "Guess I'm just not hot enough. Fuck, I'm really into him, Dave!

He's so fucking beautiful, and we click so well! What the fuck is
he doing? I know he loves me, but why does he do this shit?"

"He's done this before?"

"Yeah, seems like whenever we go out dancing. He's so popular
and usually knows everyone and look at him! He can get the
hottest guys to come over and start dancing," Alán said. "Every
time, afterwards, he tells me it's just dancing. I'm not interested
in any of them, he says. I believe him, but I get left, like tonight,
standing on the side of the dance floor holding everybody's
drinks!" he said, throwing his hands up in desperation. "It fucking
pisses me off!"

It looked like more than dancing to me, but I also didn't want
to be preachy or argumentative.

"Yeah, man, I'd be pissed, too. That sucks. Why'd you decide
to leave tonight?" We were walking through the empty central
market area, and there were only a few other people strolling
around. It was a nice, warm Mexican night, and I could hear the
ocean waves not too far off.

"Just couldn't stand there and watch it anymore," he said,
shaking his head. "I want to be the guy dancing with him out
there! Fuck! He just leaves me there, standing by myself. I bet he
still doesn't even know I left!"

I slowed for a second. "You didn't tell him you were leaving?"
This was going to be more drama than I expected. Sooner or
later, Ivan would figure out something was wrong, then he'd start
panicking. Well, most people would anyway. Ivan might just snap
a quick "sad-face" selfie and post it up to Facebook.

"No, I just decided to leave. He'll figure it out. I'm sick of
being treated this way. If he wants to hook up with the guys from
Austin, hey, go for it," he said, looking away, hiding his anger.

We walked on toward the beach and reached the promenade
along the water's edge. The promenade was crowded, with all
the clubs emptying out. I was starting to feel anxiety about
what was going to happen to these two when they got back to
their place. To change the subject away from Ivan, we stopped

at a taco truck and grabbed some food. I was starving, and there's just nothing in the world like a three-pack of chicken tacos off a Puerto Vallarta taco truck.

I think the tacos finished off Alán's night, and he abandoned his plan to walk along the beach. The sky was starting to get light, and the street cleaners were out in force, bringing the city back to stasis for another great day in paradise.

Alán's apartment was just up the street, and I was going to have to try and find a cab back to my little paradise. He offered to let me stay at his place, but that sounded like way too much work, plus I can only imagine what was waiting for him later.

We walked up to the building where his apartment was and said our goodnights. I gave him a big hug and told him if he needed anything to text me. Promises to see each other on the beach later on, I turned and started my hunt for a taxi. It was a beautiful morning, and I could see the waves crashing on the beach. The scene was so perfect, I sat on a small wall along the sidewalk and just watched the waves for a few minutes.

Just to see, I pulled out my phone.

"Yo Canada! You still up?"

He was.

SATISFACTION OF EXPECTATIONS

Chapter 23
CREATING EXPECTATIONS

I'm just guessing, but it looked to me like Ivan and Alán were a mismatch. Their circuit party romance created a world of fiction where fantasies about each other were allowed free reign. Each created a perfect person in their heads, custom tailored to fit what they perceived to be their own needs.

In their heads, everyone saw the same amazing love they saw. It's why Ivan and Alán couldn't help taking pictures of their romantic love and spreading the pictures far and wide. That way, everyone could witness the same beauty they saw; two beautiful soulmates, joined at long last, after a few inconvenient false starts with others.

Funny that each picture they posted to Instagram was two different pictures, one an expression of the deepest love the universe has ever created, seen only by Ivan and Alán; and the second, a semi-annoying, roll-your-eyes image that makes the rest of us wonder who they're trying to convince.

A strong relationship is based on reasonable expectations. In successful partnerships, the partners have a reality-based perception of each other and see each other for their flaws, their failings, as well as their positive side. The expectations come from an understanding of their humanity and their failings. With reasonable expectations, a spouse or partner can successfully satisfy the other partner's needs. If their needs are reasonable and their partner meets their needs, everyone is happy.

The problem is, the more modern people try and squeeze into the traditional paradigm, the less realistic the expectations are. The traditional expectations don't match up well with modern culture. The expectations from the previous generations aren't in line with today's expectations and, in an attempt to shoehorn a relationship, fantasy ensues.

The fundamental problem with fantasy relationships is the expectations the fantasy places on the partners. Fantasy relationships create unreasonable expectations for:

- How my partner will act
- How he will treat me
- His level of commitment toward me
- His life goals
- His belief system
- Where I fit into his life
- How he feels about family
- What he likes to do for fun
- His politics and faith

These worlds of fantasy are remarkably complete. They span so much more than just how a lover may feel about his new partner. They extend to the activities, locations, careers, and life goals. A partner imposes these expectations on the other partner to conform to their fantasy.

Conforming to the fantasy is impossible. You can fake it, like developing a Southern accent, but at the end of the day, you're a separate person, already shaped and molded. It's a sure sign of life in a fantasy land when so much of a person's character changes dramatically with their new "most incredible man."

Suddenly, basketball becomes the most amazing sport, ignoring the fact that you despised it the other twenty-something years of your adult life. A lifetime dream of moving to LA and living in Hollywood is thrown to the side as Oklahoma City becomes the capitol of culture, center of cinema, and just a darn good place to raise a family. Oh, and that degree in marketing?

Well, I'll get back to it after I get through every issue of *Good Housekeeping*.

The fantasy is pervasive and the expectations unsustainable.

You might have guessed by now, but I find this world of self-imposed fiction to be ridiculous. Despite my strongly held belief that these partners live in a fantasy world, I've also sometimes paused and wondered at how things look from the view of Prince Charming and Cinderella. If you stop to think about how they feel, and how the world looks to them, it's hard to argue that their happiness, the actual feeling they feel, isn't real.

Maybe at some deep level these deluded lovers know their relationship is based on unreasonable expectations of each other, but there's certainly no manifestation of that at the surface. Instead, it's all smiles and selfies.

Even though I might shake my head in disgust at the newest "This.is.the.life" picture of two mismatched lovers, I ask myself what am I missing?

"Is it better to be happy in a complete fantasy, or to see the fantasy for what it is and not be deliriously happy?"

I posed this question to friends and got some surprising answers back. The question goes to the heart of the type of relationship each one seeks.

Do you seek a Disney relationship with narrow black ties and blue checkered aprons, and to hell with the reality that my fictional Prince Charming is actually an alcoholic, dead-end couch potato? I'll take the damn hazy castle on the hill any day!

Or, do you think it's okay to "settle" for a real live man who's slightly shorter, snores, forgets my birthday sometimes, and leaves his dishes in the sink? It might not be a castle, but we have a nice view of the ocean, and it's close to a great coffee shop.

I began to wonder if the answer to this question gave insight about the success rate of my friends' relationships. Lexi, one of my closest friends whom I talk with every morning, has a pattern of pursuing men who won't commit emotionally or whom she can't have. Lexi would rather live happily in the fantasy. She believes the intensity of the fiction can be sustained indefinitely. Likewise, another close friend, Brian, whom I also talk with every day, voted for Prince Charming. Brian says that even a fictional relationship with such a great catch is better than "settling for reality".

In both cases, they tend to have the worst breakups. In Lexi's case, there's a repetitive track record of short, intense relationships where she convinces herself these unavailable men are actually available (and straight), including me!

This observation jives with my experience as a divorce lawyer, too. The more "amazing" and "incredible" the other person was, and the more talk about being soulmates, then the quicker the end comes. When I heard Katie Holmes say she and Tom Cruise would live forever in the honeymoon phase, I knew it was over. Her expectations just couldn't be met in the real world.

It still doesn't mean these lovers aren't in complete bliss while their fantasy is intact, though, and that's a pretty damn good feeling. I suppose that's why they do it. That feeling is completely legitimate and real. They truly feel blissful and that the world is perfect, at least for awhile. How can you not want to feel that way?

As with any drug, though, there's a hangover. Gotta pay the piper sooner or later, and when the fantasy comes crashing down, that's when I'm most happy I avoid fantasy relationships.

Relationships based on romantic love tend to come to a head at about six months, sometimes up to two years, according to the experts. Most fail. Incompatibility that leads to cheating, intolerance for character traits, repulsion of flaws or just general disillusionment are generally the common culprits. Essentially, when saying how amazing each other are gets old and the conversation is on autopilot, reality is setting in. Every conversation can't start with "you're the most incredible man I've ever met." Sooner or later you have to talk about the groceries, bills, and feeding the cat.

Still, those first six months must be pretty incredible.

Chapter 24
CHEATED

I'm no saint, and can't say I've never cheated on a partner. I have, several times. I'm not proud of the fact nor that I lied about it to someone who, reasonably or not, expected monogamy. Before I share this next story, then, I want to say up front that I don't fault Tony for having needs that I couldn't meet. I've walked in those same shoes, brother, and I can't pass judgment on you. That doesn't mean it didn't hurt, though.

It was Thanksgiving, and I rented a suite in Aspen for me and Tony, and a couple friends. This was while we were still dating, a real live couple, saying "I love you" and "you're the most incredible man I've ever met." All that good Disney shit.

There's usually no snow in Aspen that time of year, but we lucked out, and it dumped the week before. Parts of the mountain were open, and there weren't many people in town; perfect combination for a long weekend of awesome boarding.

The friends I invited up, Mark and Adam, were fun people, too. Mark and Adam lived in DC where they met three years ago. Adam was a former congressman who now worked on K-Street as a lobbyist for the pharmacy industry. He was 45, in great shape, and an amazing athlete. He'd come out late in life and had a family from a marriage that had ended after he left Congress.

Mark was a lawyer fresh out of law school, working for the State Department in the appellate division. He graduated in the top ten from Georgetown. Not only was he a smart, upcoming lawyer with a bright future, he was ridiculously handsome and funny, 27 years old, about six feet tall with a wrestler's hard body, dark-haired, and scruffy. Mark was always laughing and having a good time no matter what he was doing.

I met them at the Black Party in NYC a couple years ago. They were staying at the same hotel I was, and I found them on Scruff the day I checked in. We all three hook up, then hung out for most of the rest of the weekend. It was a blast going to the Black Party with these two since they were as much into the leather scene as I was and were equally uninhibited, but what happens at Black Party, stays at Black Party. That story will remain untold for the moment.

Aspen is a different, however. Adam and Mark hit it off with Tony, but then Tony was sexy as fuck, and Mark and Adam couldn't help but miss that. They also knew that I wasn't much of a prude and there was a good chance we'd all end up playing around together. They were right.

We boarded most of the day, ate great food, and I showed them around the town. We did cocktails at the Caribou Club and later the Oxford Hotel, then went back to our place at the Little Nell, at the base of Ajax mountain, and jumped into the hot tub.

Sex with Mark and Adam during that weekend was good, but awkward since Tony and Mark seemed to click and left Adam and me on our own. This didn't jive with my expectation of my relationship with Tony, so I was a little put off. Also, Tony seemed unusually preoccupied with his phone the entire weekend.

Back in Seattle, Tony was distant that next week, but we had plans to go to a big birthday party on the weekend, so I was hoping we could get things worked out after that. The party was fun except we argued on the way home, and it ended with crying and uncertainty. Tony and I climbed into bed together and had sex, despite the argument. I held him close, but couldn't sleep. We cuddled as he quietly snored.

At about 4:00 a.m., Tony's phone went off with a text. I wondered who was texting him at that time of night, so I checked his phone. Maybe I shouldn't have; maybe I should have just closed my eyes and ears and blocked it out of my head, but I didn't. It was Mark, my friend from DC.

I read the texts they'd been sending even while we were in Aspen. They'd been carrying on a secret conversation the whole time about how much they wanted each other. Tony even told Mark he was the "most incredible man he'd ever met". They talked about how they were going to tell me and Adam this weekend, break it off with us, then they could be together, finally. Mind you, Tony and Mark just met the week before.

Man, my heart dropped. I felt sick. I couldn't believe what I was reading. This was the guy I'd said "I love you" to this morning, the guy I showered with and had sex with just hours ago. The whole time he was planning on dumping my ass for someone I thought of as a friend.

I woke him up, told him to get dressed, and threw him out of the house.

He cried a lot over the next couple days, and he begged me to stay his friend, but he never said anything about taking him back. He'd made up his mind that Mark was the man he wanted to be with, not me.

How hard was that, to try and stay friends with someone who'd been so deceptive and caused such heartbreak? It was the right thing to do, though. Truth be told, we made better friends than partners, and fate is funny sometimes.

Mark and Tony hooked up one more time the next weekend before they were done with each other. Mark flew up to Seattle, and Tony took him out clubbing. I think Mark probably saw Tony in his true element and realized that he and Tony were at different stages of life, despite the obvious physical connection. I doubt Tony even remembers Mark's last name at this point. I do.

My story is like so many others who've walked into my office over the past twenty years, eyes still red, clutching papers in their hands. Their world was just shattered so dramatically they had to call a divorce lawyer. This is the last place they want to be.

Rarely, a person will seek my help as a divorce lawyer because he's ready to move on and wants things wrapped up legally. These clients have already gone through the stages of grieving and reached the realization they want more from life. This group may feel a little sad, but what I see in their faces is determination. They want this done, and done fast. "He can have whatever he wants, it doesn't matter to me," and "I don't need any support from him. I just want to move on."

Most of the time, though, it's infidelity; broken promises to be loyal, devoted, committed, monogamous. Unrealistic expectations, set as far back as memory, shattered by someone's uncontrolled urges to fuck someone new.

It's always the misaligned expectations. This couple's great catastrophe was destined to occur simply because of the expectations our culture sets on the institution of marriage. There's no escaping the collapse of these expectations when they're grounded in pure fantasy and the fiction of a perfect world, perfect love, and perfect people. We're just not perfect, and there is no perfect love.

The world has taught us that everything will be well and good if we just follow the beaten path of these expectations. If we just follow in the same steps as our parents, the same steps our friends and family must follow, we'll live happily ever after in perfect Disney, *Leave It to Beaver* fashion. Keep your foot in the same footprint on this path of expectations, and it'll turn out perfectly. Use the same Bible, get married at the same place as your parents, wear grandma's wedding dress, play the same silly wedding games as every other couple, and life will be complete, right?

From the moment we can walk and talk, these expectations are hammered into our brain. We establish gender roles and assign toys accordingly. Our parents begin asking about boyfriends and girlfriends as early as preschool. We chuckle at little Jonny because he held hands with little Emily in kindergarten today. We flock to Hollywood movies about beautiful people who find that one special person, finally, and begin a wonderful, monogamous life with them. But, when do you see a blockbuster love story where the handsome man is on his knees, ring extended, looking expectantly at the beautiful woman and the woman says, "I do, but we need to have an open relationship"?

Growing up gay, this expected path to happiness was particularly problematic, and the pervasive pressure to conform tore me down mentally. Low self-esteem and isolation resulted. My dad was always telling my mom they needed to toughen me up and that I was going to turn out to be a sissy boy. I tried to meet his expectations by kissing as many girls as would let me in kindergarten and first grade, before I got into trouble and the school threatened to kick me out. My dad? He was as proud as could be and, for a while, was pacified that I was on the expected path. I played football, tennis, swimming, wrestling, and even squash, just to try and earn validation from him and stay on this path.

I didn't conform, couldn't conform, and would have to do my best at faking it, praying all along the way something would change and I could meet everyone's expectations. Movies and TV assaulted me with relationships that were foreign; Sleeping Beauty was a pretty story and all, but it was never going to be my story. My story was deeper, darker, more convoluted. My story was Maleficent.

If you're straight, imagine growing up where all the media, all the movies, songs, and TV shows were variations of Brokeback Mountain. Everywhere you looked, there were two hot gay men finding each other, making out, cuddling, holding each other, saying sweet things, walking around in their underwear, maybe being torn apart by some terrible, tragic event. Would you resonate to that image and those stories? Or would you feel maybe disinterested and disconnected from the whole premise?

I was disconnected from Disney movies growing up. Love stories were interesting in the abstract, and I cried at some, but I could never put myself fully into the shoes of the lead characters.

My feeling of disconnectedness increased as I became more self-aware of my sexuality. As I came to terms with being gay, I stopped trying to force myself onto this path and started to view the whole path critically. I rebelled against religion, my parents, and my education. I was an outsider, and I knew it. I was never going to fit my stride in those footsteps.

As is common with young gay men when they realize they live outside the social contract, I descended into self-destructive behavior. The rules didn't apply to me because I was already damned to hell, so why not smoke, drink, do drugs, and be a dick to my teachers and parents? All my life, these people had been trying to force me to be someone I wasn't, and it was destroying me, so fuck 'em.

Deep down, I still prayed that, one day, I'd be straight and could rejoin the expected path.

You ask me why people cheat on their partners and lie about it? Why perfectly good and well intentioned people promise monogamy, then lie, cheat, and steal their way through a relationship, defrauding the very partner they profess to love?

It's the pressures of the expected path. Who can live under that pressure? Can you? Really?

Chapter 25
ENFORCING FIDELITY

In traditional relationships, expectations are so misaligned with today's culture that it's virtually impossible for a partner to meet them. To further pressure a partner to comply with our antiquated expectations, we create rules. The more antiquated and misaligned our expectations are, the more numerous and draconian the rules.

An expectation-based rule might be as functional as, "Tom will always take the dry cleaning" or as structural as "no dancing with other guys." Of course, the structural ones can be the most convoluted and difficult as the power struggle between the couple plays out with different anxieties.

Make no mistake, rule setting is an expression of the power struggle between the partners. Rules limit behavior and create a basis for what the couple defines as appropriate conduct. Often, though, these rules come from one partner who's feeling threatened and who wants to curtail the behavior of the other partner. A power struggle ensues over the creation of a rule where one partner may decide to give up a certain degree of freedom that he would otherwise enjoy to pacify the other partner.

For example, I don't know any couples who sit down at the beginning of the relationship and have a detailed discussion about interacting with ex-boyfriends or guys who hit on them at the gym or what do to with your Grindr and Scruff profiles. These rules develop circumstantially and after the fact, usually. An ex-boyfriend texts and wants to hang out, and now you have a discussion about what works and what's not okay. You find your new partner sending messages on Scruff, and now you have a conversation about whether the two of you will use online programs and what sort of profiles and conversations are allowed.

Hopefully, these discussions are just that, discussions, but more often than not the circumstances that lead to rule creation arise from disagreements or even fights. Rules are also created as a last resort to saving the relationship.

One rule after another and the Fidelity Police takeover. You can have a Grindr profile, but it has to say you're partnered and you aren't looking for a hookup. Your conversations can't be sexual. You can use Scruff for keeping in touch with long lost friends (i.e. tricks), but not to hit on guys nor respond to guys hitting on you. Fuck it, give me your phone, I want to read your messages.

It's a Whack-a-Mole of rule-making. Every time a new situation arises that creates a fear of losing a partner, we whack it with a new rule. This way we're always trying to close off options for our partner's behavior.

In some relationships, the ridiculous parade of power-struggle rules becomes comical. You can have oral sex, but they can't cum in your mouth. You can jerk off in the showers at the gym, but no touching. You can't give out your real number, give out mine. Our only rule is no barebacking. I like that one. That rule pretty much says the couple has thrown in the towel, and there're no boundaries left.

The power struggle shown in the process of developing these rules is a blood sport. There's a strong feeling of, "You can't have anymore fun than I'm having!" Rules get established because an event comes along that challenges one of the partner's sense of security, and the challenged partner feels the need to "lay down the law".

"Laying down the law" results in the new watermark for what's permissible and what constitutes infidelity, but that's viewing this watermark from the position of fear. The rule-setting spouse or partner wants to be sure there's no risk of the other partner having so much fun that he decides to leave. The new "law" caps the fun for both partners.

Problem is, this doesn't work. Life is filled with a countless, nearly infinite, variety of possible events and circumstances and no rule, none, can possibly contemplate the vast set of circumstances a partner might find himself in. You can Whack-a-Mole all you want, but those damn puppets are gonna keep popping up. This ever-expanding Book of Rules quickly devolves into a Cheater's Guide to Cheating.

In the world of traditional relationships, unsustainable rules fill the Cheater's Guide to Cheating because the expectations set in a traditional relationship don't align with modern culture.

Chapter 26
TYLER AND DAN

Springtime at the park arrived, and volleyball season was in full swing. Sunday afternoons the Pink Net Club gathers at a park close to capitol hill for some volleyball, beer, and sun. It's always been an informal group, with new people every week, and the volleyball isn't so much competitive as it is just a chance to socialize and have a relaxing Sunday afternoon.

This Sunday, Tony introduced me to a couple he met at a dance club, Tyler and Dan. Tony was raving about this couple for a solid two weeks, telling me how they were so awesome together and what great quality people they were and how sexy he found them. My perception, knowing Tony, was that he was worshiping the relationship these two super hot guys had, loving, dedicated, and healthy. Again, Tony believed his sole purpose in life was to find the perfect partner, and in Tyler and Dan, he thought he saw the exact type of relationship he craved.

I'd never met these guys before. They hardly went out and kept mostly to themselves, but as we talked, we discovered we had a few friends in common and liked some of the same stuff.

They were a handsome couple, two of the sexiest men I'd seen in Seattle, Dan was blond, about 6', and so fit he could have been a model, but Tyler was even sexier and more my type, dark hair, dark eyes, scruffy with a muscled body and hairy chest. His idea of relaxing for the weekend was kayaking through the sound.

At first, Tony kept me at arm's length with these guys. He probably thought my constant dose of reality would ruin the illusion he'd created around them. Of course, he was right, but if it hadn't been me, it would have been someone else, no doubt about it. Regardless, I was banished from Tony's social life for a few weeks while it was the Tyler and Dan hour.

Eventually, Tony came back to me with little or no explanation of why he wasn't running the park with Tyler or going to yoga with Dan, and I figured it was wisest to leave it alone. My questions were answered soon enough.

One weekend, I was hanging out on Grindr, cruising for a hookup or at least someone interesting to talk to for a few hours when I stumbled upon a headless profile pic of a flawless, muscular body with an amazing, broad, hairy chest, "Blacksheep". This guy was probably getting hit on by every guy in Seattle with that pic, me included.

"Hot pic man," I messaged.

I went merrily about my business of checking out other profiles and responding to messages. There was little chance he would respond, and even less chance he was real.

"Thanks, bud. You, too."

Hmmm. Well, this was interesting, but I had to remind myself this guy can't be real. He's just too hot.

"Thanks. More pics?" I shot back.

He sent over three other mirror selfies, progressively more revealing. I sent three back even more revealing than his. Let's see what he did with that.

"Damn, bud. You're amazing!" he sent back.

The conversation took off, exchanging more pics, describing what we liked to do, how we liked to do it, getting excited and worked up, then it was time to close the sale.

"Looking?" I typed.

"Got a BF. We only play together, but fuck, man! I'd love to play with you 1-on-1!"

I was confused by this equivocation. Was he saying we could only do a group, or was he saying he was going to break his rules with his partner and hook up with me on the side?

"I'm down for 1-on-1 if you want," I sent back.

"Ugh. I wish, bud, but we know some same people. Gotta be discrete."

"I'm not telling anybody lol."

"Yeah, but you're good friends with Tony . . ."

Ahhh. Yeah. This happened a lot. Tony was probably the best-known gay in all of Seattle, and I was his sidekick. Annoyingly, people would try and buddy up to me to get to know him, hoping somehow to get into his pants by association. They figured he and I were hooking up and, if they suggested a three-way, "you know any buds?" that I'd bring Tony along for the fun. I can say without hesitation that not only did this never work, not once, but it was the quickest way to be certain I never spoke with them again.

It was unclear what this headless selfie meant by mentioning Tony.

"Yeah, but I don't tell him about my hookups," I lied. We almost always told each other, but we also always kept that information to just the two of us.

"Let's see what my BF thinks and maybe the 3 of us can have some fun," said "Blacksheep" after a few minutes.

Sounded like "Blacksheep" might be hooking up outside of his relationship, but he wasn't sure about me yet because of my relationship with Tony. All good. I'd be up for a group with him and his husband.

A few more days of flirting, talking dirty, and working on schedules, and we settled on Thursday night, their place, 9:00 p.m. I didn't say anything to Tony even though we were together at the gym, dinner, my place, every day.

"Blacksheep" was kinky, one of the kinkiest guys I've talked to, not so much into leather, but bondage, domination, control, and other things. I've got a dark side, and it usually exceeds most people's interest, but not "Blacksheep". He had me beat hands down. For some reason, he started opening up to me about it.

Thursday rolled around, and I was getting excited. "Blacksheep" sent me some headless pics of his husband, and I was shocked at how hot they both were, perfect bodies I'd never seen around Seattle before, but still no faces.

Their house was in an older neighborhood with classic, turn of the century homes and big yards, hip and trendy, but with an element of being established. Pulling up in front, I saw a manicured, two-story house from the early 1900's, and a nice, clean yard with big trees. Everything about this place screamed "traditional couple".

I walked up to the porch, pushed the doorbell and shuffled my feet. Since I hadn't seen faces yet, I was bracing myself for "butta face" meaning "You've got a nice body, but your face. . ."

The door opened, and I sucked in a breath. It was Tyler, and standing a few steps behind him was Dan. Even though we'd only met once, I recognized them immediately.

Nearly speechless, I stammered my way through a hello, shook hands with both of them, and finally regained composure. "Nice to see you guys again. It's been since we all hung out with Tony at the park that day, right? Small world."

They'd obviously prepared for this conversation, as Dan and Tyler glanced at each other, and Dan said, "Yeah, we like Tony and all, but he's more of a circuit queen than we are. He's not our type of guy for a hookup either." There had to be more to this story than just that. Tony was everybody's type for a hookup.

More small talk and Tyler said, "We think you're ridiculously sexy, man. Want to come upstairs?" Fuck yeah, I did.

In their carefully manicured bedroom, with everything perfectly placed in the right spot, we started making out and stripping down. Dan and I were face to face, while Tyler was behind me. Clothes were coming off in a flurry. Naked, I could feel Tyler pressing up against my back, rock hard, as he wrapped his arms around me from behind. Dan was an amazing kisser, soft, varied, and so intense he made me feel like we were all alone. As he pressed his naked body against mine, I could feel how large he was, too.

Tyler moved to the bed and laid on his back, legs spread slightly. Dan and I moved to where he was stretched out and Dan climbed onto the bed next to him. Putting my hands on Tyler's hairy, muscled thighs I knelt down beside the bed and began rubbing my scruffy face against the inside of his leg, moving upwards.

Tyler preferred being a bottom and was verbal and loud. He obviously liked rougher play, and I was happy to help him out. Dan was more of a watcher, and the few times I tried to bring him in he shook his head, but his eyes were wide as he appeared to be on the verge of ejaculating the entire time. Finally, Dan got involved and fucked Tyler on his back while I used Tyler's head hanging backwards off the side of the bed, one hand against the back of his neck. Dan and I made out while we were both inside Tyler.

After we'd all gotten off, I went into the bathroom to clean up. Tyler followed me in and as I started taking a piss he put his finger to his lips to silence me. Coming up behind while I was pissing he lowered his face down to my cock. So turned on, I didn't care about anything except how it felt.

Small talk so Dan could hear us, we got cleaned up, then came back to bed. No one moved to get dressed.

"Fuck! That was the hottest sex we've ever had with anyone," said Dan, lying on his back, arm over his head. I have to say it was some of the hottest sex I'd ever had, too, even though they made me use a condom while I fucked Tyler and when Dan fucked me.

"Hell yeah, it was," I replied while rubbing Tyler's hairy chest. "You guys have three-ways often?"

"No, not often at all. We're picky and discrete. Plus, we just started hooking up with other guys in Seattle. We have a rule that we don't send face pics," responded Tyler. "And we have to decide together. The guy has to be hot, discrete, safe, and clean."

It sounded like these two had worked out the details in depth. It also sounded like Dan was the source of these rules, since my experience with Tyler so far led me to believe he didn't stick to them well.

"Did you guys ever hook up with Tony?" I asked. I thought I knew the answer, but decided to toss it out there.

They looked briefly at each other, then Dan turned to me and said, "Naw, we didn't think it was a good idea. He's hot and such a sweet guy, but he's not what we were looking for." Again, my intuition was going off. My guess is Tyler is very much into Tony, and Dan wasn't going to let him anywhere near that kid, not even in a three-way. Tony's looks and popularity were probably intimidating to a quiet, private person like Dan, and even though Dan was a super model in his own right, Tony was a notch above.

We laid there quietly, got aroused again, and went at it one more time before, after two hours, I was back in my car headed home, shaking my head at how hot the night had been.

The next few weeks were a whirlwind with Tyler. We talked by text all day, exchanging stories and pics and making plans for the next time we'd get together. I learned that Tyler and Dan had plenty of rules about hooking up and that Tyler was selective about which rules got enforced. For example, there wasn't supposed to be any communication with guys that couldn't be shared between the two of them, but Tyler was constantly cleaning up conversations, deleting problematic exchanges, and having me send "dummy" texts that could be shared with Dan. There were plenty of problematic texts.

Dan didn't want Tyler sharing any of his kinky side with anyone. He didn't approve of Tyler's interests but had agreed to allow some of it when they did three-ways. As of yet, that expression of Tyler's interests hadn't happened. Tyler had some interests that I doubt Dan would ever be able to satisfy, or Tyler could suppress.

It wasn't even a week before Tyler and I went to lunch. It had to be someplace he didn't think anyone would know him. After lunch, he asked if I could drop him back at his office since he'd walked over. We climbed into my car and in ten seconds were making out, Tyler was undoing my pants. Not a half hour before, Tyler was telling me there was no kissing allowed and no sex outside of a pre-approved three-way.

Later that week, Tyler and I met at my place for "lunch" and things got crazy. He finally got to explore parts of his kinkier side that Dan didn't share. I fucked Tyler hard that day, but with a condom. They had a rule, you see, that when they hooked up with others, it always had to be safe, but it was also always supposed to be together. I'm not sure Dan would have appreciated the finer points of Tyler's rule adherence.

Sex got more and more wild as our "lunches" stretched from weeks to months. Tyler and I shared specifics about what got us excited, then we got together and tried it out. As time wore on, the Rules fell like dominos. By the end, the only requirement was that Dan could never know.

We never again had a three-way. Dan decided he didn't want to. I never found out why, but Dan and I have probably only exchanged five words since that night.

I eventually told Tony when he became highly suspicious of me disappearing for "lunch" three times a week, for a couple hours. Predictably, he was angry, saying that Tyler and Dan were his friends, not mine, and that my meetings with Tyler were betraying Dan. Then he asked if he could hang out with us for lunch.

Our intense conversations and sex only ended when Tyler and Dan moved to the middle of nowhere New Mexico later that summer. I can only imagine how Tyler is feeling boxed in, unable to express himself and presumably a small group of available alternatives. Dan, I imagine, is probably as happy as a clam.

Chapter 27
CHEATER'S GUIDE TO CHEATING

The Cheater's Guide to Cheating is so chock full of rules and expectations, it becomes inevitable that the partners fail to comply. Hearts get broken, relationships end and the cycle begins all over again. Rules may work for a while, but the changing conditions of any relationship always present new situations that these rules can't so easily solve. The old saying "rules are made to be broken" can't be any truer than in the context of the Cheater's Guide to Cheating.

All these rules are intended to prescribe the boundaries of fidelity. Fidelity isn't the same as monogamy. We define fidelity as "keeping your promise to a person, cause, or belief, demonstrated by continuing loyalty and support." These ever-changing rules are a form of promised behavior. They define the behavior that meets a partner's expectation of fidelity. Fidelity, or the promised behavior, may include monogamy, but more and more, my observations are that the Cheaters Guide to Cheating never starts out with, "For the rest of your natural life, you will only have any and all types of sex, or sexual contact, with me, alone." You practically have to be a lawyer to draft this shit.

A situation presents itself that causes drama between the partners, say one of them kissed another guy at Circuit in Barcelona, a massive gay circuit party; no rule in place previously, but certainly unspoken expectations. Whatever the hurt partner's motives may be, a fight ensues about whether that's okay.

Some couples gravitate back to, "hell no, that's not okay," but most begin the lawyer-like process of creating a rule built for exceptions. A rule like, "we can make out with other guys, together, while we're on vacation." So let's see, how many arbitrary qualifiers, and conditions made to be broken can you count in this rule? Interestingly, these rules are almost always the creation of the partner who was left out.

If the origin of the rule is the partner who feels threatened, you have to ask, what exactly is the threat? Maybe he feels like he needs to chain up his guy tighter so he doesn't lose him to a better kisser. Just maybe, instead of creating a limitation, this injured partner is actually creating a permission, the permission to kiss another guy!

Why would the injured partner be looking to give himself permission, in addition to limiting his partner's behavior? Perhaps it's because he's just as hungry as the other partner for something new and exciting, something different than their daily grind together. Perhaps it's that they don't want to get left out of all the fun.

Rule-making isn't all bad. It provides structure to a relationship and satisfies expectations between the partners. Every relationship has rules that can be an effective tool for success. It's the nature of the rules and the motive behind creating them that can be problematic. In my experience, the best rules are the simplest ones. It's also best if we recognize strict compliance can be impossible and that a good rule still allows for freedom and individuality. Finally, the best rule is the one that's created before there's a conflict, and sometimes even before there's a relationship.

Most couples fear opening the door of their relationship even just a crack, because it might spell their doom. They fear their loved one might find someone better, and they'll lose everything they have and everything they worked so hard to build. Obviously, in my experience as a divorce lawyer, I see this fear get realized all the time. As a sexually active gay man I see it, too. My world is no different when it comes to this hyper-possessive fear.

Many times, though, the individuals in a couple, consciously or not, feel the need for more. Their relationship has settled into a routine, with defined roles and predictable sex, if they're lucky. If they're not, disillusionment has set in, and the fantasy they created in their heads begins to unravel. In the first scenario, the couple may survive by recognizing their needs and coming up with a non-threatening plan to meet those needs. In the second scenario, though, the relationship is done, and they're too passive or scared to end it.

If a couple has settled into a routine, both partners are probably hungry for new experiences. It's naive to think we don't want something exciting. Why does it comes as a surprise to anyone the individuals of a couple might want to try something new and different with someone other than their partner?

So when one partner strays and makes out with some beach boy in San Diego, certainly feelings are hurt, part of the fantasy dies, but I believe the injured partner, in crafting a new rule, is looking to make a little room for his own adventures, maybe for a make-out session with the hottie from Denver.

Do they discuss the other consequence of their new rule, that it might actually facilitate new adventure? No, the rule is almost always couched as a limitation instead of an exploration. "You can't do this" and "you can't do that" should be converted to, "let's try this" and "let's explore that."

Instead of creating a Cheater's Guide to Cheating, the couple should maybe be drawing up a Beginner's Guide to Kinky Sex!

Chapter 28
FLOATING UNDER THE STARS

Society has fixed expectations for traditional relationships, especially for marriage. These expectations are the same for all of us, though there's some small variety within cultures and communities. This set of expectations and their accompanying rules for enforcement create a paradigm.

A paradigm is a typical pattern, or model, that provides a rule structure. A paradigm of relationships is the model of behavior and expectations society which imposes on the structure of boyfriend, husband, wife, etc. A paradigm is the ultimate rule book.

For the longest time, I battled meeting the expectations of a traditional relationship paradigm. Growing up gay didn't jive with this paradigm, and by the time I got to college, my early ventures with men had to stop. I stopped seeing my high school fuck buddy and started dating women, lots of women. I joined a fraternity and became "that guy," with his baseball cap backward, bragging about my conquests.

I enjoyed sex with women, sometimes, but I think most of the excitement came from thinking that maybe I wasn't gay after all. I mean, I just had sex with the hottest girl in the sorority, how could I be gay? At moments, it almost felt like I was on the expected path of the paradigm and, man, that felt good. I was part of the club!

There was always a nagging pull, though. One of my girlfriends had a picture of a nearly naked man running down the beach plastered over her bed in her sorority house. We had the most awesome sex in her room because I could look up at that poster and imagine I was with him. Ripped abs, big chest and huge arms; I could just make out the head of his dick through the tiny towel wrapped around his waist.

I dated her longer than any other woman, I think, because of that poster.

To stay within the traditional paradigm, I turned down some pretty amazing advances from men in college, too. In the dorm shower one time, this beautiful guy from California who lived a few doors down climbed into the shower stall with me saying the other one was broken. We were friends and had gotten drunk together plenty of times and even came close to having a three-way once, but there was never any indication he was interested in me, until that day.

Chad was blond and outgoing, with a surfer's body. I was speechless when he just jumped in with me and began showering. With a smile, he looked me up and down, before grabbing his shower gel and starting to soap himself.

It was too much. I got erect, and it was obvious; there was no way to hide it or escape, but so was he. He reached over and started to stroke mine and pulled me in close to kiss him, but I couldn't do it. I was petrified someone would walk in and see two sets of feet in one stall, then it would all be over. I would be the campus fag.

I grabbed him and pressed him against me, my face against his. I could feel his hard dick against my stomach. Overwhelmed with fear, I bolted out of the shower. I guess I pulled him to me so that he'd know I was interested and that it was okay that he was interested, too, but I also couldn't do it. During the next couple years of college, we still hung out occasionally and, years later, I saw him at a medical school graduation. He came over, and we hugged. He was still a big handsome surfer guy, and I couldn't help but hold him just a half-second too long. That's when he introduced me to his wife.

It wasn't until I was 22 that I finally threw in the towel, so to speak, and accepted that I was gay and was gonna stay that way. I broke down and went to a gay bar I'd heard of. I meant to get laid by whoever was willing. I didn't care. It was time.

Gay bars back then weren't in the nicest parts of town. The parking lots weren't well lit, and there weren't a lot of drink specials being advertising on blinking signs out front. This place could've been mistaken for the side door to a restaurant; no windows, no signs out front, not even a name, just the street number plastered over the door. I drove around looking for the place for half an hour before I noticed guys go in and out of this nondescript entry.

It took some serious resolve to get out of my car and cross the street, but after sitting there another fifteen minutes, I got up the courage and walked in, sat at the bar, and ordered a Bud. I was so scared my eyes must have looked like dinner plates. Some Goth-looking guy, not unattractive, was staring at me, obviously interested. It made me uncomfortable so I quickly slammed my beer and fled the scene without so much as a wink and a nod.

Next day I was on a plane to Hawaii for two weeks. It was the best trip of my life because it was the first time I was honest and accepting of who I was. I remember floating on my back in the pool at the rental house, staring up at the amazing stars you can only see far away from city lights. Contemplating the infinite nature of our universe and how tiny and small we are with our little problems and insecurities, I floated there for a long time thinking how free I was, finally free.

Is that a strange feeling? I didn't hookup at that first gay bar; I didn't even talk to anyone, other than the bartender. Looking at me, there was no difference. I still saw the same person in the mirror. But the sense of freedom was overpowering, like a rubber band wound so tight, all knotted up, finally released, yet not the same since a rubber band could be wound up again. I could never return to being bound that way. At least not completely.

What was I finally free of? What was making me feel like a prisoner all those years? Everybody's expectations; it was the traditional relationship paradigm. I'd finally let go of all those expectations. I just cut loose from what people thought I should be and decided I was going to be who I was. I was no longer going to try to travel on the expected path.

All those years of fighting to get onto the expected path and years of fighting against it, the constant push-pull of what everyone thought I should do and be, were done. That path had never been my path and had led to so much heartache and disillusion that the freedom I felt now was truly transcendent.

Some straight and gay readers out there may be thinking, Yay, good for you Dave. Glad you came out and finally accepted who you are. Yawn. You miss the point.

This expected path is just as toxic, just as limiting, just as much a prison for you as it was for me, regardless of whether you're straight or gay. Your moment of freedom from these stupid, antiquated expectations will be just as powerful as mine was. My moment of liberalization had nothing to do with the fact that I preferred sex with men; it had to do with breaking free from the suffocating expectations heaped upon me from my first memories. In my case, those expectations included the expectation I would find a nice girl, but it was so much broader and encompassed so many other pressures society places on us.

Free from the Disney paradigm, I could set my own rules, make my own path through life, and create my own expectations. It took a few weeks to determine how I was going to do that, but when I did, I made one of the biggest mistakes of my life.

I photocopied the expected path, painted it pink, and decided that was the path I was going to take. The rubber band began to twist and knot again.

Chapter 29
TEN YEARS TOO LONG

After my great realization and liberation, life clarified itself in some ways and became opaque in others. Freed from the guilt and pressure of the expected path, I could now go my own way, but what way was that? We humans crave structure and predicability. How was I supposed to act? What was I supposed to do? I was grasping for a new paradigm that would give me stability and meaning.

Upon returning to Seattle, I immediately started looking for sex. I grabbed the only gay newspaper I knew of and started answering personal ads. We didn't have any online options since "online" hadn't been invented yet. It was the personal ads, a gay bar or bushes at the park. I felt safest with the ads.

I only went to meet three people from those personal ads, and one was Danny. He was a big, 'str8' acting, auto mechanic deep in the closet. We latched onto each other for dear life.

It was a mistake to jump into things with Danny so quickly, and it was a mistake to go looking for sex in personal ads, not that there's anything wrong with random hookups (more on this later), but I wasn't emotionally ready and hadn't decided on my own version of the social contract. Without thinking through what rules I had, or moral compass to follow, I was at the mercy of chance opportunity. I may have fallen in with the heavy drug crowd, or big-time drinkers, or the wide world of promiscuous unsafe sex in an age of AIDS. Maybe I was weak, but I lacked a star to navigate by. In a way, Danny saved my life. In another, I was still locked in a cage.

Without a paradigm, but knowing the expected path wasn't mine, I grasped for structure and found it in the same old expected path, but with a gay twist. I would just swap out the husband and wife at the top of the wedding cake for a husband and husband, and we'd call it good.

I defaulted to the same toxic, ill-conceived, antiquated paradigm I'd just escaped.

Danny and I committed to being "exclusive" right up until we weren't just a few short months later. Fights, crying, stalking, and high drama, and we agreed, again, to be monogamous, but to have three-ways occasionally, but both of us were horny, young, and newly out. After a couple years of picking drapes and china, dinner parties with all the important gays, and learning how to make cosmos, Danny began traveling for work.

I'm pretty sure this was a choice on his part, but I didn't argue too loudly. He was becoming unbearable to live with. He ate junk food, watched TV all the time, and was condescending toward me, bordering on violent. I looked forward to my time alone in the house.

Believe it or not, this dragged on for ten years. I look back and shake my head at the stupid things we'd do to try and adopt the expected path with a gay twist. There were times I was happy with Danny, and I still love him, but we should've just been best friends and worked on developing our own path.

He cheated. I cheated. We never talked about it, but it was no mystery when he was gone for six months at time. I was competing in triathlons and going to gay dance clubs on the weekends. I looked good, better than Tony ever did. I got a lot of attention even without Facebook, if you can believe it.

One day, Danny said he was out of town, but he wasn't. I had a friend at the house. Danny came home, and it was all over.

Chapter 30
CHEATING ON TRAVIS

Since my job is management, I feel like I need to be in our Tacoma office once a week to meet with our employees, make sure everything is working smoothly, and just be present for a day to help link the two offices together character wise.

Occasionally there's some down-time when the Tacoma staff is busy and I'm not, so I sneak out and go to the gym. It was one of these slow days when I snuck off to the LA Fitness up the street from our office. The little red dots on my iPhone app icons drive me nuts, so I've gotten into the habit of going through and clearing them all out whenever I have a chance. Today, as with most days, there was one on the Grindr icon so I logged in to respond and clear out the messages.

As soon as you log in, Grindr places your profile in the "online" screen and lets everyone know how far away you are from them. No big deal; it's a good way to meet new people. Today was no exception. I changed, started my workout, and got a few exercises in when I stopped and checked Grindr again, red dot. There were a few new messages, including one from a profile named "Navy DL". I checked his pictures and wow! Headless pic of a ridiculously hot guy sitting on the couch playing a video game. Holy shit, I thought. That guy is smoking hot. Hello, Tacoma!

"Hey. You're close," said his message, and I was. His profile said I was about a 1000 feet away.

"Yup. At the gym. Hot pic. What are you up to?" You could see where this was going. Navy DL (short for "down low," meaning he needed to be discrete) was working, but was looking around for later. Unfortunately, I was heading back up to Seattle in a bit so couldn't meet him but I did favorite him, so maybe we could connect sometime in the future. We said we'd stay in touch, but reality is most of the time these near-misses disappear forever. Not this one.

Every so often, I host a game night at my house in Seattle for friends and their friends. I keep it small and manageable, so usually no more than eight people. We play games ranging from spoons to truth-or-dare and, depending on the substance imbibed, things can get a little out of hand.

It was a game night in November, about a month after the message from Navy DL, and I invited over some friends I hadn't seen in awhile. I usually invite people who don't know each other since it's kind of cool to introduce good people to other good people. Tonight, Tony was there, of course, my friends Jeff and his partner Bobby, my friends Rick and Thomas, both single, and a friend I hadn't seen since a trip to Las Vegas last spring, Travis, and his new husband, Andrew. They'd met shortly after Vegas and had a ceremony over the summer. Love at first sight, soulmates, Prince Charming, and let's get hitched on Sunday.

Andrew was tall, dark-haired, blue-eyed, and brownish, smooth skin. He had a perfect form with broad shoulders, tapering to a narrow waist, nice arms, and a six pack you could see quite well through his shirt. His husband, Travis was shorter, thicker, with a rounded face, still in good shape and handsome. There was a time when Travis and I played with the idea of hooking up, but it hadn't happened.

Travis owned a specialized car dealership and did well at it. He was always throwing big parties and taking extravagant trips. Andrew worked for the military in security and had recently relocated to Seattle to live with Travis. They were a cute couple, always affectionate and overtly sexual. Travis knew what a hot catch Andrew was.

Travis and Andrew were traditional, spending a lot of time with their families, babysitting their nephews and nieces and talking about having kids of their own, but not just yet. They set up house together and talked about themselves in that annoying, imperial "we". "We went to San Diego to visit our mom", "we just got a new car", "we love Chinese food", and the required, "we don't believe in sex outside marriage". Right.

Game night was fun, and everyone had a great time, enjoying lots of cocktails and playing Cards Against Humanity, a game that can devolve into a sexually charged situation. Between rounds, I got up to make more drinks and checked my phone; no particular reason, just grabbed it and saw some red dots. I had Grindr messages, so I opened the app real quick and saw it, Navy DL's profile right next to mine on the "online" screen. He was "56 ft" away. That's when it hit me, even though I'd never seen Navy DL's face, the body was unmistakeable; it was Andrew.

Oh damn! I thought. It's not too big of a deal that a partner in a committed relationship keeps up a Grindr profile. It certainly doesn't mean he's cheating, but it's a bit of a surprise with a couple that holds themselves out as married and traditional. It also struck me as odd that Andrew was apparently logged in, too. I mean, Travis was right there!

I decided to message Navy DL. Should I recognize him or play dumb? I went with recognize him; that seemed most likely to draw a response since it would be hard to deny the fact that we were in the same room.

"Hey Andrew! We should work this so we win the next round! I'll tell you what I write down for my answer :)" I messaged him. I made the drinks and came back to the game. It might take Andrew a while to see my message and the plan I'd proposed wouldn't have worked anyway, but it was a non-threatening way of letting him know I recognized him.

We played a while longer before the chance to see if he'd gotten my message came up. I was back in the kitchen for more drinks and was able to check my phone. There was a red dot on the Grindr icon. Opening it, I saw a message from Navy DL.

"Hey. Don't tell Travis PLEASE! Talk more later."

Game night went off without a hitch and no more Grindr texts between me and Navy DL. A few days later, I heard from Andrew, and we chatted some and he assured me he only used Grindr to check out hot guys and find pictures for private time. What was he supposed to say? What do they always say? I pretended to believe him and ignored the obvious; why was it "DL" and a headless, shirtless pic, unless there was something to hide?

We kept talking, though, and Andrew told me he was bored most nights and wanted to hangout with Tony and me some time, so I invited him over to watch TV with us and relax. He jumped at it.

There's only one TV in my house, and it's in my bedroom. I'm not a big TV fan and usually only watch football when Tony's not around, and sitcoms with Tony like Modern Family. The night when Andrew came over, we all three lay on my bed and watched Modern Family, over and over. No one wanted to leave.

Here I was, in my bed in nothing but gym shorts, with two of the hottest guys you I could imagine; not everyone's type, many people thought Andrew was too pretty, and Tony too short, but damn! I could feel the sexual tension in the room as "innocent" contact became more and more overt, and finally, I leaned over and kissed Andrew. He reciprocated and reached over to Tony and began rubbing his chest. Tony leaned in and put his body against Andrew's.

An hour later, clothes being pulled back on, Andrew seemed uncomfortable.

"Well, now I'm just one of those cheating husbands, I guess," he said, but without much remorse. What do you say back to something like that?

"Travis doesn't need to know, man. Dave and I aren't going to tell him, that's for sure," said Tony as he pulled on his shoes. Those damn things were so old, ratty, and smelly it was amazing Tony could stand them. Didn't seem to bother him at all.

"Fuck, I hope not, man! I'd like to keep this just between us, okay?" said Andrew. "If it's just between us, maybe we can do it again sometime." There it was. Andrew wasn't so much embarrassed as he was trying to set up the next session, and I'm not so sure he was trying to set it up with me.

I walked them both to the front door and Andrew left first. Tony stuck around for a few minutes to stress that he didn't like doing three-ways, and was upset at me for putting him in "that situation". It was such bullshit since he pushed me to invite Andrew over, and it wasn't the first nor last time Tony and I would have sex with other people together.

Over the next few weeks, I heard from Andrew a few times, and he and I got together one more time one afternoon in the middle of the workday. I'm pretty certain Andrew was hooking up with Tony, too, since I knew they went to a concert one night and movie another. Andrew and Travis wandered out of both of our lives within a couple months, until we ran into them at a dinner party later that winter. Five of the guests jumped into the hot tub after dinner, including Andrew and me.

It was a fun night, but somehow we got onto the subject of another couple breaking up because one of the partners got caught hooking up with someone else. Andrew piped in with his sanctimonious bullshit, "What a scum bag! I can't believe he'd cheat on his partner that way after everything that guy's done for him! What the hell was he thinking?" He was thinking about having a hot three-way and hoped his husband never found out, I thought. But the hot tub grumbled with agreement.

"I don't understand gay men," Andrew went on. "Is monogamy too much to ask for? They're always hooking up with each other and don't care about cheating on their partner!" Our eyes met.

Apparently, I wasn't doing a good job of hiding my look of disbelief because he promptly shut up.

I was single, so at least that part isn't my fault, and when I first hit on Andrew, I didn't know he wasn't single, so you can't blame me for that either, but by the time we did actually hook up, I knew he was married and chose to ignore that fact for two reasons. First, Andrew is amazingly sexy and has the one of the hottest bodies in all of Seattle. Second, I knew that Travis was cheating on Andrew, too.

EMOTIONAL INVESTMENT

Chapter 31
EMOTIONAL INVESTMENT

In addition to the availability of alternative partners and excessive expectations, traditional monogamous relationships also fail due to a lack of emotional investment between the partners. Lack of emotional investment is the third strong indicator that a relationship is doomed.

Emotional investment is the process of giving and receiving between partners. You're emotionally invested in someone if you strike a balance between giving and receiving things like attention, support, and love. Balance is important, as both partners should be demonstrating an equal level of emotional commitment to each other. Giving and receiving are equally important to the survivability of the relationship.

Emotional investment must be mutual and at equal levels for it to stay a positive force in a relationship. If there's any hint of manipulation or excess in giving or receiving, the situation is out of balance and resentment may set in. If you only receive and never give, there's a problem with your emotional investment in this relationship. If you only give and never receive, then you've become your partner's enabler, and you need to question his emotional, as well as financial, investment in this relationship.

Moderation in all things; excessive emotion will have the same negative consequence as not enough. Lack of balance results in major disappointment for whoever invests more.

What I've observed in almost every divorce case is one or both of the spouses lack emotional investment. One spouse doesn't have any substantial commitment to the other. They've gotten out of balance in their degree of emotional investment, or they both completely lack any emotional investment in each other.

The later scenario often happens where a couple sticks it out for the kids. They politely co-exist, but demonstrate no emotional investment in each other, instead directing it all to their kids. Delaying divorce so a couple can raise children in this sort of emotionally vacuous environment is almost always a bad thing. Children learn from watching their parents, and the example you set for your kids by existing in this loveless relationship is impacting the types and quality of relationships they will seek out.

Based on my anecdotal experience, there are five indicators that a marriage or relationship is destined to fail due to a lack of emotional investment:

1. **Poor Communication—** If your spouse or partner doesn't respond to your texts or give you a clear answer when you talk, it's an indication he lacks an emotional commitment to you. Even if a spouse can't give you a full answer, if he has an emotional investment, he'll shoot you a quick note instead of just ignoring you.

2. **Absent—** Maybe it's a work event, a book release party, or just a plan to meet for Christmas shopping, if your spouse doesn't show up to support you, he's emotionally closed off. People who care will make it happen and show up.

3. **A Spouse Gives More Than He Receives—** A sense of entitlement settles in when one spouse feels he doesn't need to reciprocate the same level of love, attention, and support the other spouse shows. He never buys gifts, pays for dinner, nor feels the need to say thank you anymore.

4. **Excuses and Indecision—** Making plans with an emotionally unavailable partner is like trying to catch

smoke. His excuses mean he's not open to long lasting <u>love</u> nor intimate connection.

5. **They Talk About Football All the Time—** This is only partially tongue-in-cheek. I'm a football fan, too, but it's a hard cold fact, when the Seahawks lose on Sunday, our phone rings like crazy on Monday. Every time. Emotionally detached partners and spouses spend an inordinate amount of time with distractions like football. Go Gators!

In speaking with people in failed marriages, I'm struck by how early emotional investment fails and how long a couple will endure in this state before they decide to get a divorce. It's almost like this is the first thing to go, and they don't seem to miss it much.

Chapter 32
A STAIRWELL IN BARCELONA

Barcelona Circuit is an event not to be missed. You have to see for yourself this week-long gay version of *Where the Wild Things Are* to believe it. Hundreds of thousands of gay men from all over the world descend on this beautiful, crown city of Europe for some of the best DJs, dance parties, and beach parties anywhere. At the pinnacle of this week is the water park party where, for a day and a night, Barcelona's largest water park is closed off for a giant circuit party, the likes of which you've never imagined.

Since this was my second trip to Circuit, I talked up the water park party to my traveling friends for months. The six of us rented a nice apartment on Las Ramblas, and some other friends were staying at Axel Hotel (advertised as "straight friendly") up the street. Of the ten people in my group, there were only two of us who were single. The other four couples were from all over; Toronto, London, Miami, and Dublin. Just me and one German were on singles duty.

All the couples had varying degrees of rules of conduct. One was all the way open, as far as I could tell, and another was completely closed. The other two had the typically convoluted rules you never want to ask about because they're too complicated and you just don't believe them anyway. "We only hook up together, except on vacation, and only after we talk to each other first, and never bare." Right. Good luck with all that.

I love all these guys, and I enjoy meeting up with them at various places around the world. This Barcelona trip was at the end of a cruise for some of us and just a weekend trip for others. It was great to be able to come together for a few days and do something crazy like the Circuit pool party.

No fear of me being pulled into a three-way with any of these couples, though. Not only would that be messy, but they're not my type. I only wanted to hangout and share this experience with my friends.

I just didn't realize how diverse the experience was going to be.

It was Saturday night, and one of the scheduled parties was a "gear" party, where party goers wear their favorite fetish gear. Gear could be a leather harness, which is a series of straps that wrap around the shoulders and sometimes go all the way down to the crotch, or motorcycle gear, rubber, wrestling singlets, and military outfits. Think of it as a halloween party without the sense of humor. People take their gear seriously.

I wore a bulldog harness and jeans, boring, but I also had on a black jock strap just in case it turned into that kind of party.

Herding ten people into costume, cabs, through the line to get in, then to the bar is half a night's work. Lots of complaining about outfits that night, since some of the guys weren't into fetish and were fighting the idea hard, yet we managed to get everyone into some novel gear, through the parade of getting to the bar for a drink, and started to enjoy ourselves. My favorite DJ, Mickey Wolf, was spinning. Not only is Mickey hot, he's a friend and he added me to his guest list that night. Nothing like walking past a long line at Circuit, to the front, and saying in a slightly bored tone of voice, without making eye contact, "I'm on the guest list." Boom! I'd arrived, and the party could commence!

Inside, the music was going, and there wasn't a shirt in sight in this crowd of thousands. The lights were barely on, except for on the strippers gyrating on the boxes around the dance floor. Amazing bodies, handsome faces, where do they find these guys? I'd get the answer soon enough.

My group danced together for most of the night, but trips to the bar or the bathroom would dwindle our number as some wouldn't return to our spot, at least not right away. I was starting to feel the urge to peel off and make my rounds through the crowd to see what was out there. No offense to Mickey, but there's more to a gear party than dancing. It was time to find a hot guy to make out with.

People ask, how do you know if someone's gay, and I always answer, it's the eyes. Gay men show their interest with a look. The look lasts a little longer, is deeper and is engaging at a sexual level. As I walked around the club, I got that look all over the place, as men showed they were interested in me. Most of them, though, weren't my type.

I made eye contact a few times with some sexy men, and even danced with some, but so far no one at the "gotta have it" level. That is, until I was lingering near the stage, talking with Mickey for a few seconds. He and another DJ were doing a "spin off," taking turns playing, rather than going for one huge, long block of time. That way, he had a few minutes for a hug and a hello. Mickey is hot as fuck, but has a great partner to whom he's deeply devoted.

While I was standing there with Mickey, the dancers switched shifts and those ending their shift walked by. It was impossible not to stare at their perfect bodies, covered in sweat and almost nothing else. I could use my imagination, but I didn't need to.

A Spanish-looking dancer, 5'10, maybe 23, muscular, scruffy, with some chest hair and obviously well endowed, glanced at me as he walked by and stutter-stepped, almost crashing into the dancer in front of him. A little laugh and he kept walking, but he looked over his shoulder and checked me out, up and down and smiled. Right before he walked around the corner and through the curtain, he turned fully around to face me and gave me a nod.

Mickey noticed me staring. "Holy fuck!" I said, and he laughed.

"You should go talk to him!" he said in halting English. Mickey is German. His was all the encouragement I needed.

How does one hit on a stripper at Circuit? These guys are flown in from all over the world and have their choice of any man they want. Sometimes, the man they want is the one with money, who can pay for a night together. That didn't interest me in the slightest, no matter how hot the guy was.

I slowly walked toward where the Spanish-looking guy disappeared, trying to act as if I was just strolling along, wherever my feet felt like going, and glanced through the curtain. There he was, just a few feet away acting like he was just drying off in the hallway with no one else around. He saw me, and smiled, and kept rubbing the towel over his body and legs for a few seconds. Then he gave a nod, like come in here. I looked around to see if anyone was watching, and ducked though the curtain.

I moved up to him, close. He pushed his body into mine and we started making out. Arms wrapped around each other, sweaty, nearly naked, it didn't take much imagination to see where this was going. It also didn't take any imagination to see his cock. It was out to the side of his jockstrap and fully hard; nice indeed.

The hallway was dark and empty now, but soon there would be people walking through since it was the way to the "green" rooms. The dancer pulled me to the end of the hallway, toward a back exit door, in a stairwell. There, he pulled down my jeans, leaving my jock strap on, and spun me around.

It felt like hours later, but I'm sure it was no more than twenty minutes. Herodoto and I swapped numbers and made a vague plan to meet after the club closed at 6:00 a.m. He was Cuban, from Miami, and was just here for Circuit and didn't have to dance again until tomorrow night at a different club. Herodoto was one of the hottest, most sensual men I'd ever met. The world was pretty beautiful at that moment. God, I love Barcelona.

It was a good thing, too, because I was about to walk into a full-on hornet's nest.

Spent, content, loving the music, feeling like the wolf at the front of the pack, I made my way through the crowd, stopping to dance with a few people I knew along the way. It's funny, but after being out now for twenty years, I can't go anywhere in the world without running into people I know. Makes the planet feel more like a family.

My group was no where in sight, and I was getting concerned. They could have left me and gone home already, but it was 3:00 a.m., which is early in Barcelona, and that seemed unlikely. I wasn't worried about myself. I'm completely fine taking care of myself in pretty much any city of the world. I was more worried that they'd gotten bored or weren't having a good time.

After a couple laps around the dance floor, I spotted them, standing by the upstairs bar in a group, looking animated, and not in a good way. I made my way up the stairs and approached the group. There was obviously a fight going on between two of them.

Carlos and Stephen were a couple from Toronto whom I'd met years ago on a gay cruise. Carlos was forty-five and a cardiologist with his own nationwide practice, and Stephen was thirty-three and the CEO of a technology company that focused on developing security for complex computer systems. Obviously, they're successful, type-"A" personalities, and I love them both, but perhaps not right at that moment.

"You're a fucking asshole!" yelled Carlos, jabbing his finger at Stephen. "You can find your own way home, fucker, and when you get there just go ahead and pack your shit." He was red in the face, not bothering to try and restrain himself. It was only a matter time before we got the attention of security.

"Dude, what are you talking about? I was just kissing the guy! It's no big deal! It's not like we're doing anything!" Stephen shouted back. "I don't understand what your problem is!"

Carlos and Stephen were the one monogamous couple on our trip. As long as I've known them, this was a hard rule, not to be broken nor infringed upon. They'd been together for twelve years so far and according to them, they've never hooked up with anyone outside their relationship. Every time we got together, though, my impression was this rule was more for Carlos than Stephen.

"I saw you guys together. Don't give me that bullshit. If I hadn't followed you up here, you guys would have been fucking in the stairwell." A little too close to home, I bit my lip and blushed, wondering if someone had seen us.

Carlos' demeanor was verging on irrational, and he'd had too much to drink. I started to worry this argument was about to turn physical, and we'd have a situation on our hand. I stepped in.

"Hey, we're gonna get kicked out of here or worse. Let's break this up or take it outside, okay? Nobody wants this to get ugly here, right?" I didn't know if I was throwing red meat at the pack, or if they'd listen and pull back from the edge of this cliff.

"What a fucker," said Carlos, turning to me. "Do you believe this shit, Dave? After twelve years, he's sneaking off with some trashy European boy to fucking cheat on me." If nothing else, I'd temporarily redirected his attention.

"Fuck it, man. Come on, Carlos. Let's go get a drink and talk." Since he was already too drunk, I had absolutely no intention of getting him another drink but rather was hoping to get him away from the confrontation.

Carlos followed me, but before he did, he turned to Stephen and said, "You need to get the fuck out of the hotel tonight. Go stay with your trashy little circuit boy." I thought he might poke or push Stephen, so I moved myself between them.

"Let's go, man. I got you," I said, and we headed across the upstairs bar to the stairwell. Thankfully, security was still nowhere in sight.

"That fucking prick, man. I'm done. I'm sick of his bullshit. He's always pulling shit like this!" Carlos said as we made our way down the stairs to the main dance floor. I didn't have a plan except to separate the two of them and, at the moment, was at a loss for what to do next.

"So what happened up there, bud?" I said, pulling him toward the back wall so we could hear each other over Mickey's music. I think I had the gist of the argument, but thought it might be a good idea to get Carlos talking about it.

"Just the same old bullshit, man. We were dancing, and Stephen started hitting on this guy next to us. They got close, and he said he wanted to go get a drink." Still angry, sadness was also showing through. "He went off, but not toward the bar, so I watched, and I saw him and that guy go upstairs, that fucker."

"Oh shit," I said.

"Yeah. So I followed them, and sure enough, there he was, standing at the bar, making out with this trashy european slut!" His voice raised, face red, anger was back for a visit. "Fucking asshole snuck off so I wouldn't see him! Why'm I still with this fucker? I fucking hate him!" Carlos launched his water bottle against the back wall.

I glanced around hoping no security people saw. I sure didn't want to get caught up in a situation where they thought the two of us were fighting. My Spanish was nowhere near good enough to try and explain this dynamic over the booming music.

I managed to get Carlos calmed down to the point where he wasn't throwing things anymore, but he was pretty set on leaving the club. Herodoto might just have to wait until tomorrow, but the thought of him slipping away was making me not happy with my friends Carlos and Stephen. It was now 4:30 a.m. and my night was being ended by a drunken pair of middle-aged children.

Our group had fragmented and wasn't likely to get back together. Since I had no idea where anyone was except the two of us I texted our friend Thomas to let him know I was taking Carlos back to his place at Axel.

Once we were safely in a cab winding its way through the convoluted streets of old town Barcelona, Carlos told me he and Stephen had been in and out of counseling for years, working through their jealousy and apparent disinterest in each other's lives. Sounded to me like it wasn't going too well. Carlos had no interest in Steven's issues, he just thought Stephen was a dick. Stephen didn't listen to him, Stephen wasn't intimate with him. Stephen worked late and went out after with friends. Stephen was always checking out younger guys.

These two were going through the motions of being in a relationship and protecting that status without making any legitimate effort to improve it or consider why their relationship was in the shitter in the first place. To the divorce lawyer, it sounded like this horse died years ago, and they just kept kicking it, too scared to leave the corpse and move on.

Chapter 33
TRADITIONAL VS. MODERN EMOTIONAL INVESTMENT

In a modern relationship, there's emotional investment, too. How is it different, though, from a traditional relationship? We still expect please and thank you and attention to our needs. We still give and take. We still have expectations that our partners will communicate, reciprocate, and show love and affection. So what's different?

The difference is the level of investment that we expect. Imagine two towers of block, representing the partner's level of investment. During the romantic love stage of traditional relationships, both towers are twenty blocks high; so high they teeter back and forth. The level of investment, and the level of expected return on that investment, is high.

For any relationship to be stable, the levels of emotional investment must be in balance, and here, at twenty blocks high, they're indeed in balance. This relationship, even though it's in the romantic love stage and based on fantasy, is stable!

As we know, though, romantic love is a fiction and reality sets in sooner or later. Sometimes, it sets in for one partner, but not the other. His tower of blocks begins to dwindle, while the other is still at twenty blocks high. His emotional investment in the relationship fades. Now down to five blocks, this partner's tower is dwarfed by the expectations of the other partner's tower of twenty blocks, and they're out of balance.

With one tower still at twenty blocks and the other now at five, this relationship is no longer stable. The expectations don't align, and it's only a matter of time before this couple fails.

What about the modern relationship? How are the towers of blocks different for partners in this new structure?

The answer is, in the modern relationship structure, the towers start smaller. In a modern relationship, the emotional investment during the romantic love stage is still elevated, say ten blocks, but these expectations, while not completely rational and reasonable, come nowhere near the expectations of the traditional relationship.

The emotional investment at the romantic love stage of a traditional relationship includes expectations based on the Disney paradigm that aren't contained in a modern relationship such as monogamy, servitude, and a trajectory toward marriage. Blocks like these are missing from the modern relationship tower.

Since the expectations are more reasonable and the emotional investment more realistic, the sharp reduction from twenty blocks to five blocks, or even ten to five blocks, is unlikely. The fantasy of romantic love isn't so extensive in a modern relationship because the expectations aren't based on the Disney paradigm. Instead, these expectations are based on the needs of modern society.

Modern relationships still fail, though, after the romantic love stage, and they still fail because of different levels of emotional investment.

The failure of an emotional investment comes from the expectations of a partner about reciprocating actions. In other words, a spouse's standard for what he expects the other person to do for him, or give to him is more than the other spouse ever intended to give.

The key to emotional investment is balance and equity between the partners.

In the traditional paradigm, we overburden our central relationship. We look to our partners for all manner of support, from sexual satisfaction to self-esteem and personal growth. These demands for an emotional investment are too much. In the modern world, people sustain themselves, they don't rely on their parters. They're independent and have their own lives separate from their spouse or partner. They don't want nor expect their partner to provide for them.

Therefore, the level of emotional investment where a modern couple strikes balance is lower than the level for a balance in traditional monogamous relationships. The spouse should still fully expect his partner to communicate, and to show him respect, and to say thank you, but he should no longer expect to fully, 100%, support him and his lifestyle.

Since it's a question of balance between the two towers of blocks, both modern and traditional relationships still fail when the emotional investment between the partners is out of whack. Partners should still expect certain things from each other, but when one partner stops reciprocating, it's time to kick him to the curb.

An interesting side observation is that, often, emotional investment disappears about the same time as romantic love ends. Once the fantasy fades and the reality of true personalities and the daily grind sets in, emotional investment disappears. This isn't always the case. Romantic love can convert to adult love and emotional investment continues. The towers can reduce in parity and remain in balance all the way down to just two or three blocks if that's all the partners expect of each other. It's not the number of blocks that's important; who are we to judge a couple's expectations? It's about balance.

I often see couples who are all about each other, roses, chocolate, cuddling on the couch, making dinner together, while they're in the romantic stage. This changes once Prince Charming's football team loses one too many games, or he has one too many scotch on the rocks. The spell breaks and the emotional investment evaporates right along with the romantic stage of love.

Chapter 34
CHAMPAIGN AND ROSES

By the time 6:00 a.m. rolled around I was just getting back to my apartment on Las Ramblas and was pretty beat. Overall, it'd been a great night, despite the drama caused by Mr. and Mrs. Leave It to Beaver, and I headed to bed with a smile. I was in Barcelona, spent the night dancing to Mickey's music, got fucked by one of the hottest men in the whole city; what more could I ask for?

My phone lit up with a text. It was Herodoto.

"Where are you, sexy fucker?"

Damn it! I didn't think I'd hear from him! Herodoto was so far out of my league and had his choice of men. Plus, he'd already had me. Men are always on the hunt for something new. It's part of our DNA, yet here he was, trying to hit me up. Could this night get any better?

"Had to babysit a friend. Just back to Las Ramblas. Where you staying?"

"W at the port. Want to hang?"

You're kidding me, right? I lead a charmed life, and I have no idea why. One day, the bill for all this good luck is gonna to come due, and I'm gonna get hit by bus; a big one with a lot of fat people on it.

A few minutes later and I'm in a cab on my way to the W; nice place to put up the strippers. This was a mystery I'm not sure I wanted solved.

Herodoto met me downstairs in loose jeans and a plain white t-shirt. He looked infinitely comfortable. Greeting me with a warm hug and a quick kiss, he led me up to his room. Once there, we started making out. He's a fantastic kisser.

Before I got there, Herodoto ordered up some champaign and OJ, along with a fruit plate. There was even a flower. I smiled broadly when I saw all his effort, feeling special. Just take me now, Jesus; it just doesn't get any better.

Cuddled up on the couch we sat and watched the sun come up over the Mediterranean, sipping champaign and talking about Barcelona, the beach, Miami, Cuba, stripping. It was fantastic to just hang out and share things with this handsome, thoughtful man.

We finally curled up and slept for a few hours, but around 2:00 p.m., my phone started going off with texts from my worried friends. It was time to start getting around and text them back. Herodoto was still curled up in my arms sleeping gently, his broad, muscled back pushed against my chest. Pulling him in closer to me, I kissed the back of his neck and whispered, "Hey, handsome."

Herodoto stirred and stretched his body against mine. "Good morning, mister Dave," he said, in a raspy whisper, grabbing my arms and wrapping them more tightly around his body. I nuzzled my head against his. We lay like that slowly coming out of sleep.

After a while we got up together and showered. The showers at the W in Barcelona are the size of an entire room. Herodoto washed my body, shampooed my hair, and gave me a soft neck massage. We had slow, gentle sex in the shower, then ran to the bed where it was wild, fast, hard, and sweaty. It was amazing. Herodoto would come all the way out, then push back in deep and fast, all in one continuous stroke; and he was not small, maybe the biggest I've been with.

Based on the texts, my group wanted to meet at the beach. They knew me so well, they didn't even bother to ask where I was.

"Hey, what are you doing today?" I asked Herodoto.

"No plans. Just have to be at the club at 11:00 tonight. Why?" he said as he pulled a loose white tank top over his head.

"Wanna come to the beach with me?"

A big smile spread across his face and his brown eyes lit up. "I'd love that," he said.

"And I'd love to share it with you, handsome."

The W sits on one of the best beaches in Barcelona but I didn't bring a suit, and Herodoto was much smaller than I, well, his waist anyway. The shop in the lobby had a few and we headed out to find the boys.

You can't walk along the beach with a guy as handsome as Herodoto and not hold hands. You should've seen the looks we got. Straight, gay, old, young, almost every head turned, but the best reaction was when I saw my friends as we walked up to them on the beach. Stephen saw us at first, but whatever he said to the group made them all turn in unison and look in my direction, some of them sitting up. I smiled a little inside.

After introducing everyone, Herodoto and I spread some towels, and cuddled up. Across the towels and lounge chairs, I could see Carlos and Stephen were still full-on fighting; they just weren't doing so openly. Backs to each other, no communication, and angry faces all told me the powder keg was sitting awfully close to the fire.

The consensus was that the night had been a good one. Other than Carlos and Stephen, everyone reported a great time, and we were ready for the next one tonight in a town south of Barcelona called Sitges. Herodoto was dancing on stage, but was gonna try and find time to be with me, too. That made me very happy.

My new Cuban friend was goofy and smart and determined to be successful in life. Stripping was great money and he was exceptionally good at it, but he knew it wouldn't last and was already planning a different future in Miami. Very much a family guy, Herodoto loved to talk about his brothers and sisters and all his extended family back in Cuba, but most especially his mom. I felt like I knew her personally by the end of the day.

We alternated between cuddling on the beach and playing in the water most of the rest of that day. We even rented paddle boards, and Herodoto taught me the basics. I had to show off and do a headstand that ended tragically as the board went one way, and my body went the other, but before the crash, I managed to get up on my head, inverted, and stay up for at least a ten-count before splashing down into the warm, blue waters of the Mediterranean. I think he was impressed.

It was a comfortable day with one of the sweetest guys in town. It ended with a walk back to the W where he invited me up one more time. Clothes thrown to the floor, I enjoyed his body on top of me and inside me and in my arms, then I was in a cab back to my place on Las Ramblas. On the way home, I realized I felt like a teenager around Herodoto and reflected on how easily we slipped into this day-long relationship. Spontaneously, I called the W and ordered a dozen white roses for delivery to his room. I liked Herodoto and hoped I'd get to see him again.

When I got back to the apartment, I learned Carlos had thrown Stephen's iPhone into the wall and stormed out. He was planning on flying back to Toronto in the morning.

Part IV
FORCE OF TECHNOLOGY

Chapter 35
TECHNOLOGY'S EVOLUTION OF MODERN RELATIONSHIP

Right now, a new social structure is developing, shaped by an unprecedented revolution in technology. Looking at the modern forces impacting our daily lives, it's hard to deny that technology is changing our culture faster than it's ever changed before. The ability to instantly communicate with anyone in the world, the increased productivity, the amazing ways technology provides to entertain ourselves, the personal growth opportunities, the ability to stretch your mind in directions never before possible, and the tremendous economic possibilities all operate to drive an enormous and pervasive change in our lives, including in our sexual relationships.

How fast things are changing can be seen in the rapid growth of the technology industry itself:

- Facebook was founded in February, 2004. Ten years later, in July, 2014, there were 1.317 billion monthly active users and the company's worth is estimated at $190 billion.
- Google was founded in September, 1998. Sixteen years later, people use Google for 3.5 billion searches every day or about 40,000 searches every second. As of September, 2014, Google has a market capitalization of $360 billion.
- Apple's iPhone launched in June, 2007. Seven years later, 41.4% of all cellphones in the US are iPhones. As of

October 2014, Apple has a market capitalization of $576 billion, making it the most valuable company in the world.

Of the five most valuable companies in the world, three are technology companies (Apple, Microsoft and Google). These three companies have a combined market value of $1.335 trillion, and an average age of 29 years old. By comparison, the other two most valuable companies rounding out the top five were both founded in the 1880s, and average 130 years old.

Seeing this explosion of an industry, it's difficult to argue that technology isn't impacting every aspect of our lives. These companies only came into existence recently, comparatively speaking, and they're just getting started. Their expansion into our daily, personal lives will only accelerate.

One of the social structures most impacted by this stunning explosion of technology is our relationships. An evolution in our relationships is happening just as fast as the growth of this industry, yet little is said about it. There's a presumption that relationships have always been this way, always will be this way, and can't be impacted by any changes in society. All three are flat-out wrong.

What's the nexus between this industry and the evolution of sexual relationships? How's technology driving the changes in our relationships and the types of relationships we enter into? Technology is driving this change in three ways:

- Creating new avenues for social interaction and creativity
- Evolving characteristics conducive to the use and expansion of itself
- Creating work environments within the industry and in supporting industries that further develop a progressive nature

Society has evolved continuously since humans began to congregate in villages and tribes. Under constant pressure from external factors and from internal evolution, yesterday's rules and constructs become obsolete and transform into a drag on further development. Outdated rules slow development and progress, and thus get ignored and become irrelevant. It's like a law in town purporting to reduce traffic congestion; "Pigs and other farm animals shall not be allowed on the streets before 10:00 a.m."

Societies that adapt and modernize these rules are the successful ones. A quote misattributed to Charles Darwin says, "It isn't the strongest of the species that survives, nor the most intelligent. It's the one that's most adaptable to change." Even though Darwin didn't, in fact, say it, I think it represents the fundamental principle of evolution.

Relationships are no different. Our world is changing, thanks in large part to technology, and our relationship structure is changing right along with it. The constant push-pull between the "we've always done it this way" crowd and the "let's try something new" crowd reaches equilibrium, and a new normative is developed which is useful, right up until it's not.

Being in the middle of this incredible period of change in sexual relationships clouds our perspective of its extent. Much like being stuck in all the trees, we can't see the forest; a new sexual revolution is underway, driven by the force of technology, and it's happening all around us.

Chapter 36
PIGS IN BLANKET AND FOLSOM FAIR

Folsom Street Fair in San Francisco is a leather and fetish weekend-long party held in September. The main event is a street fair where the city blocks off most of Folsom Street and vendors set up tents with their fetish-oriented gear, live demonstrations and sex exhibits. It's perhaps the largest event of its type and certainly holds the title for being the most well-known.

It's not for the faint of heart, however. There's plenty of nudity and open sex acts, along with flogging exhibits, "puppy pounds," and more fetish outfits than you'll probably ever see anywhere else. You'll see plenty of men in nothing more than jock straps or even just a cock ring on occasion. There'll be bare-chested women and a few who are completely nude, men on leashes, men gagged, and porn stars all over the place who are happy to get their dicks out for a picture with you.

Essentially, there are no rules for Folsom, with participants trying to out-do each other's extreme outfits or behavior everywhere you look.

This is just the outdoor festival.

The indoor scene is just simply sex, and the foreplay leading up to sex. At the main dance party, the dark room area is almost as big as the dance floor. This is why you go to Folsom.

It was my first time to Folsom Street Fair. I'd been to other parties of the same vein, so I wasn't surprised at what I saw, but I was interested in the widespread acceptance of the extreme behavior. Other parties, like the Black Party in NYC, are closed off, private, and almost exclusively for gay men. Folsom is open, public, and there are plenty of straight people walking around enjoying the fetish scene, too.

People didn't seem to be shocked by anything at Folsom; interested, and maybe chuckles at certain exhibits, but festival-goers were comfortable with the scene around them. It was my first time wearing just a harness, baseball cap, and a jockstrap in public, but after about twenty minutes, I realized it was no big deal; pretty incredible.

I went to the street fair with a group of friends from Seattle and San Francisco, including Jason and Chris. We had a great time exploring the exhibits and trying things out and meeting new people. After a few margaritas from the street vendors I was feeling pretty good that afternoon.

My friend Cameron, who's an officer in the Navy, and I were flirting with this couple from San Francisco who lived around the corner. The couple was just getting ready to invite us back to their place when I looked to the right, toward the stage, and there was Robbie in a harness, military hat, and leather pants, about fifty feet away.

Robbie has an amazing body. He's not massive, or even a big guy, but he's lean, muscular and well defined. He has broad shoulders and a slightly hairy chest that fits perfectly into a harness, framing his muscular upper body.

It's hard to describe how sexy he looked at that moment. Nothing else in the world mattered right then as I stared at him. He must have felt me staring because he lifted his head and looked straight into my eyes. Cruising me up and down, he stopped talking to his friends and turned his body toward me.

That was all it took. I dumped my drink and started walking toward him. He mirrored me, never taking his eyes off mine, and started walking, too. When we met, it was raw, rough, and intense. I pushed my mouth over his and held his head close to mine so that even if he wanted to back away, he couldn't, but he didn't. Instead, he grabbed me by the waist and pulled his body hard against mine.

For a few moments, the world stopped and the crowd on Folsom disappeared. Standing in the street with the sexiest man in all of SF in my arms, I lost track of everything else around me. Starting to get aroused, I could feel his body responding, but since a jockstrap wasn't adequate coverage, I backed away before it got more intense.

A small crowd stopped to watch, and when Robbie and I pulled apart a few started clapping. The moment passed; we smiled and kissed again.

"I thought you had to work," I said, fixing his military cap.

"Yeah, I decided to take off a few hours this afternoon and come over. I gotta be back at 4:00," he responded, my arm still wrapped around his waist. "How do you like Folsom?"

"Crazy. Never seen anything like some of the exhibits. That puppy pound was pretty nuts," I said. A puppy pound is a little fenced off area where guys who like to dress as puppies hang out while their masters go off and enjoy the festival. The puppies play around, sniff each other's butts, and piss in the corner.

He laughed. "Not my thing, but to each his own, right? I'm glad I ran into you. I knew I would," he said with a sly smile.

"I'm glad you did, too. Made my day."

We stood there talking for a few minutes, pulling each other close for a kiss every once in awhile. The conversation surrounded Folsom and the parties, music, outfits, etc. I knew Robbie was into leather, but I had no idea how amazing he looked in it. I couldn't take my eyes off him.

It was a little after 3:00 p.m. and Robbie said he needed to get home and change for work. I asked if he wanted me to go with him, but he said he'd be running around and I should stay and enjoy the festival.

"Can I come see you later?" I asked.

"Are you kidding? Come by at closing. I'd love to spend another night with you before you gotta fly out," he said as he grabbed my crotch and leaned in to lick my face.

Recalling our first night together, I pulled his head close to mine and whispered into his ear, "Can I fuck you?"

Robbie's smile filled his face. He winked and turned to walk off. Turning back to my group of friends, I caught Jason's eye. He was standing there with Chris, both with a look of amused disbelief, then it dawned on me.

Jason and Chris were friends with Tony, and Tony still didn't know about Robbie and me. From soaring in the clouds, my heart crashed into the pit of my stomach.

Chapter 37
NEXUS: SOCIAL INTERACTION AND CREATIVITY

The first way technology is providing the nexus for the evolution in modern relationships is through the development of creativity and individuality. Creativity and individuality have been around since before the explosion of technology, but never before have the tools, resources, and connectivity of technology been available to drive and enhance these two characteristics.

The more technology facilitates the development of creativity and fosters individuality, the greater the need for a modern versus traditional relationships. Individuality and creativity run counter to the traditional paradigm of marriage and monogamy.

This isn't the first time that the opportunities created by individuality and creative thinking have driven the marriage rates down. Prior to the turn of the nineteenth century, during the dawn of the industrial revolution, marriage rates also collapsed, but not nearly to the extent that they have today. This period of the dawn of the industrial revolution gave rise to a new level of expressionism in art and music as well as fewer traditional marriages. This was the age of Monet, Debussy, and Bohemia.

Today, thanks to technology, we're working more creatively, and the way creative people go about creating is different. This shift is more than exchanging typewriters for computers or art tables for graphic design programs; it's a complete pivot in the creative process.

Never before have our creative hands been so free to engage in new forms of art and music. The tools made available through technology allow almost any image, sound, or structure we can envision to become reality. Freed from linear thinking, creation is more organic and free flowing than it ever could be with typewriters or paint brushes. This creativity comes at a low price, as many of the apps available for creative expression are under five dollars.

Modern technology, with its increased access to people, art, and ideas from faraway places, helps us become more creative not only by exposing us to a variety of styles and ideas, but also by allowing us to think more abstractly. You can now collaborate with someone across the globe who has a completely different culture, background, musical style, etc. than you. This immediately puts you at a distinct advantage when it comes to creating new art and ideas.

While the technology generation is expressing its individuality through music, clothing, body art, piercings etc., it's also expressing its individuality online. The use of Facebook walls, personal blogs, Soundcloud, Instagram, and the myriad of other technology-based options available allow this group of talented people to express themselves on the fly 24/7. Nearly any random thought they might have throughout the day can be shared instantly with a wide group of "friends" or followers. As a result of the positive feedback they receive, these individuals grow even more sophisticated in their use of technology and expression of individuality.

Technology has made creating art and experimenting with novel creative tools much easier by providing more time in which to engage in creative outlets. The Internet has reduced our daily allocation of task-time and freed up hours and energy to pursue art and ideas. Technology is creating new avenues for social interaction as well.

The process of human communication has evolved over the years, with game-changing inventions triggering revolutions that move communication to the next level. The evolution began with the invention of the first written communication, where mankind could capture a thought and preserve it over time and distance. Communication leapt forward with the invention of paper, enabling an even broader reach of recorded thought. Electronic transmission of thoughts and ideas expanded communication like never before with the invention of devices like the telegraph and the telephone. Today, communication is undergoing perhaps the most epic shift since the invention of paper with the creation of the Internet that makes the instant transfer of all types of information from one place to another a reality. Technology is providing the next leap in communication by changing how we connect and add to the world of ideas.

In his book, *The End of Big*, Nico Mealy describes the wide-ranging implications of the digital revolution. "Radical connectivity – our breathtaking ability to send vast amounts of data instantly, constantly, and globally – has all but transformed politics, business, and culture, bringing about the upheaval of traditional, 'big' institutions and the empowerment of upstarts and renegades."

I don't know about upstarts and renegades, but the term "radical connectivity" is perfect for describing the impact communication is having on our relationships to people. It describes the velocity with which we can communicate and transfer information. It's the velocity of communication that's different. While services like Grindr, Scruff, and Facebook provide the mechanical means for communicating, they, themselves, aren't what's changing the nature of communication. It's the velocity of communication enabled by technology.

It's a common argument that online communication and text messages supplant other means of communication. Experts argue that we've forgotten how to communicate face-to-face because all our communication is through the use of modern technology; however, research demonstrates that the use of technology to communicate is enhancing, and adding to the volume of communication, not detracting from it.

Research by Barry Wellman, at the University of Toronto, supports the conclusion that the use of social media has actually augmented our personal relationships. Wellman's research indicates that people who use social media and other technological tools for communicating, have just as many off-line discussions as those who don't. The difference is that modern communication is faster and more frequent.

More frequent communication is creating a radically more interconnected society, where the velocity of the exchange of ideas, information, and communication is enhancing every aspect of our lives, including our own sexual relationships.

Decades ago, our social networks were decidedly local. The network was made up of those within arm's reach; our neighbors and nearby friends and family members. More recently, we've become, in Wellman's words, "glocalized," simultaneously involved in both local and long-distance relationships.

Our devices have changed the way we communicate with each other as well, enabling instant communication from wherever we are, whatever we're doing. We live in a world created by technology, where ideas, expression, and opportunity can explode regardless of who offers them or where they originate.

This velocity of communication is allowing us to form completely new types of relationships with people we would've never known or met face-to-face.

Chapter 38
GETTING A BRAZILIAN

When you give someone your cabin number and tell them to come over at 5:30 p.m., there's a better than even chance it's never gonna happen. I know that sounds counter intuitive, but the truth of the matter is that most of the time, people flake out. They find someone better, lose interest, or were just being nice in the first place.

Earlier in the day, when I told the hot Brazilian to come back for round two at 5:30 p.m. and that I'd try and put together a hot group, it was a long shot that he'd come over. By the time 5:00 p.m. rolled around I'd lost interest and forgotten all about it. After two hours sleep the night before, my brain was operating at half-steam.

I closed the shades, stripped down to nothing, and flopped onto the bed for a disco nap before dinner.

It seemed like hours later when the door opened and my roommate Nick and two friends Mark and Andre came in. The fact that I was naked on top of the bed didn't bother me at all; just not shy that way.

Their voices were whispering and laughing, and I felt someone crawl into bed behind me and put his arm over me. A few seconds later, someone else slid into bed in front of me. Both were wearing nothing but their swimming trunks. I recognized the one in front as Andre because of his beard and muscular body. Sandwiched between these two men, I wrapped my arm around Andre and pulled him close, and we all three cuddled up into a ball.

I think they thought I'd freak out with people crawling into bed with me naked, but instead, I just cuddled up nice and tight and kept on sleeping. Almost immediately, I could feel Mark getting aroused.

Nick jumped into the shower while the three of us lay there. It felt amazing. I just met these two on this cruise and fell in love with them. They were fun, handsome, kind, and Canadian.

Even though I could feel Mark hard behind me, and despite the fact that I was fully naked, it wasn't a sexual cuddle. I knew these two played around with single guys on the cruise; in fact, Mark wasn't shy about giving me copious details, and I also knew there was mutual attraction between us, but something waved me off pursuing a hookup. Frankly, they were such awesome friends, I didn't want to change the relationship with just a quick rubbing one out together. There was a connection with Mark and Andre and this cuddle, quiet, close, intimate, said everything about my feelings.

Nick came out of the shower, wrapped in nothing but a towel, and was surprised, I think, to see us still in bed together and not fucking. "Alright, boys, hate to break up this little love-fest, but it's gonna be dinner time in a few and you all need to get dressed," he said, standing at the end of the bed, still wrapped in a towel. We didn't move.

There was a knock at the door. It didn't register as anything but probably another one of our group coming to get ready for dinner. Our room seemed to be a mandatory stop on the way to anywhere for our group of about ten people.

Nick moved to the door and opened it. No movement from my bed; I wasn't gonna let these two go if I could help it.

Whoever it was walked back in with Nick. They were standing at the end of the bed talking, but one of them was speaking halting, simple English. It didn't register except as a curiosity. Instead, I was thinking how warm Andres' body felt pressed against mine, breathing on his naked back.

I heard the sounds of someone undressing, then Nick say, "oh shit!"

My brain finally blasted into awareness as I put together what was happening. This was the Brazilian, and he was greeted by a sexy, young guy in nothing but a towel and walked in to see me naked in bed with two other big muscle men. Naturally, he was stripping down as quickly as he could.

It was Nick's "oh shit!" that finally made my brain go "clunk". I had exactly the same reaction when I hooked up with this Brazilian and an Aussie earlier in the day and he pulled down his swimming suit. It was exceptionally nice.

Eyes open, jumping out of bed fully naked, poor Andre scattered to the floor. At the end of the bed was standing a newly naked, beautifully built, dark-haired muscle man from Brazil who speaks almost no English. Nick was standing to the side, still staring at the Brazilian's quickly swelling penis. The Brazilian had a big smile.

Confusion reigned.

"What th . . .," said Andre from the floor.

A laugh came from Mark.

"No! Wait! Come . . . here!" I said as I grabbed the Brazilian's shorts that were now down around his knees, and began pulling them up and trying to get him to move out of the bedroom. I grabbed my shorts and pulled them on backwards.

"You finish?" he said as I pulled/pushed his still mostly naked body out of the bedroom, the smile draining from his face, a look of confusion setting in instead.

"No! Oh shit. They're just friends. I didn't . . . No, we were just cuddling! I didn't . . ." It was surreal. I was trying to explain the inexplicable to someone whose English vocabulary could be printed on a condom wrapper. Even if his English had been perfect, how could I hope to explain four guys in various states of nakedness, in bed together, when I told him to come by for a group?

The urge to laugh was overpowering.

I managed to get him dressed and, as gently as I could, pulled him into the hallway. I tried explaining that it wasn't a group and that I'd fallen asleep and was so sorry. There's no way he understood anything except that it was an embarrassing situation and there wasn't going to be a group. His face finally settled into a look of frustration and resolve, and he turned and walked off down the hallway.

What are the odds? On a gay cruise? Apparently, pretty good.

Chapter 39
CYBER CUDDLING

One game-changing technology for the development of new or existing relationships is the video call. This technology is rapidly becoming the *de facto* means for communicating between long distance partners and initiating new relationships that go beyond text messages. Another emerging trend is the use of FaceTime to verify the identity of people you've spoken with online since up to 12% of Facebook profiles are fake. This statistic is even higher with dating and hookup applications.

For existing long-distance relationships, the use of applications like FaceTime provides a much-needed connection to your absent partner. In our global economy, it's not uncommon to find a couple separated by long-distance either temporarily or on a permanent basis. Perhaps one person has to move for a job and the other needs to stay put for a while.

This exploding technology isn't just for people at the career stage of life. An estimated 75% of college students have engaged in a long distance love at one point or another, and about three million American adults in relationships live apart. Most of this crowd makes use of video technology on a regular basis.

Research shows that FaceTiming your distant loved ones can minimize the difficulties of a long distance relationship. Microsoft's Idea Lab conducted a survey of Skypers and found that 96% of respondents said the video call gives them a closer connection to their far away partner.

It's not only about a closer connection; 61% percent of users said video calling improves their romantic relationships, and 47% credit the technology with "keeping the love alive" while far apart.

Who hasn't seen the FaceTime or Skype screenshots of two lovers enjoying a little cyber cuddling? In that cute Instagram picture, they each lay in bed, in various stages of undress smiling or laughing, one big picture and one little overlay in the corner.

My first use of video calling technology was in the late 1990s. I'm not sure how I met this couple, Danny and Mike from Auckland, New Zealand, but over the ICQ chat program, we decided to try and make a video call work. After weeks of trying cameras, software, cables, and microphones we finally managed to make a video call from Seattle reach all the way down to New Zealand.

The pixels were the size of your thumb and the video rarely matched up with the audio, but we communicated. As long as we didn't move much, I could kind of make out what Danny and Mike looked like. A new friendship was born from those video calls, and I still talk with Danny at least once a week, although he now lives in London, and we communicate via Facebook. We still haven't met in person.

Over the years, I've been in a couple of long distance relationships and we made use of these tools to stay in touch and stay relevant in each other's lives. The awkwardness of the communication drops off relatively quickly, and you're able to engage at a high level of connectedness.

The frequent, visual, and instantaneous sharing of each other's life enables you to remain "present". This way, when you're able to have face-to-face contact again, there isn't a gaping hole in your friendship. In today's world, sharing can be accomplished even if you're separated by hundreds or thousands of miles.

This technology has made long distance relationships much more manageable. When something good or bad happens at work, one partner can notify the other immediately by texting him. If he sees a great pair of Bruno Magli on sale, just Snapchat it to the other. The gym is ridiculously crowded, and the guy with the arms is there, iMessage it. Want to let your partner know you're at his favorite pot shop? Send him your location and let him imagine what you've got planned for the night.

While users can't touch, hug, or kiss via FaceTime, they can gaze into each other's eyes, blow kisses, as well as other intimate activities. In fact, according to Idea Lab, 29% of FaceTimers admitted to taking part in a "naughty" call. While it's unclear what exactly that means, some things seem better left to the imagination.

This technology has radically changed these relationships. Some would have died from distance, others would have drifted into the red zone. Still others would never have existed at all.

Chapter 40
GAYS GOT TECH FIRST

When I first started practicing law, I ran ads in one of the local gay papers for a general litigation practice, including criminal defense cases, and was active in the GLBT community. One of the types of cases I regularly got hired on was the "sex in the park" case. This was during a time when gay men went looking for a hookup in a local park, after sunset, and the police would hunt them down and give them a ticket. The penalty for these crimes varied from just a fine for being in the park after hours to indecent exposure and listing on the sex offender registry.

These were dark times for gay men, with the world shaming you, punishing you for being who you were. Sure, these guys shouldn't have been looking for sex at the park, but the world left them few alternatives for meeting other men like themselves.

I never went to the parks looking for sex. It was tempting but just too risky, but when I first came out, the choices were few-- parks, personal ads, and the bars. I met Danny, my first boyfriend, through personal ads.

As happens with many gay relationships, Danny and I exhausted our sexual interest in a short period and opened up the relationship soon after we started dating. By this time, I'd discovered the AOL chatrooms. Chat rooms were a whole new world, and a new sexual revolution was sparked by this mechanism for finding sexual partners.

The functionality of this form of communication was limited compared to our capabilities today, but so much more advanced than what we had before. Suddenly, I could have a conversation with someone safely, privately about hooking up, and explore whether we were compatible over a period of minutes, days or weeks. We could swap pictures by email, although scanning pictures (there were no digital pics yet), attaching them to an email, and being able to open the pictures (different formats required different programs to view) was a significant technical challenge at the time. All of these functions were emerging technology that needed to be mastered if you wanted to hook up.

Our sex drive pushed gay men to master all aspects of technology. Nothing motivates someone quite like sex, and closeted gay men would do anything to find a hot, sexy, compatible man. Not only did we dive into technology with everything we had, we mastered it in a way that put our talented people at the top of the industry.

That's not to say today's tech CEOs all got their start in gay chatrooms, but our gay world filled up with tech language, money, jobs, and successful people overnight, thanks to this huge, sex-driven leap into the digital communication age. You don't have to look far down the list of the top ten technology industry CEOs, board members, or chief technologists to find an overwhelming representation of gays and lesbians.

We wanted sex. If we were gonna find the hottest guy in town to fuck, we had to master chat, email, photos, file sharing, Internet access, and all the other computer maintenance issues that come with living a digital life. We had to know about storage, memory, processors, and baud rate. What do people do with such specialized and advanced knowledge? They build on it.

With their leap ahead of the straight world, gays jumped into programming, web development, hardware design, and every other type of digital specialty out there. Our community, being close and private already, made for a synergy between talent, need, and resources. Millionaires were made in the span of just a few years, and I'm not just talking about the talented programmers, but also their bankers, supporters, and even employees.

Sexual desire drove skill development that opened doors to exciting futures. Opportunity was created to shape this new industry, one like no other in the history of the world.

AOL chat rooms gave away to hookup specific websites, like Manhunt, as well as social networking sites, like Connexions and Facebook, but even as these alternatives made it easier and easier to find partners, a mastery of the technology increased the likelihood of finding the hottest guy. A feedback loop developed where the talents we developed in AOL chatrooms created Manhunt, where we discovered even newer tricks and talents, which we used to create the mobile apps Scruff and Grindr.

Today, mastery of these app-based hookup tools increases your chance of finding the hottest guy. Eventually, these skills will drive the development of the next tool for finding a hookup. A twenty-something flipping through Grindr may decide he can do things better and develop some as-yet undreamed of new way of finding the next Mr. Incredible.

Do you know how valuable this twenty-something is to the tech industry? If you're in the business and you aren't nodding your head right now, turn in your resignation and start looking for a career in insurance. This highly motivated, skilled kid with few preconceived notions of how things are "supposed to be" may just develop an idea that turns into the next Facebook or Google. Where do you think these monster ideas come from, a staff meeting?

Brilliance is punctuated, not a process. The flash of a great idea happens in just one person's head. While it may take shape and be perfected by a process with the contributions of other great minds, that initial, "Oh hey!" moment sparks in just one mind at a time. Without that spark, nothing happens, no matter how great the talent sitting around the table.

Chapter 41
HUNTING TWENTY-SOMETHINGS

In 2010, Steve Jobs famously mused that, for technology to be truly brilliant, it must be coupled with artistry. "It's in Apple's DNA that technology alone is not enough," he said. "It's technology married with liberal arts, married with the humanities, that yields the results that make our hearts sing."

Most technology companies recognize the value of the twenty-something's "spark" and actively seek out these internally motivated people. As I noted earlier, technology companies pursue individuals with these characteristics:

Curiosity
Creativity
Challenging the status quo
Independence and confidence
Positive balance of time

When they manage to hire one of these sparks-in-waiting, smart technology companies continue to foster these traits with specifically tailored policies and benefits. They recognize that these characteristics are the source of the brilliance these twenty-somethings bring to the company. Sticking one of these assets into a windowless room, eight to five, Monday thru Friday, with a nice 401k program will stifle their creativity and cut off any hope of generating that spark of brilliance.

While it'd be nice if these twenty-somethings would always come up with that big idea making their employer billions, most of the time they don't, obviously. Instead, their contributions are measured in baby steps, creating a new button for an app, scripting simple and elegant code, designing a more intuitive interface, efficient use of a small screen, or even engineering of internal components to be more sleek. These may be little "sparks," but they eventually add up to amazing new products and profits.

Smart technology companies seek out and foster these twenty-somethings. All the talent and energy aren't directed solely at developing the next hookup app. The skills they develop push the creation of many other solutions to life's daily challenges and tasks. Online banking, with instant deposits, Uber, flight tracking, health monitoring, and ordering pretty much whatever you want, all have been advanced, in part, thanks to the talents of people developed in pursuit of a hookup.

Why is it so hard to imagine the broad impact of these skills also deeply impacts the types of relationships this generation enters? As we've seen, statistically speaking, this generation is predisposed to modern relationships, but the subgroup of twenty-somethings who grew up using technology to seek out and develop relationships are even more inclined to be assets to a technology company.

It's an unfair generalization, but the point is illustrative: if a twenty-something is in a traditional relationship, with the traditional trappings of 2.5 kids, white picket fence, married to his soulmate, and a wedding complete with grandma's wedding dress and reception games, is he more likely or less likely to think outside the box and come up with a spark of brilliance? I believe he's less likely.

I think a powerful indicator of someone's potential success in the tech industry is his choice of relationships. The threshold isn't whether he's married; the question is, what kind of relationship does he have with his partner, if he has a partner at all? Does his relationship fit perfectly within the traditional paradigm, with predefined expectations? Or does he form relationships with their own structure, where the expectations are tailored to the individuals in the relationship?

My observations in San Francisco, the habitat of technology, is that most couples are in modern relationships, where the structure is determined by the individuals. I'm sure there are traditional relationships existing in the traditional paradigm in San Francisco, too, since I also saw some around town, but the vast majority of people I met were building their own paradigm. The younger the person was, the more likely he stayed well clear of the traditional paradigm.

You might think I'm describing people who only work in the tech industry in San Francisco, but the truth is, the entire city lives and breathes technology. It's so deeply rooted in everything throughout the city, it's hard to miss as an outsider coming in. It drives the economy, the government, transportation, and entertainment. The mentality that develops as a result of the technology industry permeates everything else; bankers, lawyers, Uber drivers, and bar-backs.

The twenty-somethings in San Francisco are focused on careers, health, community, and friends. Some are partnered; many aren't. If they have partners, the relationship looks different than others in other places. Exclusivity exists, certainly, but isn't prominent, and the relationship itself isn't the primary focus of life for this group. Their sole purpose in life isn't to find the right partner.

In San Francisco, this generation doesn't subscribe to the traditional paradigm. That couldn't be clearer. I met a few new couples who were swept up in the moment of romantic love and were existing in the Disney world of perfect soulmates. Still, I found even this group to be more realistic with their expectations of each other and their relationship. They often were waiting longer to live together, share expenses, or make other major life changes. Overall, even in the throws of romantic love, couples in San Francisco were more realistic about the structure of their relationship plans.

A feedback loop develops; individuality drives the tech industry's success, which in turn empowers the individual and encourages independence and creative thinking, which in turn continues to drive the tech industry's success. Further and further, these two entities, the creative individual and the tech industry, intertwine into a synergy where they need each other and drive each other's advancement.

Chapter 42

COVERING TRACKS AT FOLSOM

Jason and Chris knew Tony from Seattle. I don't remember if it was from the gym or some other place, but we'd all hung out together in Seattle on a few occasions.

On that first trip back to San Francisco, the one where I'd brought Tony along, we met up with Jason and Chris for dinner at their condo in Mission. Top floor of an old row house, their place is personable and warm. Chris has a thing for modern art, and some of the best pieces he's collected over the years were on display.

The dinner party was small with just one other couple and Chris' boyfriend, Mickey. Meeting him was an interesting experience and caused me some anxiety. I expected a degree of resentment or anger from Jason that Chris invited his other man to dinner with guests, but there was nothing of the sort. Jason was open and friendly, and Mickey was relaxed, engaging, and attentive to Jason as well as to Chris.

Jason and Chris also knew Robbie since, well, everyone in San Francisco knows Robbie. They didn't know that Tony and Robbie dated until that night at dinner, however, when Tony started talking about all the time he'd spent in San Francisco over the past couple years, while dating this guy.

Jason made a big deal of imagining the porn Tony and Robbie could make and how big a hit the video would be. He went on and on about how sexy Robbie was. Jason also didn't understand why he worked as a bar-back, and was suspicious that maybe Robbie was doing porn. I held back the fact that Robbie worked as a video editor for a porn company. Chris also remembered meeting Robbie and made a big deal about how Robbie asked him to spot him at the gym one time and that his body odor was overpowering. Of course, that part of the conversation got my attention, since one of the things I found irresistible about Robbie was his masculinity.

Robbie and I didn't mean for anything to happen between us, at least not consciously. That first night in San Francisco, our plan was to hang out and chat about things we shared interest in, like science fiction and Game of Thrones and stuff like that. We're both geeks, but deep down, just based on the conversation we had before, there were feelings on my part, and I think maybe on his too.

While Robbie and Tony dated, Tony had flown Robbie up to Seattle a few times. I only got to meet him once, toward the end of the relationship, when Tony brought him to the gym for a workout. I'd seen pictures of him before, but I was unprepared for how masculine and handsome he was in person or how infectious his laugh was. He was a total man's man in every way.

Up to this point, Tony's exclusion of me from his life with Robbie had been complete. While other Seattle friends went to dinners and played volleyball in the park with him, I was banned. It took a huge fight, after which Tony and I didn't speak for two weeks, to lead to an invite to workout together, just once, briefly, before Tony whisked Robbie off to other more important social events.

Things were casual and cordial throughout the workout. Robbie obviously knew what he was doing and picked out a few exercises to show Tony and me. Robbie was strong and fit having been a personal trainer in his early twenties, but I was still stronger. That didn't stop him from trying the heavier weights I was lifting, though, and he basically followed me through my routine using my weights. Tony couldn't lift what Robbie and I could so Robbie and I ended up spotting each other several times. The more time I spent near Robbie, the more attraction I felt. Worse yet, I was starting to like him.

Tony was my best friend, and there was no chance of me hitting on Robbie, but that didn't stop me from feeling this way. He was incredibly attractive, funny, and intelligent, and I had a hard time not feeling something.

Near the end of the work out, I was spotting Robbie on bench press, standing over him, his head near my shorts, arms spread wide to grip the bar. He was pushing a heavy set, the front of his gray, sideless muscle shirt sweaty from the intense workout, his face straining to push the weight. I could smell him, and it was fucking amazing; a mix of sweat, body odor, and sex. At that moment, my attraction overpowered me, and I started getting aroused.

He was struggling with the last couple of repetitions of the set, while I encouraged him. The gray shirt was pushed to the side and his muscled, lightly hairy chest was fully exposed.

"Come on, man. You got it," I said quietly, so only he could hear me. "Push it. Fuck yeah." He glanced up at me and pushed extra hard. "One more. Fuck yeah, Robbie." He saw the bulge in my workout shorts right in front of his face. At that point, he could've tossed the weight up and stopped right there, but instead he went for one more repetition. He didn't have anything left for that weight, and it forced me to lean over him and pull the weight up myself, my crotch just a few inches from his face. It was more than I could take.

I had to back away from him the rest of the workout, but I didn't forget the look he gave me and how it made me feel. I had seriously conflicting emotions about Robbie from that point to this very day.

After our first night of intimacy at that San Francisco bed and breakfast, we both realized that no one could know we were meeting up. If Tony found out, it would kill him, and we both still cared for him, but secrecy was an unsustainable strategy; an end game was needed. Would we stop seeing each other because of Tony, would we tell him, or would he find out from someone else? It was the last of these three possibilities that scared me most, and looking at Jason and Chris right now in the middle of Folsom Street Fair, it was this possibility that might actually happen.

"What the fuck?" asked Chris as I walked back over. I knew what he meant, but was hoping in vain he might just forget about what he'd just seen.

"What do you mean?" I said, acting like nothing happened. Jason laughed.

"Dude, that was Robbie! I didn't know you guys even knew each other. What the fuck was that all about?" demanded Jason. I don't think Jason was trying to protect Tony, just interested in the drama about to unfold.

Like a kid with his hand in a cookie jar, I had to come clean and do my best to buy some time because now, that was all I was gonna get. No matter what, it was only a matter of time before our relationship got back to Tony.

"Look, Robbie and I have hung out a few times. It's no big deal, but I'd appreciate it if you didn't say anything to anyone, especially Tony," I said.

"Well, we don't stay in touch with Tony, except seeing his posts to Facebook and daily Instagram selfies. It just seems a little weird after everything that happened with him. Are you guys dating?" asked Chris.

"No! I just see him every once in awhile when I'm down here. Look, it's no big deal. Please don't say anything to anyone, okay?" Even I could hear the pleading in my voice.

"Hey, don't worry about it, Dave. I don't care what you do, man. I just wish I got to watch that sometime! Damn, man! How do you always end up with the hottest guys?" laughed Jason.

"Fuck that, man. Not true. Hey, I need another drink. You guys want to come?" It was my attempt to change the subject. It worked, and we moved toward the bar. It was a temporary interlude, I knew. Jason and Chris would later talk about what they saw, decipher it, and get a few delectable minutes of gossip at brunch over the next few weeks, "Hey you won't believe what happened at Folsom!" Word would spread.

Chapter 43
NEXUS: EVOLVING FAVORABLE CHARACTERISTICS

The second way technology is acting as the nexus for the modern sexual revolution is by driving the evolution of characteristics that are favorable for its own growth and expansion. Technology is causing the evolution of skills and characteristics that promote further use of technology.

Using technology develops skill sets that enable a person to use more technology. A positive feedback loop is created where the user is rewarded for learning more about technology. He gets better and better at all the various things that technology requires to get him the things that he wants.

Since so much of life and our success is now tied to the use of technology, the more competence a person has with this skill, the more successful he'll be in his pursuits. His job may or may not be directly tied to technology, however his personal life probably is.

Think of it as a ten story library, where the study rooms are on the first floor, but the books you need are on the tenth floor. A person adept at technology gets to use the elevator because he knows how to operate it. The more he uses it, the faster it goes, but the person who's not tech-savvy has to use the stairs. This person trudges up and down ten flights of stairs for every book, every time he needs one.

At the end of the day, when these two individuals turn in their research papers, there's no comparison. The one using the elevator inevitably has a better written and better resourced paper than the individual who trudged ten flights of stairs for every book. The extra time available to the tech savvy researcher thanks to the use of the elevator enabled him to craft a better product. His ability to rapidly find new supporting material and authority gives his paper more credibility and therefore a better grade.

The advantage conveyed to the tech savvy person who knows how to use the elevator is undeniable. It leads to more success, personally and professionally. With more success and the positive feedback from being tech savvy, the person invests more of his time into technology, thereby increasing the speed of the elevator.

The positive consequence, or reward, of using technology is the evolution of characteristics conducive to the use and expansion of technology itself. The person trudging the stairs is left behind long ago as a new competition develops between tech savvy individuals and the speed of their elevators. The more you're rewarded for using technology, the more you want to use it.

This positive feedback for the use of technology also exists in the creation of technology. The more technology impacts our lives, the better we become at developing and using it. The better we become at developing and using it, the more technology impacts our lives.

It starts early with the development of basic skills. We hand preschoolers iPads and iPhones to play with, while teaching them the basic skills of interacting with a machine. We allow children to freely explore touch screens loaded with a wide variety of developmentally appropriate interactive media experiences designed to enhance feelings of success. We provide opportunities for children to begin to feel comfortable using a mouse and keyboard and to use websites to look up answers with a search engine. Children who readily pick up these developmental skills are at a distinct advantage over their classmates.

It's easy to nod in agreement with observations demonstrating the integration of technology in our jobs, education, and the daily tasks. We easily agree that using technology in these areas puts us ahead in achieving our goals. The more we learn about technology, the more successful we'll be in our careers.

For some reason, though, we balk at imagining technology impacting our sexual relationships, our partnerships, and our marriages, yet these are so clearly impacted by the same natural selection and evolution principles we see in our jobs, education, and daily tasks. The person who has to take the ten flights of stairs is just as disadvantaged in his relationships as he is submitting his paper.

The technology we create is also at the same time recreating our relationships.

Chapter 44
SELFIES

I doubt there's anyone out there with a camera phone who hasn't taken at least a few selfies. Statistics indicate that most have taken naked or nearly naked selfies, too. A smaller percentage have also made some NSFW videos for private sharing.

There's nothing inherently wrong with taking selfies, since they can serve many purposes, some good and some not so good. Selfies can help us monitor progress of body improvements, help show off new clothes, or record a special event or meeting. Sometimes they're just there because we're happy!

Some people view selfies as the dumbing down of the populace by the Internet. Others view selfies as an expression of a person's individuality, just not the expression they think they're conveying. Like Alan and Ivan, they think they're sharing every step of their glorious Disney love affair with adoring fans, but they're actually screaming for validation from a bunch of Barcalounger-bound Instagram stalkers.

While most therapists see selfies as a "sign that we're going to hell in a narcissistic hand-basket," Mike Langlois, a psychotherapist and social media expert, sees them as a chance for us to "transcend the ordinary for a moment in time, to celebrate the self, and share with a larger community as a form of infinite game."

Still other experts believe many people who regularly take selfies aren't so much celebrating themselves, as they are arguing that they're worth being visible. Many selfie-addicted twenty-somethings grew up in a world that told them they were the wrong size, color, gender, sexual orientation, or body type. They look around the world and see others with power and prestige, and compare that to the sense of emptiness and invisibility they feel. For these experts, selfies are a demand for attention and a shout, "I'm relevant!"

A selfie-addicted twenty-something might be able to force his way into relevance with a nice set of abs and "love.my.life" puppy pictures, but he's still fundamentally invisible. The image pushed out to the world of Instagram isn't who he is as much as it is who he'd like to be. Still insecure and fearful of exposing his humanity, this twenty-something masks his true-self with carefully thought-out and staged caricatures, fearful of rejection if the world discovers who he *really* is. One day he's a happy child laying the grass with his dog, another he's a thoughtful intellectual, staring out into the ocean, and yet another he's a jock with his baseball cap backwards rooting for a football team he can't even name the coach of. It's an empty exercise bound to end in unhappiness.

We all have *that* friend who takes a shirtless selfie every day on Facebook and Instagram and over whom the world swoons; "I'll dump Brad Pitt for you", "Can I lick your pecs?" "You're my new best friend" come the comments. Everything is an accomplishment, his every act destined for greatness, the planet orbits around his life. This need to be seen, to be relevant, is like a drug addiction. The validating comments drive even more manufactured selfies, all the while pushing the true person further and further into the shadows. The real person with flaws, insecurities, and humanity looks nothing like the supermodel with the perfect relationship and perfect boyfriend we're shown every day. That's a shame. As my friend PJ Ferguson told me while discussing selfies, "we are who we present ourselves to be, and so feel completely unknown."

These selfie-addicted twenty-somethings prefer a world of fantasy all the way around. They tend to be the ones who's relationships are pure fiction, who live their lives in a constant state of romantic love, and who, like Tony, bounce in and out of relationships with the "most incredible man I've ever met." Fiction is normative for these individuals and they're rewarded for it with a constant stream of encouragement from their 5000 Facebook friends. So fearful are they of reality they'll do everything to mask who they really are.

This isn't to say selfies are always bad. There're many great reasons for selfies, including putting up a recognizable picture so people know who you are, and sharing progress photos or event photos like pictures from a ski trip, but what's hard to understand is the need to snap a pic every time you try on a new shirt, or climb into your car at the dry cleaners. Do I need to see you picking up the two dress shirts you own?

Posting a selfie every day is pure narcissism. What can be so important that you've got to pose for a pic every single day? Easy answer is, nothing. The sole purpose for daily selfies is a desperate cry for validation.

Selfies have become synonymous with the twenty-somethings; they've perfected it to an art form, but twenty-somethings also have a lot to prove in life and daily selfies are an attempt to do just that. They need to prove they're attractive (with the number of "likes"), prove they're smart (put some glasses on, carry a book), prove their relationship is perfection (holding hands, strolling down the sidewalk), and prove they're masculine (playing a sport other than beer pong, maybe canoeing). You may think your audience loves seeing five pictures a day of you grocery shopping, musing over the price of produce, but maybe you should have stopped at the messy hair selfie from earlier.

Technology's impact on our lives is not always positive. Like all evolutionary forces, there are successes and failures. The ability to generate a whole new perfect persona, and stifle your humanity behind staged selfies is without a doubt a failure.

Chapter 45
NEXUS: DEFINING THE WORK FORCE

The final way technology is providing the nexus for changes in the modern sexual relationship is through its hiring process, and employee policies.

The technology industry is creating work environments, within itself and in supporting industries, that further develop a modern character. The tech industry actively seeks individuals with certain characteristics, stimulates their growth, and rewards them nicely for the results of their creativity and independence. Once again, principles of natural selection weed out the individuals incapable of certain technical skills and create a footrace within the tech industry to learn more, use more, and maximize technical skills. Individual success in the tech industry is accelerated through a positive feedback loop between technical skills and personal satisfaction.

The tech industry is a massive part of our economic workforce and is growing disproportionately every year. Recent estimates indicate that about 4.2 million workers, over 3% of the nation's payroll workforce, work directly for technology companies. The United States now accounts for more than 55% of global information and communication technology research and development. As an indication of where this growth is headed, global revenue from public cloud computing services will grow four times as fast as information technology spending generally, increasing by 27.6% year-on-year basis.

What makes a person successful in other non-tech related industries is different than the character set required to make individuals successful in the tech industry. Many experts point to the following characteristics of today's successful people:

Work extremely hard
Curiosity and eager to learn
Challenge the status quo
Extremely creative
Good at networking
Don't fear failure, embrace it
Possess a strong sense of self and personal development
Goal-oriented
Independent and confident
Positive balance of time
Optimistic

The relative importance of these traits varies from industry to industry. For example, in the law, we may value hard work, networking, and a focus on a goal more than in other fields. In the legal profession, creativity is frowned upon and balance is difficult to achieve. Independence is also not a highly sought after trait.

In the technology sector, success is driven by a shorter, more focused list:

Curiosity
Creativity
Challenge the status quo
Independence and confidence
Positive balance of time

Employees entering the technology industry are younger (18-30) and grew up with computers, iPhones, and the Internet, and are now taking their place in a world where the only constant is rapid change. Their enthusiasm for technology, and creativity in problem-solving, combine to make these individuals ideal employees for technology companies looking for the "next thing".

Tech companies challenge the status quo through their very existence. They're looking for better, more productive, and less expensive ways of doing the same things other industries do. For example, look at Uber, a ride share app that's on the way to retiring the taxi industry. The creators of this app used creativity and independence to attack an entrenched, outdated industry and make the world a better place for consumers.

Thinking outside of the box and challenging existing ideas is also a huge value in the tech industry. With the rapid fire changes in technology, opportunity for the next "big idea" is everywhere. There are no limits to what people can do in this field, and the more they're encouraged to think differently and critically, the better chances they have of hitting a home run.

Not only do tech companies seek people with these traits, they also work hard to foster them. Even Google's bathrooms contribute to this culture. Above the urinals and on bathroom stall doors you can find coding tips and puzzles.

Companies like Google recognize that people are more creative and more productive when they're given independence and life balance. Google employees get free food, fitness facilities, massage rooms, hair dressers, laundry rooms, and on-site doctors. They're encouraged to manage their own time and work remotely. The payoff shows up in increased innovation and productivity, low turnover, low sickness rates, and high employee satisfaction.

What's fascinating is that these traits line up nicely with the personality characteristic of the younger generations entering the technology industry.

According to a 2007 study by Pew Research, this age group (18-30) is different from previous generations:

- They use technology, such as text messaging, instant messaging, and email, as a primary means of networking with people.

- A "Look at Me" generation--Extensive use of social networking sites like Facebook and Instagram allows expression of their individuality with descriptions of interests and hobbies.
- Their embrace of new technology has made them uniquely aware of its advantages and disadvantages. They say cyber-tools make it easier for them to make new friends and help them stay close to old friends and family.
- They challenge the political status quo by siding with the growing number of immigrants, believing immigration strengthens the country. They also lead the way in their support for gay marriage and acceptance of interracial dating.
- About half say they've either gotten a tattoo, dyed their hair an untraditional color, or had a body piercing in a place other than their ear lobe. One-third have tattoos.
- One-in-five say they have no religious affiliation or are atheist or agnostic, nearly double the proportion of young people who said that in the late 1980s.
- They're more comfortable with globalization and new ways of doing work. They're the most likely of any age group to say that automation, the outsourcing of jobs, and the growing number of immigrants have helped, not hurt American workers.
- Asked about the life goals of those in their age group, most say their generation's top goals are fortune and fame. Roughly eight-in-ten say people in their generation think getting rich is either the most important, or second most important, goal in their lives. About half say that becoming famous also is valued highly.

How this tech generation feels about itself is also interesting. They view themselves as a distinct group of individuals with values and experiences different than previous generations. They're optimistic about their future and the future of the planet;

however, they express much more concern about social freedoms and the global condition.

These young people are relatively content with their financial lives. An amazing 78% say they're satisfied with their standard of living and 82% say they're satisfied with the kind of work they do. The same percentage (82%) say when a person reaches the mid-twenties; it's important to have a good plan for what they're going to do with the rest of their lives.

The majority of the tech generation say getting rich and being famous are important goals for people in their age group; 64% say getting rich is the most important goal in life for their generation. More than half of this generation say the first or second most important goal in life is to be famous. Only 12% say helping people is their generation's most important goal.

Because of their age and stage in life, work is less central to their lives. Almost half are still in school and presumably haven't settled on a career path.

Individuals in this generation also believe they have more sexual freedom, live in a more exciting time, and are more able to bring about social change compared with young adults twenty years ago.

A strong majority of this population (75%) say they're more likely to have casual sex than were young people twenty years ago. Only 7% say their generation has less casual sex and 17% say they have about the same amount.

These characteristics impact the relationships they enter. Most of these individuals have never been married (85%); 62% believe having a good marriage is hard. Among the unmarried, 57% say they definitely want to get married and 28% probably want to marry. In the 1990 Time/CNN poll, 25% of 18-25 year-olds said they were married; this compares with 15% today. That's a 60% decrease in marriage rates for this age group in just one generation.

Individuals from the tech generation are among the least likely to attend church regularly. Less than one third attend at least once a week compared with 40% of those over age 25. A staggering 16% say they never attend.

It's this generation's relationship with technology that's truly unique. Young people have adopted new technologies and are using them to both expand their social networks and maintain contact with their families and friends. More than any other generation, the tech generation recognizes the positive aspects of the technology revolution; however, they also readily acknowledge its drawbacks.

We don't call them the tech generation for nothing. Where the individuals in the tech generation clearly stand out is in their deployment of real-time technologies, such as instant messaging and text messaging. More than half say they sent or received a text message on a cell phone during the 24-hour period before they were interviewed.

The workforce these tech giants seek to employ is one they created with their own products. Now, natural selection has allowed the most tech savvy, creative, and independent people to rise to the top and be considered for employment by the companies that drove their interest in field in the first place.

This is a workforce that's used the library elevator for its entire life and wouldn't even know where to look for the stairs.

The qualities and traits this industry develops are the same qualities and traits that give raise to a modern relationship:

Curiosity
Creativity
Challenge the status quo
Independence and confidence
Positive balance of time

If you view these qualities as forces that produce a relationship between equals, individuals who aren't attached to the Disney paradigm, then you see that the drive to succeed in the world of technology aligns with the drive to create modern relationships.

Part V

MODERN RELATIONSHIPS

Chapter 46
COSMIC CABBIE

After a long fucking week, it was time for an escape from the craziness of Seattle to my new second home, San Francisco. Life gets crowded with obligations, appointments and demands, and I reach a point where the only thing that'll keep me sane is to cut and run and head out for an adventure. After battles at work and battles in relationships, it was time to book a trip to San Francisco.

The flight is nice and short, and there's usually no issue getting in and out of SFO, but today was destined to be different. After the short flight, we sat on the runway for an hour and a half waiting for a gate to open. My discount carrier only had one gate, and the plane at our gate had mechanical issues. SFO wouldn't assign us a new gate, and the carrier didn't want to back out the broken plane, in hopes of fixing it and getting it loaded for its own departure.

On top of that inconvenience, my inbox contained several items of bad news from work. Friday night, stuck on the runway, there was nothing I could do except sit there and stress out. I'm one of those people who has to do something to relieve stress. Forcing me to sit in a cramped seat with nowhere to go, locked in a metal tube, was creating more anxiety on top of the real stress that actually did exist. I was an unhappy passenger in 3C.

My friend, Bradley, and I were planning a dinner at a new place he picked out. By now, I knew we'd lost whatever reservation he'd made at some exciting, exotic, fabulous Bay Area restaurant. It's nearly impossible to get into a good restaurant in San Francisco without a reservation, that is, if you want to eat anywhere but a taco truck. Plus, the guys who owned my Airbnb apartment were expecting me to check in around 8:30 p.m. My delay was probably screwing up their night, too. I had no way of reaching them at the moment so, in my head, they were pacing up and down a long hallway, pulling at their hair, mumbling, "Where is he, dammit!"

As soon as the plane door opened, I huffed my way to baggage carousel 12 and waited some more. At least I was off that damn plane! On my other trips, it was comforting to step off the plane at the same gate, same baggage carousel, and feel like I was coming home. Even though SFO is a massive international airport, the terminal we arrive at is small and feels like a little town. Not tonight. My usual feelings of excitement and renewal were replaced by anxiety and frustration. Bag finally in hand, I headed for the taxi stand; no line and into a cab I went, just in time for World Series traffic. Awesome.

My cabbie was a young Middle Eastern guy who greeted me at the curb with a broad smile on his chubby face. While he loaded my luggage into the trunk, I tossed my backpack into the back seat and climbed in next to it, quickly grabbing my phone to get the address and keep myself occupied for the twenty or so minute ride into the city. I didn't feel like conversing or socializing, but instead just wanted to sit there fuming about how I wasted an hour and a half and everybody's plans were ruined.

My cabbie, who looked to be about twenty-five years old, however, had a different plan. In a cheery voice and a thick Middle Eastern accent, he asked about my flight. I grumbled out a five second version of my runway stint.

"Flight was good, but we sat on the runway for an hour and a half waiting for the plane at our gate to be fixed and pulled out," I replied curtly.

"You know, you're the third person this week to tell me the same thing!" said my cabbie, sympathetically, pushing up his round glasses in the rearview mirror. "At least you got here safely. That's what counts, right?"

Had me there. I nodded and sat quietly for a few minutes as he negotiated traffic out of SFO and onto the highway.

"Which route would you like me to take? I think Ceasar Chavez might be best, but maybe you know a faster way?"

I'm always suspicious of this type of question from cabbies. I'm afraid that the cabby is banking on my ignorance of the city to use a longer route for a bigger fare. As many times as I've been to San Francisco, I still didn't know the best way to get from SFO to the Castro. It seems like such a strange highway system through the city, and I can never wrap my mind around the layout as it relates to that highway. I mumbled that I wasn't from here, but I was hoping we could avoid the baseball traffic as the game had just ended.

"Oh! No worries. All that traffic is going the other direction. At least we're not going downtown! That place is a parking lot right now," he informed me knowingly. He asked where I was from and what I was coming into town for. Seattle! He'd heard great things about it, always wanted to visit.

As we moved down the highway I began spotting San Francisco landmarks, like Sutro Tower, and started to relax. I asked where he was from--Morocco. Well, that was different. After a couple years in LA, he came to the Bay Area and never looked back. We talked about Morocco, my time in Tunisia as well as in southern Spain and the amazing wines that come from that part of the world, then joked at the irony of being in the heart of wine country talking wistfully about Spanish wines.

My Moroccan cabbie described for me why he loved San Francisco and how different it was from other places, in character, architecture, climate, and community. He finally settled on, "Yes, my friend, it's the people. The people here are happy and friendly." He pushed up his glasses again as he smiled at me in the rearview mirror.

I nodded in agreement. The people here are different.

"They sure make me feel at home in this town," I said.

My cabbie then proceeded to tell me why he loved the city of San Francisco over cities like LA. He compared how closely everybody lived together and how you're almost forced to get to know your neighbor in San Francisco. In LA, there's so much space between houses and so much distance between the communities that you never feel like you're in a neighborhood, but here, because all the houses, apartments and condos are piled on top of the other (it's the second most densely populated city in United States) you have to know your neighbors and you have to deal with each other. A real sense of community develops, according to my wise cabbie.

Indeed. I sat silently for a moment and watched the individually painted row houses roll by my window, pink, blue, yellow, with one-of-a-kind accents, each looking like a perfect toy house, each one someone's proud creation. From the time it was built a hundred years ago to the happy resident today, an unbroken line of care and love.

As we approached the intersection of 18th and Dolores, my cabbie laughed and pointed out the line of people in front of BuyRight. It was a chilly night, 10:00 p.m., and the line for ice cream wrapped around the corner of the block. I laughed along with him. Crazy people! It's too cold for ice cream! But we both wanted some. Best damn ice cream in the city.

Through the light, half a block, and we arrived at my apartment.

By the time my cab pulled up in front of the address I'd given him, I was a different, happy person. Bradley didn't care that we missed our reservation and had a new adventure planned for us instead. The guys who own the apartment were just watching the game and relaxing and didn't even realize I was late. They showed me around and introduced me to the lady of the house, a seventeen-year-old orange tabby named Stella. Stella and I would become great friends over the next few days. The world was just fine despite my delay, and most important, I arrived safely.

The wisdom of cabbies.

Chapter 47

ELEMENTS OF A MODERN PARADIGM

Humans are creatures of habit and structure, and we instinctively crave both. Most people find their lives adrift without some structure to live by. The first thing we do when presented with a new test is to look back and see how it's been solved before. Authoritative texts on behaviors and expectations like the Bible and the Koran tell us how to live. They tell us what food to eat, who to marry, and how to procreate (and sell our children into slavery). They define the morality of justice and war. We cling to these structures to give our lives purpose and meaning.

It creates uncertainty and anxiety, then, to be adrift in a world of relationships without a compass or structure that tells us how to create and sustain a relationship. The old paradigm isn't working, and is creating more harm than good at this point, but we don't have anything to replace it with. What would a new paradigm look like?

Any new relationship structure would have to provide significantly more freedom than the existing one of marriage and monogamy. It would have to allow for shorter-term relationships, relationships without some grander purpose, along with a different level of emotional investment.

The new structure should meet the needs of the partners and encourage love and compassion. It should recognize these needs as something evolved and distinct from the previous generation.

Any new structure must also provide a higher degree of individuality and allow for creativity in the forms of relationships a person might choose. For example, a new paradigm should allow for open relationships and group associations and friends with benefits. These friends with benefits relationships are pervading society more and more, satisfying the needs of people in ways not approved of before. Because of their growing role in our relationships they must be included in any new structure if that structure is going to be successful.

The old paradigm was cumbersome and overloaded with outdated expectations. Everything in life was scripted out for you, from dating, to engagement, to the wedding, and everything that followed. The new one should be stripped down to the bare essentials and should leave behind all the expectations, pressure, and pomp of the old, or it will also be doomed to failure.

Modern couples may or may not have living together as a goal. That expectation comes from the sharing of farm duties and consolidating living expenses. Romance is better kept alive by living apart. People realize you don't need to pile the everyday household upkeep demands on your partner. These mundane, tedious tasks kill a relationship and convert it into a functional arrangement. That may be just fine for some or even necessary for others, but as a fundamental element of any new relationship paradigm, it fails.

I love having someone in my bed overnight. I love being able to roll over and cuddle up for a few more hours of sleep or sex. It's comforting and convenient, but our relationships don't need to be validated by seeing each other seven nights a week. In reality, both partners probably want some alone time, too.

During a divorce, couples with kids often fight over every single minute of parenting time, jealously hoarding that time regardless of any other consideration. I hear, "I can't live without my kids!" all the time, and "My kids need me!" To be validated as a parent, they feel they must fight for every overnight and parent-teacher conference.

After a period of successful transfers of the children, though, with parenting time going smoothly, the non-custodial parent begins to enjoy his time off! This isn't to say he doesn't want to be with his kids. Rather, it's the chance to do his own thing or simply relax quietly at home that can be just what a hard-working parent needs. Few will admit it openly, but giving parents this break can make everyone happier all the way around, including the kids.

This applies to intimate relationships, too. Our partners are amazing, awesome and we love them, but the truth is, sometimes we need to do our own thing.

The idea of "what's yours is mine, and what's mine is yours" is also a non-starter for the modern paradigm. This is such an antiquated, dysfunctional arrangement, I don't know where to start. It wasn't too long ago that marriage was "paid for" with a dowry, and it wasn't so much about building a life as it was owning one.

A dowry was the money, goods, or estate a woman brought to her husband as payment for the marriage. It was meant to serve as a form of protection for the wife against the real possibility of ill treatment by her husband. A dowry was a conditional gift that would be returned to the wife if the husband divorces, abuses, or commits other grave offenses against her. Barring any of these conditions, a dowry became the property of the husband. The wife owned no property but what the husband allowed her.

This consolidation of property under the control of the husband is still practiced in some places around the world. In others, its ghost lives on in the concept of a marital estate.

The marital estate is often made up of houses, cars, retirement accounts, rugs, furniture, jewelry, pets, and other items of real and personal property. During a divorce, we pull apart the marital estate and divide it between the spouses. In many states, courts begin with the presumption that the marital estate should be split evenly, but allow for arguments for an uneven distribution. In other states, the law directs an "equitable" distribution, meaning the judge looks for a "fair" way of dividing up the estate. In a shrinking number of other states, the fault of a party in a divorce is a factor in determining how to divide the estate.

Clients come into my office and are often amazed at the consequences of their vows at the altar; "When did I say she gets half of everything?" Yet, that's a potential legal implication of binding yourself to another person by way of marriage. You could say it's in the fine print, except there's no print. The rules are so convoluted that you need people like me to dive though your pile of goods, assess the marital value, the law, the judge, the other lawyer, etc, and do my best to get you the most "stuff" I can.

What a horrible idea! If I want to give somebody something, I will, but to have this be the default operative is ridiculous. There are many reasons marriage rate is going down, but I think one clear reason is, younger people are more independent and have their own careers and reject the idea that a wedding entitles their spouse to what's essentially a land grab.

A pledge to take care of someone does have an important place in some relationships. For example, a couple may want to have a large family and decides, together, that one of the spouses is going to give up his career and be a stay-at-home parent. That partnership, of having and raising children, could seriously disadvantage the spouse giving up his career, and the law should protect him, but the idea that this arrangement should be imposed on all married couples is nonsense.

The factors that made it advantageous to pair for life have also disappeared. The vow "till death do us part" is nothing but a well rehearsed mantra, and in most marriages today, it's a heavy expectation that goes unmet.

A better alternative is to recognize that all relationships are transitory. They all come and go and maybe come back again. Even relationships defined by blood undergo transitions throughout life. Your relationship with your parents has probably changed several times, same with your siblings. They come and go in intensity, impacted by fights, births, illness, whatever. All relationships change over time.

Recognizing that your intimate relationship will change may help it last longer and be more fulfilling. It's an honest approach, without the pressure of the old paradigm's lifetime commitment. Being honest and realistic about expectations can only improve your relationship.

Rather than have the expectation that they'll enter a single, lifelong relationship, an approach many individuals are taking is to expect a series of meaningful relationships at different stages of life as needs change. This structure is also called "serial monogamy".

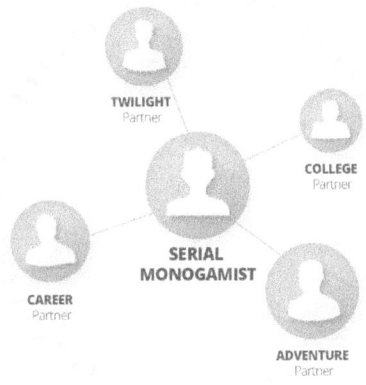

Figure 4 - Serial Monogamy

Economist Alvin Roth, Nobel Laureate, suggests that since we live longer and child-rearing takes up less of our lifespan, we may want to be with different people for different stages of our lives; that 'new forms of polygamy-over-lifetime relationships' may be more satisfying.

"Relationships can last for two or five or twenty years," says Hollywood actress Cameron Diaz, known for her unconventional relationships. "I don't believe in sharing your bed with someone your whole life."

The world has changed since the days of the plow and chicken house. While the needs of individuals have changed, the nature of our expectations of marriage and relationships haven't. It's time to make these changes and adapt a new relationship structure that meets the needs and expectations of people living in the twenty-first century. We can make our bed and decide who to share it with, a man or a woman, with several of each or, sometimes maybe no one at all.

Chapter 48
DINNER WITH BRADLEY

Bradley texted that he was happy I arrived and was heading over for dinner. Bradley is recently single after a two-year relationship. He was diagnosed with stage-two melanoma about eighteen months ago and underwent several rounds of chemotherapy, surgeries, and radiation treatment. They say you're never cured of cancer, especially melanoma, but Bradley's doctors thought they got it all. At only twenty-four, he would spend the rest of his life avoiding the sun and being constantly vigilant of any changes in his body, a hard pill for Bradley to swallow. Before his diagnosis, he was a world-class biker and spent all day on his bike, in the sun, without sunscreen on his neck which is where the melanoma first developed.

As a result of his treatment, Bradley had no hair, lost a tremendous amount of weight, and had a massive scar on the back of his neck. He was just now starting to regain some of his former weight and strength. When I opened the door of my new San Francisco home and saw my friend standing under a street light, I caught my breath. I tried to cover my shock at his drawn face, hallowed eyes, and lack of hair anywhere on his head, but he still noticed.

I hadn't seen Bradley since before his diagnosis, but we stayed in touch with frequent texts. He's part of a group of friends who text each other every Friday morning. The man I remembered was cocky, stocky, quick to laugh, and quick to anger. He was always the center of attention, but in a good way, friendly and open to everyone. We met when one of his races came though Seattle and my partner at the time, who knew him from high school, invited him to stay with us.

People who've stood face to face with death have a depth of being us regular humans can't begin to understand. Standing there at my door, exposed to my surprise at his condition, he smiled wryly, spread his arms, and said, "I love you, Dave." I was broken.

The hug was deep and long, and I cried, then laughed. He came inside, and we started catching up. An hour later, famished, we headed out for Bradley's adventure dinner. Into the Mission District we went. As we walked, we talked about his work, his bikes, his ex-boyfriend, and playing Wii. All of the sudden, he pulled up short, turned to the building we stood in front of, and said, "Do you want fancy Mexican or authentic Mexican?" He pointed to one restaurant on the right, then one on the left. I laughed. It was a test.

"Authentic Mexican it is!" he said and we walked up to the hostess station. A short, older, Mexican woman with a heavy accent squealed, "Mr. Bradley!" and hobbled over to give him a hug. "Why you no come visit more?" she asked, stepping back and shaking her finger at him. She turned and looked at me, then to him with a knowing smile, and a wink. "You need a table for two tonight Mr. Bradley." It wasn't a question.

Bradley and I talked all night, right util they kicked us out. Well, not so much kicked us out as told Bradley he'd have to lock the doors unless we left with the last of the crew.

We talked about his relationship and how it failed, what brought it to an end and what he was looking for now. Did you know that the rate of failure for a relationship that pre-exists a cancer diagnosis is 70%? Within the first year of getting the bad news, 70% of "committed" relationships break under the strain of this existential challenge.

Married women, in a study by the University of Utah Huntsman Cancer Institute, who were told they had a serious illness were seven times more likely to become separated or divorced as men with similar health problems. Overall, the divorce rate in the first year for patients in the study ranged up to 21% higher than the general population.

Men are more likely to abandon their partners who become seriously ill. The author of the Utah study, Dr. Chamberlain, believes that differences in male and female roles in the family can explain the trend. "There clearly is an emotional attachment women have to spouse, family, and home that in times of stress causes women to hunker down and deal with it, while men may want to flee," he said.

My own antidotal experience as a divorce lawyer confirms this often studied phenomena. Where the relationship is built on fantasy, the traditional Disney paradigm, a challenge of this type shatters the fiction and reality is too much for the abandoning partner. They retreat to find a new fantasy, without the complicated reality of terminal illness.

Bradley and I talked about some of our common friends, like my friend Tony and Bradley's best friend, Robbie, but we also spent a lot of time talking about his clients and the impact the technology industry was having on the city.

Bradley works for one of the largest client contact and sales management companies in the world as a senior account manager. His company uses a sophisticated database to create custom solutions for client and sales management. Bradley works with some of the biggest tech companies in the world.

According to Bradley, the technology companies he has as clients are creating all kinds of crazy benefits packages and employment policies for recruiting and keeping talented employees. For example, one of his clients, a major accounting software company, kept a robot-building lab where employees could go and piece together various bits and gadgets and wheels into functioning robots. The employees hold regular competitions in the lab using custom built bootcamp-type obstacle courses.

When Bradley calls on his clients, they'll discuss new processes and services provided by his company over a fierce game of MLB 2k12, or even a bike ride, although Bradley has to be fully covered by a special suit to avoid the sun. It's his job to integrate himself into the culture of the client company and then help them customize their process with his product, so if his client's representative wants to talk about processes while rock climbing in the lunch room, Bradley straps on a harness and grabs some rope.

Tech companies go to extraordinary lengths to recruit talented employees with the skill sets they desire, then make sure they get whatever they want.

- Airbnb gives all of its employees $2,000 a year to travel anywhere in the world they want. These lucky employees also get to bring their pets to work every day, go sailing together, have a pingpong table, have weekly Yoga classes at work, and get to eat organic lunches on a daily basis.

- At most tech companies today, like Ask.com, one of the perks is that there's no limit on the vacation time or paid time off. Vacation time is left to the discretion of the employee and isn't accrued or tracked by the HR department. In its employee recruitment materials, Ask.com states, "We believe the best measure of success is what you accomplish, so we don't need to measure how much time you take off to enjoy life."

- Over at DropBox headquarters, the office comes with a fully equipped music studio and game rooms, which sounds like every nerd's dream with DDR, ping pong, and gaming tournaments. Dropbox's Whiskey Fridays are infamous.

- At Facebook, innovation and autonomy are encouraged and valued to such a great extent that they're second only to Google when it comes to innovative employment practices and benefits packages. Facebook employees get free meals, have access to kitchens stocked with snacks, and the Facebook Culinary Team lets you know what's on the menu using, you guessed it, a Facebook page.

- The grand daddy of all tech companies when it comes to keeping its employees innovating and creative is Google. At Google, they get snow in California. Google floods a space in their headquarters with real snow for building forts and having snowball fights. Googlers also get a cafeteria which uses homegrown organic produce in its kitchen, bikes, volleyball courts, heated swimming pools, on-site oil change and car wash services, dry cleaning, massage therapy, a gym, a hair stylist, fitness classes, bike repair, plus an indoor slide.

- At Twitter's San Francisco office, employees get a daily catered breakfast and lunch, plus they also get weekly in-office yoga and Pilates classes as well as a Zipcar and wireless discounts.

- Zynga offers relaxation lounges with Nintendo, arcade games, Xbox 360, and PS3 gaming systems, and if you want to relax, you can go for an onsite massage, reflexology, and acupuncture. They even provide haircuts.

- In an effort to attract more women in the tech industry, Apple and <u>Facebook</u> are even offering to freeze eggs for female employees. Facebook offers up to $20,000 for egg cryogenics for female employees. The company also offers adoption and surrogacy assistance.

The recruiting tactics and HR policies of these technology companies are having rippling effects passing out to societies, changing things as fundamental as our families. Bradley is the perfect person to observe this impact since he works with a broad range of progressive companies and is tasked with keeping his clients happy.

When I asked Bradley, though, if he thought the tech industry was also having an impact on relationships in the city of San Francisco, he looked at me quizzically.

"What do you mean?" he said, as if the idea that the structure of relationships could change at all was a foreign concept.

I pointed out that the economy of San Francisco is primarily based on tech companies. These tech companies have amazing policies intended to attract and develop creativity and independence. I wondered if the creativity and independence of these employees was also being expressed in the types of relationships they sought and entered.

"You mean like who they get married to? Or if they get married at all?" he asked me.

"Yes, both, but it's a bigger question. I mean, do these traits impact the type of marriage or the type of relationship that the people in San Francisco decide to enter?" I answered back. "Because, it seems to me that a lot of the relationships, actually every relationship that I've come into contact with out here, is open in one form or another. That's not the way it is across the rest of the country. So I'm wondering if what you see in the tech industry with these liberal and progressive employment benefits and policies is also impacting the intimate relationships of the population of San Francisco. What do you think?"

He stopped for a second and contemplated. A few sips on his margarita and he responded, "Well, I think you're probably right. Most of the couples I know are open at least to play with others together. But I don't know if that's because it's San Francisco or some other reason. Why do you think it's related to the tech industry?"

"Why do you think the relationships here in San Francisco are different?" I asked him back.

"I don't know! I think San Francisco is just different! I don't know why," he said, shaking his head. "I guess I never stopped to think about why San Francisco's relationships are different. I mean, it's the capitol of the gay world after all. So I suppose it's just the sheer number of gay people in the city."

I knew that couldn't be correct. Other cities had a denser population of gays and lesbians, and while some couples in those cities were certainly open, there wasn't the prevalence of open relationships that can't be missed in San Francisco.

After another round of margaritas, Bradley was in agreement that the tech industry was the biggest difference in San Francisco's population. He was still skeptical that it could be impacting the modern relationships developing in the city; however, for Bradley, an open relationship wasn't what he wanted, at least initially. Bradley was a traditionalist. He was looking for a monogamous relationship, one that would eventually lead to marriage. In the meantime, though, Bradley was going to have as much fun as he possibly could, and was in no rush to get married.

Bradley and I had a brief romantic relationship following his visit to Seattle. My partner and I were in an open relationship at the time, but our rule was that we could only play together, so my first time with Bradley was a three-way with my partner. It didn't go well because Bradley and I connected, but my partner and Bradley didn't.

Despite the fact that the rule was we could only play together, Bradley and I continued to hook up over the next few days. When he returned to San Francisco, we stayed in touch and would occasionally meet either in Seattle or in some other city easily reachable and easily explainable.

That night after we closed down the little hole in the wall Mexican restaurant, Bradley took me back to his place, and we reignited our sexual relationship. Afterward, we lay there and cuddled as a rain storm passed through San Francisco. Wrapped in arms, my head against his Bradley's back, his body felt like half of what it'd been, and had lost the hard athletic feel from years ago, but the intensity of my feeling for him, this survivor, this fighter, this man with an unconquerable smile and love of life had deepened beyond measure.

Sometime before dawn, I quietly slid out of bed, got dressed, said goodbye to Bradley, and made my way back to my apartment.

Chapter 49
THE PYRAMID

The structure of relationships is evolving. We're leaving behind the linear paring of a man and a wife, a structure that operated to the exclusion of other relationships, and growing into a multilayered pyramid structure. This structure defies traditional assumptions where a "relationship" is only between two people, and in fact expressly includes many people at different layers.

Instead of a two-person relationship, the modern relationship may be made up of any number of people. The size of a modern relationship is dependent on whether a person has a partner, friends with benefits, and close friends. He may not have a partner but has three fuck buddies and five close friends. Another person may have a partner, no friends with benefits and two close friends. The intimate pyramid is made up of all these people.

What unites the layers of the pyramid is intimacy. Sometime it's sexual intimacy, other times it's emotional intimacy, and occasionally it's both. We're sexually and emotionally intimate with our partner, sexually intimate with our fuck buddies, and emotionally intimate with our friends. Intimacy provides the commonality between the layers of the pyramid.

The traditional linear structure required the partners to draw all their emotional support from each other. Walls were built to keep the emotional connections to others at a minimum, and involvement with former lovers was generally prohibited. Friendships had boundaries. Threats were everywhere.

In contrast, the intimate pyramid draws its strength and duration from the number of persons and variety of levels. It's a positive thing to keep former spouses or partners as part of your pyramid. Since friendships contribute more to our long term happiness than any other relationship, their inclusion in the pyramid is vital, not a threat. The liberty to explore your sexuality with friends with benefits is likewise important to our happiness.

Since the traditional linear structure only existed when you had a partner or spouse, a relationship didn't exist when you were "single". Not so in the intimate pyramid. A layer may be missing entirely, yet the relationship structure still exists. For example, you may not have a partner, and may not want a partner, but you do have friends with benefits and close friendships.

This flexibility of the pyramid structure arises from the modern day need for independence and individuality in our relationships. We're free to recognize the importance of our other relationships and create interactions that didn't fit in the linear structure. Not only is the content of each person's pyramid different, it's also fluid. People may move between the levels of the pyramid, or may leave it entirely.

Before, when the line breaks between linear partners and their relationship comes to an end, everything must start from scratch. "I've got nothing left," say divorcing spouses in a hopeless and exhausted voice. All the emotional and sexual intimacy was directed down the line to a partner, and it ends when the relationship ends. In this person's mind, they're truly left with nothing.

The exclusive investment of emotional and sexual intimacy in one person doesn't work in the modern age of technology. Intuitively, we use the tools of the modern world to "hedge our bets," such as maintaining a Plan "B" and continuing to keep relationship of all types alive with social media and texting. Subconsciously, we know that the "all our eggs in one basket" approach is dangerous and likely to result in pain and isolation. But more important, we instinctively feel the benefit of maintaining intimacy of all types with a variety of people.

The pyramid structure is a creation of the age of technology and aligns better with our modern needs and expectations.

Chapter 50
A DAY OF RESEARCH

After my dinner with Bradley, I managed to get a few more hours of sleep at my Dolores Park apartment, but Saturday morning wouldn't be denied, and I eventually had to start moving around. I got up and immediately got on Scruff. There was a hot Middle Eastern man who needed to be discrete, but was eager to meet up. Fit, about 35, six feet, he told me his relationship was open, but he couldn't stay long. We had sex, but didn't use a condom and that upset him afterward. He initially asked if I had any condoms, but I hadn't brought any on this trip.

He came twice quickly, both times without touching himself. We laid around and chatted afterward. He was unemployed and over-educated. He and his partner had been together about five years, and his inability to contribute was becoming an issue. He said they were open but his behavior indicated otherwise. I got the impression that maybe they played together and maybe they'd play separately, but that what we were doing violated some as-yet undiscussed rule.

Later that same morning, Teddy came over, a red-haired little muscle guy, about 35 years old, always laughing. I had trouble getting into it with him since he was constantly joking around and was so nonchalant! Plus, he insisted on a condom the whole time, which was distracting. He was negative, but his long-time partner was undetectable positive.

Afterward, we laid in bed talking for a long time about technology and relationships in the Bay Area. Teddy is a professor in the economics department at Stanford. He was fluent in the economic impact technology was having on the city, but he never stopped to think that the cause of this amazingly powerful shift in economics could have an impact on the structure of relationships. As it dawned on him what a baseless assumption this was, he turned into a fountain of information.

There's a significant age difference in his relationship. His partner is twenty-five years older than he and had two previous partners pass away during the AIDS epidemic. They're open, but as I said, they always play safe. Teddy likes older guys, but also likes sex more often than his partner. His interests in variety and the hunt of finding men on Scruff are things his partner encourages.

His partner, Donald, had boyfriends on the side throughout the years of their relationship, but didn't have one currently. Teddy was fine with his partner finding another one if he wanted to. Why deny each other these experiences? Teddy used his hands to create a Venn diagram by showing two circles that didn't quite overlap. In Teddy's case, he and his partner had different interests. In most places their interests overlapped. Sometimes they didn't, and things would change over time where those interests would shift. No one remains the same throughout all of life. Instead, we grow and change, and develop new interests in other things. Teddy and his partner recognized that their interests may align for a short period but will certainly drift over the long-term.

When Teddy used his hands to create two circles, he held them together and said, "When we met, Donald and I overlapped completely, or at least convinced ourselves we did. But over time our interests diverged slightly." Teddy shifted one of the circles to the right so that they didn't align completely. "And my interests changed over time too. So rather than deny the man I love something he's interested in, we decided that we'd allow each other to explore these interests, sexual and otherwise, throughout our entire relationship."

"Most of the time, we like the same things, but sometimes he's interested in things that I'm not, and vice versa. Doesn't have to be sexual," he said, and shrugged. "He's a retired director and gets into the whole filmmaking thing. He also likes asians. I'm not a film buff and Asians are great and all, but not my thing," he laughed.

"You should write a book!" I said.

"Do you think the relationships in San Francisco are all that different?" he said as he rolled over and put his arms on my chest looking at me intently.

"Yeah. The more time I spend here, the more people I meet, the more convinced I am that things are different here and that the difference is being driven by the tech industry. It's like it's been so obvious and right there in front of my face! I guess I never stopped to think that they were tied together," I said. "Now that the idea has firmly settled into my head, I see it everywhere, in every person I talk to."

Teddy needed to get back, but we exchanged numbers. He invited me to dinner to meet Donald next trip, and I was excited about that. He sounded like an interesting person to get to know.

I was starving by this point and had to run out and find some food and hit the gym. On the way back from the gym, I stopped and had some particularly bad Indian food at a place in Castro. Guess the city can't be perfect all the time. While eating, I was also returning emails and checking Scruff. One of the guys I'd been talking to earlier that morning, who was rather persistent and had a great . . . Ummm . . . picture, sent me a note telling me I should come over. I texted him back, and he sent me his address. His place was on the way back to my apartment, so what the hell?

His house was on one of those side streets that only ran between two other streets. There was no thru traffic, and the houses were nice and quiet. I rang the bell and a dark, stocky, bearded guy, about thirty, 5'9, opened the door with a big smile. His name was Harold. He lived with two other guys, one of whom, I discovered, worked with Robbie.

The sex was great and lasted a long while. We ended up going two times. Between, we talked about San Francisco and his relationships. Originally from the Napa area, Harold had a daughter with a lesbian couple who had since broken up. They were dedicated parents, all three. Harold showed me pictures of his beautiful six-year-old daughter who split her time primarily between her two moms and their new families. One of her moms was now married to a man and had another child with him. All the grandparents were active in the little girl's life, too.

Harold was newly single. He and his boyfriend broke up due to distance. The other guy lived in LA, and the travel was just too much. One of Harold's current roommates was his ex-partner's best friend.

Travis came over to my place a few hours later. He was tall, about forty, fit and lean, with a great sense of humor. Travis was a full-time nanny for a straight family with two young children, one of whom was born with cystic fibrosis.

Travis was also newly single. His last relationship had deteriorated when they purchased a property in San Francisco and began remodeling it. The investment of time, money, and the fact that neither had experience with project management exacerbated his partner's alcohol dependence, and Travis' partner slowly sank into alcoholism. Travis finally had to leave his partner and look for a job and a place to live. Chance or fate or Karma rewarded Travis as the changes in his life took him to his dream job of taking care of disabled children.

Travis' relationship had been open, but they only meet up with other guys together. They'd talked about marriage and had vague plans to do so after the condo was done. Travis has plenty of experience with straight men, for some reason, and had several married men he'd see regularly. Travis was a favorite fuck buddy for the straight scene, apparently.

As the sun went down, I took to the streets of Mission with the goal of finding some dinner. Harold was already texting me to see if I would come back over, but I already made plans and had to put him off.

My plan was to meet my friend Mark and his partner, Cade, to watch the World Series at High Tops. I first met Mark and Cade in Puerto Vallarta a few years ago, and we'd hit it off. Mark was just about the most sexually active person I knew. He and Cade had been together three years at that point and seemed to be doing great, but Mark was constantly texting me with graphic details, pictures, and videos of his near daily tricks. The great thing was, Cade didn't just support Mark in these explorations, he pretty much pushed him out the door. This wasn't a stretch for Cade either. Cade genuinely got turned on by Mark's tricks and would jump him the minute he came home from one. Like I said, Mark got a lot of sex!

Best laid plans rarely turn out and through some crazy twist of fate, my night would bounce from one emotional extreme to the next and return to me something I feared was lost forever.

LEVEL 1
THE PINNACLE

Chapter 51
THE PINNACLE RELATIONSHIP

The pinnacle relationship, at the top of the pyramid, may be a formal marriage, an informal one, or just "boyfriends". It's the dominate relationship, behaving more like a partnership than any other relationship at a different level.

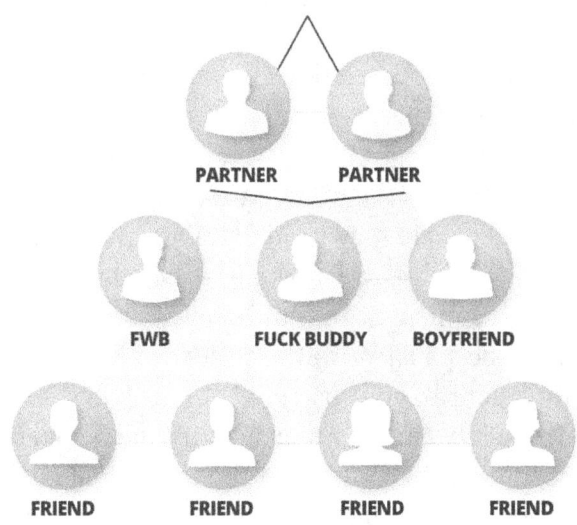

Figure 5 - The Pinnacle Relationship

The pinnacle relationship has the following characteristics:

- Highest degree of commitment
- Non-monogamy
- Fidelity
- Love (Romantic or Adult)

Highest Degree of Commitment

Commitment can be defined as an engagement or obligation that restricts freedom of action. Each member of the pinnacle relationship is agreeing to restrict his or her freedom in some way by entering this committed relationship. People tend to think of monogamy whenever someone says a "committed" relationship, but there are plenty of other ways of being committed beyond just pledging to only fuck one person for the rest of your life. Commitment can be something deeper than where you stick your dick.

The commitment observed in the pinnacle relationship can range anywhere from the vows exchanged at a wedding, down to simply honoring date night once a week. A commitment in this sense is a recognition of the other partner's needs and your pledge to meet those needs. He may need extra attention, more than most boyfriends, because of who he is or how he was raised. You might make a commitment to him to always try and be especially attentive and to be sensitive to this aspect of his personality. This is your commitment to your partner.

Commitments between pinnacle partners are deeply personal since the commitments come from the individual needs of each partner. It's these personalized commitments that set apart this relationship from both traditional relationship and relationships lower down the pyramid.

Sometimes, the level of commitment is discussed and agreed upon, such as the vows exchanged at a wedding ceremony, but commonly it's a general, undefined level such as "boyfriends".

Sometimes the couple has discussed what the expectations are for a "boyfriends" relationship, and sometimes they haven't. Regardless, there's a sense of commitment to whatever status they've assigned for each other.

Non-Monogamy

In a modern relationship based on this pyramid structure, there is no commitment to monogamy. The pinnacle couple may choose to be monogamous, or one of the partners may choose to be monogamous, but that's simply a choice by the individuals, not a formal commitment. One of the defining characteristics of the modern relationship is a lack of a formal pledge or vow of monogamy between the partners in the pinnacle relationship.

A traditional couple may default into a modern relationship structure at some point. This usually happens when the romantic love stage of the traditional relationship is over, and the couple decides they need to open up their relationship to sustain it. Maybe it's a demand by one of the partners and the other partner concedes because he wants to hang on no matter what, or maybe the couple decides that the time is right to expand their sexual activities to include other people. Either way, the horses get changed mid-stream, and the couple goes from, "Oh my God! We would never!" to "If he's hot, and we agree and it's safe, and it's on vacation, and . . ." Down the hill, we roll.

A truly modern relationship, however, begins without the pledge or commitment to monogamy. The pinnacle couple in a modern relationship may commit to a lot of different things, such as living together, or having children, but they don't commit to or make a pledge of exclusivity. It's not common to find a couple who has this discussion at the beginning of their relationship. Most wait months into it, but a growing number of people are entering relationships aware that it's not going to be exclusive.

The problem of having a discussion about monogamy months into the relationship is that the couple suffers through some triggering event that changes their status and forces the issue. Maybe there's a fight on the dance floor, or one partner discovers the other on Grindr, or one of them hooks up with someone else and it gets discovered. Whatever the triggering event may be, it causes drama for a couple, and many won't survive it.

This phase is particularly dangerous for couples. They begin the process of rule-making, and therefore rule breaking. They come up with convoluted behavior systems such as, "We only hook up together, on vacation." While this will qualify as a modern relationship based on the criteria set forth above, it's a tenuous situation and likely to lead to more drama.

On the other hand, the couples I met in San Francisco that began the relationship with no expectation of monogamy appeared the most stable and the partners seemed the most happy. I'll admit, it struck me as disconnected, but it's hard to argue with an open couple that's been together a couple of decades, and you see such affection and love between the two of them.

Fidelity

Fidelity is faithfulness to a person demonstrated by continuing loyalty, honesty, and support. Fidelity isn't monogamy. Fidelity is honoring a commitment you've made to someone else.

I think of fidelity as "followthrough". I made these pledges or commitments to you; how faithfully have I adhered to them? Fidelity isn't the underlying pledge; it's the degree to which you're honoring that pledge and being honest with your partner about it.

Many new pinnacle relationships, where the couple has been together six months or less, are typically closed to sexual encounters with others. There are no boyfriends on the side, and they don't hook up with others together or separate, so what appears to be monogamy is probably fidelity. Their early exclusivity is more an indication of romantic love and a desire to be sexual with their new partner than it is a mutual vow of life long monogamy.

Fidelity and monogamy often get incorrectly lumped together as one and the same. In a modern relationship, though, fidelity is broader than a commitment to monogamy.

Love

Of course, the fundamental trademark of any relationship, modern or otherwise, is love. Whether it's romantic love or adult love, a relationship is based on a fundamental affection for each other. You can question the depth of love in any relationship or even question its true existence, but we can't question how someone feels about another person. High-schoolers say they love each other in their first sweetheart love affairs, and partners say they love each other on their deathbeds. While the range may be different, the feeling is the same, and it's just as valid.

This is a concept I struggle with. It was hard to watch Tony's parade of "incredible" men and not sneer at the vacuous nature of his pledge to these beach boys. I lost a partner to cancer and held his head while he puked his guts up during chemotherapy, carried him a mile from a concert when he only weighed hundred pounds because I knew it'd be the last time he'd see one, cuddled up in bed with him, arms wrapped so tenderly around his skeletal body as he whispered, "This is how I want to die," and spread his ashes on a lonely trail near Steamboat. I grit my teeth at comparing that love with Tony's love for his beach boy in Mobile. I tell you what, it's hard to argue that Tony's feelings of romantic love are just as valid as the true love I had for my dying partner, but I must make that argument. The difference is his is pure fantasy, mine was all too real.

It's this adult love that distinguishes the pinnacle couple from everything below it. While we can say we love our friends, that love is certainly a different type than love we have for our partner. This isn't to diminish the love we have for our friends; that love can have extraordinary value to us. Some even argue that the love in friendships is truer and more reliable than the love we have for our partners, but it's a different type.

We all know that love has to be a two-way street or the relationship won't last. One partner may try to tough it out for a variety of reasons, but at the end of the day the lack of love eventually tears apart the relationship.

The pinnacle couples I met during my last few years of traveling love each other and are committed to each other emotionally and sexually, just not monogamously. These couples show varying degrees of affection for each other. Some are still in the semblance of romantic love, while others are more distant, acting like close friends, finishing each others sentences but rarely holding hands or displaying other signs of closeness.

A pinnacle relationship can bring great joy to life. It's someone to share things with, cuddle up to when it's cold, confide in when there's no one else to trust, and excite the senses in ways only love can color, someone to be with when things are fantastic and everything is going your way, and to support you and hold your hand when the end is near. Your partner is the person you tenderly, quietly say goodbye to.

Chapter 52

JEALOUSY

You can't talk about the modern relationship without also talking about jealousy. If you're not in one, your primary objection to the open structure of a modern relationship is probably based on jealousy. So many times, when discussing the positives and negatives of modern relationship structures, friends whose relationships aren't open bring up jealousy.

"I could never watch my partner with someone else!" I immediately follow that up with, why not? I get a variety of verbiage back:

"I'd never do that to him."
"He should only want me."
"I'd get too jealous."
"What if he likes the other guy better?"

None of these objections answer the "why not?" question. They may describe a feeling, like jealousy, and a fear of losing the other person to someone they perceive as a better alternative, but their objections all stem from insecurity about themselves.

In describing the feelings jealousy creates, Irish writer Elizabeth Bowen once wrote, "Jealousy is no more than feeling alone against smiling enemies." Jealousy makes you feel insecure, inadequate, and secretly laughed at.

We all feel insecure now and then, in many different contexts. Are we good enough, smart enough, attractive enough for anyone to like us? We fear our partner, if he only knew the truth about us, could easily find someone better. It's a natural, instinctive emotion that everyone experiences at one point or another.

Jealousy appears to come from four internal characteristics:

- **Lack of self-confidence:** This is perhaps the most common cause of jealousy. If you were 100% confident in your abilities, qualities, and judgment, and could look yourself in the mirror and honestly say, "Damn! I'm a good catch!" you wouldn't be insecure when your partner found someone else attractive. You'd be confident that you're always going to be the best option.
- **Poor self-image:** Having a poor self-image can also lead to jealousy. If you think you're unattractive or physically inadequate, chances are you'll experience feelings of jealousy whenever your partner notices someone you perceive to be sexier or more beautiful, although they actually aren't.
- **Insecurity:** Feelings of insecurity are the result of a lack of confidence and poor self-image. When you lack the security of being sure of yourself, your abilities, qualities, and judgment, and when you don't think you "deserve" what you have, you feel insecure about the relationship.
- **Fear:** I think fear is the most insidious instigator of jealousy. Your lack of confidence and your poor self-image create a fear that your partner is going to find someone better than you and dump you like a hot potato. Fear sits behind jealousy and feeds it to the point of destructive behaviors. Fear is often shielding deep-seated feelings of possessiveness, insecurity or shame.

If you step back and consider these four character issues, you come to one conclusion: jealousy is a comparison of yourself to someone else. A jealous person is constantly comparing himself to other available alternatives. We've been taught since we were in kindergarten to compare ourselves to the other kids around us.

Somebody else has a better house, a more beautiful body, more money, or a more charismatic personality. Jealousy is the natural child of these comparisons.

Comparisons can also lead to unhealthy views of success and failure. After a terrible storm and flooding, an elderly village farmer was moodily regarding the ravages of the flood.

"Hiram!" yelled a neighbor, "your pigs were all washed down the creek!"

"How about Thompson's pigs?" asked the farmer.

"They're gone, too."

"And Larsen's?"

"Yes."

"Humph!" said the farmer, cheering up. "It ain't as bad as I thought."

I wish I could be the perfect Buddhist and say comparison is always a bad thing, but I think it serves a purpose in some contexts. For example, I can compare myself now to myself at a previous point in time, and it can help drive me to self-improvement. Last week, I ran the park in 21.5 minutes. This week, I want to cut that down to 21 minutes. Or at work, in September I got hired on five cases, but this month I want to try and get hired on seven.

Even comparisons to other people can be productive and drive us to make positive improvements in ourselves. I can't go to an empty gym because I need the motivation of seeing other people who lift heavier or have a better form or have a better body than I do. Am I jealous of them? I suppose I am at that moment, but in my mind I think, I can do that, too, if I work at it. I have the self-confidence to know I can improve and reach their level, or better.

If jealousy is a comparison of yourself to someone else, by having confidence, you win that comparison; jealousy fades.

Each person is unique and incomparable. Existence only creates originals. Once you understand this, the need for comparison disappears.

Chapter 53
SAFE SEX AND REALITY

Looming large over the evolution of modern relationships is the question of safe sex. Promiscuity, defined as the practice of having casual sex frequently with different partners or being indiscriminate in the choice of sexual partners, carries a heavy judgment in the gay world. The unspoken suspicion is that someone who likes sex is HIV positive; however, this prejudice is evaporating quickly and giving new life to gay sex, and consequently, new relationship structures.

I came out in the era of AIDS and HIV. I remember being in college, and the intense, disgusting frat-boy jokes made about AIDS and gay men and thinking AIDS was just about the worst thing possible. I was petrified of it, but not petrified enough to use a condom when I had sex with women. After college, when I finally came out, I practiced safe sex initially, but once I started dating Danny, we stopped.

One of my first volunteer projects after passing the bar exam was writing wills for people living with AIDS at the local AIDS Project. There was a waiting room full of people looking to get their affairs in order and pass their things on to the people they loved, sometimes partners, sometimes friends, but where they had no one left, often charity. It was a sobering experience to sit with these dying men who believed their time was short and talk about who should get their lifetime accumulation of stuff.

I was there for the various benchmarks of the epic AIDS battle, but the powerful feelings related to that struggle have diminished over time, and it's especially hard to convey their full force years later.

I'll never forget going over to this man's house, his family surrounding him in his bed, and writing his will in his bedroom because he was too weak to get up. He was probably no older than thirty and was so handsome from the pictures spread around his room. There was one over his bed of him on the deck of a sailing ship, just a pair of jean shorts on, muscled, fit, and smiling, but here before me was someone completely unrecognizable from the photos, a weak skeleton of a human being, unable to care for his most basic needs. His face was sunken, his hair mostly gone, eyes so slow to move.

The family waited outside the room while I asked my questions and prepared his final documents. When I stepped out and said it was okay to come back in, they were huddled together, crying hard. Documents done and witnessed, I got back into my beat up old Volkswagen and broke down in a torrent, crying so hard I couldn't drive. The man passed away only a few days later.

While in law school, I roomed with my fraternity brother, Greg. Greg and I were always good friends even though he was a class behind me. During law school, it was hard to sustain that close of a friendship. I couldn't go out or get crazy like I used to, and our friendship was limited to saying, "hey" at breakfast and every once in awhile catching a Seahawks game together.

Since we were roommates and living on top of each other in my tiny little house in First Hill, it became difficult to hide my lifestyle from Greg. Once I started seeing Danny and Danny was sleeping over, it became impossible, and I had to sit down with Greg one day and tell him I was gay. Greg took the news much better than I thought he would and basically said he'd known for a long time and was fine with it. He seemed strangely relieved by my announcement.

Not too long after coming out to him, Greg and his girlfriend, Rachel, said they were leaving town for a couple weeks. Neither wanted to talk about it beyond telling me they'd be gone and asking if I'd watch their beagle, Sam.

When Greg and Rachel finally came back, it was with a U-Haul from Wyoming filled with furniture, clothes, artwork, the things of someone's life. There was so much stuff, it took him and Rachel a few days to unloaded everything into my basement. The next Sunday afternoon, the Seahawks were losing to the Broncos and I finally got to talk with Greg on my own.

Distant and sad, he sat there in silence watching the game. We both like the Seahawks, but losing to John Elway is one of those humiliations you can live with. Something else was going on.

"Alright, man. I'm worried about you. What the fuck is wrong?" I finally blurted out during the game.

He stopped watching the game and stared at the ground for a few seconds, his eyes welling with tears. Suddenly, he sat up, shook his head and took a deep breath. "My dad passed away a few weeks ago," he said, looking at the ceiling. "He died of AIDS."

Greg opened up like never before. All the fraternity bullshit aside, he told me that as long as he could remember, he'd known his dad was gay. That's why his parents got divorced. Apparently, it was a pretty ugly divorce where his parents involved the kids, and there was a lot of nasty stuff said that alienated the kids from their dad. Greg told me how hard it was growing up hearing gay slurs from his mother. He loved his dad and when his mom lashed out at him this way, she might as well have hit Greg with a closed fist. The pain was palpable.

Greg flew back and forth to be with him as AIDS settled in for the final battle. He was the only one of his dad's kids who did.

All that time, all those years, Greg lived with this stigma, quietly feeling the pain of the insults as our fraternity brothers made fun of "AIDS faggots" and other stupid bullshit mean little boys say. Here was Greg, taking care of his dad, sitting with him until the end, just loving the man who'd given him life.

These men were real, and their stories were real. AIDS and HIV are still real. This all actually did happen. I have to remind myself of how terrible it was sometimes and how lucky we are to live in the time that we do.

Nothing pisses me off more about my community than the attitude some gays have toward HIV positive people. Some men don't want anything to do with positive men, not as friends, lovers, family members, nothing. I know it comes from fear, and I have compassion for that, but these are awesome human beings have amazing stories to share and lives to live just like you, and your fear is harming you, and it's harming them.

The truth is, HIV still progresses to AIDS, but rarely. People do still pass away from complications related to AIDS, but rarely. Medications can now keep positive people from progressing to AIDS and can keep their viral load undetectable.

An undetectable viral load means that this positive person can't pass on HIV; it's impossible. That's the science. No matter if they cum in you 1,000 times, no matter if they bleed into an open wound you have, no matter what; undetectable means it's safer, in fact, to have sex with them than a random person who claims to be negative. I gotta say that again just to be clear, if you want to be sure you never become infected with HIV, you should have sex with undetectable positive gay men only. How's that for the shoe on the other foot?

This is because 20% of people who have HIV don't know they have HIV. So, if you hook up with someone who says he's negative, he may be wrong. It's not that he's lying about it, that's a different story, right? It's just that he's mistaken about his status.

HIV is also easily managed these days, and most positive people can quickly get to, and maintain, a zero viral load for years. Getting positive people to this zero viral load is perhaps the quickest way to bring this epidemic to an end; that, and getting everyone tested, so there isn't a 20% "surprise".

Gay men who are paranoid and discriminate against positive men need some loving and education, but even then, if they're still paranoid, now they have the option of preventing their infection by going on PrEP.

Pre-exposure prophylaxis, or PrEP, is an FDA approved way for people who don't have HIV, but who are at potential risk of getting it, to prevent an HIV infection by taking one pill every day. The pill, called Truvada, is a combination of two other medicines, tenofovir and emtricitabine, which are most commonly used in combination with other medicines to treat HIV.

When someone is exposed to HIV, these medicines work by keeping the virus from establishing a permanent infection. According to the Center for Disease Control, if a person consistently takes Truvada, it's been shown to reduce the risk of HIV infection by up to 92%; however, other studies are demonstrating that it's, in fact, a better preventive measure than condoms. Yup, let's re-read that one, too. PrEP may be more effective at preventing future HIV infections than using a condom.

Many health insurance companies have done the math and figured out that if someone requests PrEP, it's cheaper (despite the over $1,000 month cost) to fully cover the preventative treatment than to run the risk of incurring the cost of a lifetime of treatment for HIV. Also, the patent for these drugs runs out in two years. Cheaper generic versions will be hitting shelves near you soon.

The era of HIV and AIDS isn't over, and certainly, there're still some bad STDs floating around that can only be prevented through the use of a condom, but it's a different world today. I don't think this new generation of twenty-somethings has any concept of those dark days of shame, fear, and death all around our community. If they think going in for a test now is scary, try it twenty-five years ago when there was little hope, and a positive test meant a terrible, lonely death.

So what constitutes "safe sex" has changed in the last few years. Studies have shown zero risk of infection from zero viral load, positive men, and the advancement of PrEP as a nearly perfect preventative measure changes the meaning of "protection". The safest sex for someone who's negative and doesn't want to become infected with HIV may be taking PrEP, and having sex with a zero viral load, positive guy!

While it's too early to declare victory in the fight against HIV and AIDS, these new studies and treatments are opening doors for our community that have been slammed shut for decades. As awareness spreads about these new studies and the availability of PrEP increases, especially when the generic version hits, a new sexual revolution in the gay community is dawning. Sex is taking on a new dimension shaping relationships, and adding to the dynamic ignited by technology.

Chapter 54
YOU CHECKING MY PHONE?

Many years ago, during my stint as a serial monogamist, I briefly dated a national champion diver. As you might imagine, Derek's body was flawless. He was twenty-six when we met at Aspen Gay Ski Week, about six feet tall, dark hair with some scruff, and piercing blue eyes. We met in the hot tub at the host hotel, the Limelight. Derek was quick witted and funny. I broke up with my last partner a couple weeks prior but, as a serial monogamist, this was long enough. I was ready for the next one.

We were instantly attracted to each other, and for the rest of the week, spent all our time together. He lived in LA, but that didn't last long. After just a few weeks, I asked him to come up and live with me in Seattle. It took another few weeks to get it all sorted out, but just two months after we said a tearful goodbye at the Aspen airport I was in LA loading his blue Jeep Grand Cherokee for the drive to Seattle.

I could probably use this story to illustrate a whole lot of relationship issues, romantic love, the U-haul mentality, living in a fiction, but this relationship was unique in a couple ways. First, it was the only relationship I was ever in where I was a victim of abuse, and second, it was the one where my partner's jealousy was overpowering and irrational.

One cold, rainy Saturday morning in Seattle, we were lying in bed and Derek was still sleeping. We spent most the night cuddled up, keeping each other warm, alternating with sex. That morning,

I watched him quietly sleeping looking so handsome and peaceful. A wave of love came over me, and I thought, this is the man I want to be with forever.

That memory is still so strong. Even though I know now it was a complete fiction and he was definitely not "the one," I'll probably never be able to forget how strong and reassuring that feeling was, or the look of peacefulness on his face as he lay there sleeping.

Almost as soon he moved in, jealousy started creeping in. One night, I took him to the Pony, a local gay bar, and made the mistake of saying how hot the bartender was. I thought I was gonna have to walk home. For the rest of the night, all I heard was that if I liked the bartender that much, maybe I should just go home with him, and he was serious.

I learned not to make those comments with Derek again.

Shortly after this incident, I also noticed that he was checking my phone. Today, most phones require a passcode or a fingerprint to access it, but back then, passcodes were the exception. Several times in the morning, I got out of the shower and noticed my phone was on a screen that I hadn't left it on.

There was nothing to hide since I wasn't cheating on him and wasn't pursuing anyone else, but I felt violated. I didn't confront Derek and, in fact, continued to give him free access to the phone whenever he felt like he needed to spy on me. Since I wasn't cheating on him, I hoped he'd be reassured as he dug through my phone, day after day, looking for something but never finding it. I was wrong.

I don't remember what exact emails or texts caused him to start making accusations, but after just a couple months of living together, Derek started accusing me of carrying on inappropriate conversations with other men. I was pretty shocked by his anger since I knew I wasn't doing anything, and I was confused at the basis for his claim. He always came back to, "I just know you are. Don't worry about how."

That was when I put a passcode on my phone. That's also when things took a turn for the worse.

It only took him a day to figure out I locked my phone, but what could he say? I noticed a significant change in him right away. He was anxious, closed down, and easily angered. He started making mean jabs at me about everything; what I was wearing, what I was reading, and most important, what I was doing all day. He didn't believe I was at work or the gym.

A week or so after I added the passcode, he secretly followed me to the gym. I've always had workout buddies, and it's rare to see me at the gym alone. Some of my workout buddies, like Tony, lasted for years. Others lasted only a few weeks. When Derek and I dated, I was working out with Tony.

Derek knew Tony and hated him. Several times during those short months of being together, Tony was the target of some pretty vicious attacks by Derek. Derek told Tony to get out of the house once and kept telling me Tony was a whore and I should stay away from him, so when Derek followed me into the gym and saw me working out with Tony, it was a formula for an argument.

Derek waited until I got home to tell me he'd followed me to the gym and watched Tony and me work out. He accused me of hooking up with Tony and secretly having an affair with him. That's when he "proved" it by pointing out that I'd put a passcode on my phone. He demanded I give him my phone and passcode was so he could look at my messages.

That was enough. I said no.

Derek flew into a rage and tried to wrestle my phone from me. I'm not sure what he thought he was doing. Even if he got it from me, there was no way he could open it without the passcode, but he went after me with everything he had.

Shocked and scared by his assault, and rather than fight him for the phone, I let the phone go after a few seconds and stepped back.

"Give me the goddamn code!" he shouted at me. His face was red and his eyes wild. The look on his face was so irrational, I was scared of him. I'd never seen anyone fly off the handle like this.

"I'm not cheating on you with Tony! He's my best friend and we were just working out together like we do pretty much every day," I said, calmly but with tears in my eyes. "You've got no right to go digging through my phone, Derek. I don't look at yours, man."

"Give me the fucking passcode, asshole!" he screamed and threw my phone against the wall, putting a hole in the drywall and shattering the glass. We were standing upstairs in the hallway in front of my bedroom. The passcode was pretty much pointless now, and I was scared for my safety.

Luckily, I still had my keys and wallet on me. I fled down the stairs, out the front door, and into the street. Derek came after me until I got outside. I ran over to my car, jumped in without looking back, and sped off.

That was the height of the drama and the end of the relationship. With the help of friends and a threat of calling the police, I got Derek out of the house, changed the locks, got a new phone, and I never saw Derek again. I arranged for a hotel for him for a week, but I have no idea if he used it.

I never got a chance to tell Derek I knew he was spying on me the whole time, but I guess it wouldn't have mattered. There was nothing rational about Derek's jealousy; no amount of reassurance from me would have put his concerns to rest. There was nothing I could have done to rid our relationship of his jealousy, except end it, and that, I was happy to do.

Chapter 55

COPING WITH JEALOUSY

It surprised and scared me when I caught Derek checking my phone, but I was also a little flattered. Mistakenly, I interpreted his jealousy as an indication he cared enough to checkup on me. Were my feelings misplaced?

Researchers believe jealousy evolved for positive reasons. They argue jealousy between mating couples discouraged desertion by a mate, bolstered the family unit, and enabled the survival of the young.

Jealousy can have positive side effects for a relationship. One partner may feel secretly flattered when the other is mildly jealous. Even catching someone flirting with your boyfriend may spark the kind of lust that helps reignite a relationship.

How do we balance the healthy aspects of jealousy with its potential for destruction? Research suggests that the key to managing feelings like jealousy lies not in eliminating them altogether, but in expressing them in the right way. Like any vulnerable feeling, jealousy can either foster or hinder intimacy. It all depends on how it's handled.

In my experience, there are five ways you can express jealousy in the right way:

- **Fess up**—Talking openly about jealousy can help prevent and manage it. Try sharing your feelings without making accusations. Request specific actions, like more frequent communication, that may help you feel more secure. The more connected you are, the less jealous you'll feel.

- **Ask for reassurance**—If you feel suspicious, use 'I-statements' and ask for reassurances. Better to talk about it than make accusations and create angry distance. If there's nothing going on, it shouldn't be a big deal to talk about it. Avoid attempts to control your partner, like making demands or hurling accusations.
- **But avoid interrogation**—If you always have to get an accounting from your partner, something's wrong. If things are innocent, your partner should routinely volunteer information; you shouldn't have to keep asking. If he's giving you information, but you always want more, you're attempting to control, and you'll push him away.
- **Know your limits**—If you worry day and night or frequently shoot off accusatory texts, then it's time for a break. When no amount of reassurance or communication relieves your stress, this relationship is toxic, and it's time to end it.
- **Cure your insecurities**—Jealousy often arises from insecurities about your worthiness as a partner. Deep down you fear if your partner only knew the truth about you then he'd leave you for someone better. Insecurities lead to fear of being replaced.

Expressing your jealousy is a fine line to walk. Jealous outbursts wear on your partner, and they erode trust and closeness, eventually driving a partner to keep secrets he'd otherwise share. Faced with a barrage of questions, a partner may become afraid to talk about what's going on in his life for fear of being misunderstood. Frequent interrogation can make him feel bullied, which leads inevitably to a break down in communication between the partners.

If your partner is gonna cheat on you, he's gonna cheat on you, and there's not a damn thing you can do about it, short of locking him up. Likewise, if he's not someone who would cheat on you, he's not gonna cheat on you. The decision to cheat is his own to make and you ultimately have no control over his actions.

These two points are fundamental in a modern relationship. The idea that "If he's gonna cheat, he's gonna cheat, and if he's not, he's not" seems like a painfully obvious point, but it's a recognition of the individuality of your partner. Whatever your partner choses to do is ultimately out of your control.

All you can do is be the best person you can be and remind yourself that he's chosen to be with you, and you with him for a reason. Your jealousy may only serve to weaken that reason. Trust in the strength of your relationship.

Trust exists in both traditional and modern relationships; the difference is the subject of the trust you're extending. In traditional relationships, you're trusting that the partner isn't going to sleep with someone else. That's the ultimate question and the true measure of fidelity in a traditional relationship. In a modern relationship, the trust is more in yourself and therefore in the validity of the relationship. You're trusting that you are, in fact, desirable, wanted, and loved. There's no reason to go looking for anyone "better". You believe in the relationship and trust that the reasons you've decided to be together are good enough to keep you together.

Managing insecurities and developing this trust requires a self-evaluation of the source of those insecurities, and they come from all different directions; childhood, abuse, body image, peer pressure, and past relationships to name a few. Another source of insecurities is the creation of a fantasy relationship during romantic love, or through the use of social media. When a partner finally sees the fantasy he's created, he realizes he can't live up to the expectations of his fictional self or fictional relationship. How can he possibly be the superstar, mega-popular and beautiful person he's created in the mind of his partner or on social media? Imagine the insecurities this supermodel-turned-human must feel.

A jealous man lives in a special kind of hell. Constantly comparing oneself to alternatives, real and imagined, is a bad business. If a jealous man drops comparing, jealousy disappears, meanness disappears, phoniness disappears. The difficulty is that you can only stop comparing yourself to others once you're able to see your own value and worth and rid yourself of insecurities. You can drop jealousy only if you start growing your inner confidence; there's no other way.

Chapter 56
TELLING TONY

I knew I wasn't Robbie's only interest; he wasn't mine either. Even in San Francisco I continued to meet other people and hook up sometimes, plus I had some friends with benefits back in Seattle. I didn't expect him to make any commitment to me, nor me to him, but he also wasn't just a friend in my mind. I was hoping it would develop into something more.

We continued to see each other after Folsom, through the holidays, but so far only on my trips down to San Francisco. Not only was it risky to have him up to Seattle, he couldn't leave because of his work. Robbie hated both his jobs. Day time as a video editor and a bar-back three nights a week was exhausting, but San Francisco is such an expensive place, his options were limited. He mentioned getting his teaching certificate, but nothing came of it yet.

My anxiety that Tony might find out was growing daily. He knew I was going out there for work, but he also knew that I was enjoying my trips. I had a hard time talking to him about those trips because he had so many questions and was getting suspicious of my evasion on certain topics. Tony was suspicious I was seeing a guy, just based on the descriptions I gave him about where I was going and who I was with; "Oh, just this guy I know." More alarm bells went off each time I dodged his questions.

Our relationship was incredibly close, and we'd tell each other almost everything, so this black hole of information about my time in San Francisco stood out like a sore thumb. It was just a matter of time before I had to tell him, but it also might mean the end of our friendship.

It started out like any other workout at gym, just a normal day of doing triceps and shoulders. Tony had a trip planned down to Alabama the coming weekend and was focused on trying to get a good workout so he could look good for his new guy. It confused me that he always thought one workout would make a big change in his body; it looked more like a Hail Mary to me.

Today, the gym was pretty busy and several people we knew were there. We usually spend the first ten or fifteen minutes saying hi to everybody, deciding what to do, then settling on whatever Tony wanted to work. Tonight, he was wearing a 'Bama football T-shirt and sporting a new haircut. I had a hard time keeping my smart-ass mouth shut.

I was leaving for San Francisco this weekend, too, but only to spend time with Robbie. We wouldn't get to spend the entire weekend together, maybe just a whole day or part of two, but it would be enough. Tony knew I was excited about this trip; he just didn't know who I was going to see.

"So you ready for your trip?" he asked me.

"So ready. Can't wait to get there," I said with plenty of emotion. It'd been a long week already, and I needed an escape from Seattle.

"What're you gonna to do while you're out there?" he said lying on the bench, grabbing some weights. I stood behind the bench to spot him in case he got too tired to finish his set.

"Got dinner plans Friday night with a friend. Then I'll probably see Greg and Scott sometime on Saturday. Planning on just hanging out with a buddy Saturday night, maybe go out to Backtracks," I said vaguely. I'm pretty sure he knew that I was talking about having dates Friday and Saturday, but that I didn't want to give him too many details.

He pushed the easy-curl bar over his head as many times as he could until his triceps failed, then he passed it to me. Tony sat up, turned around on the bench, pulled his ear phones out and said, "Are you gonna tell me who you're dating out there? I know you're seeing someone. You're a terrible liar, Dave."

I turned away nervously and moved to put the barbell back on the rack and grab a heavier one for myself. When I came back to the bench, Tony was still sitting there staring at me.

"It's Robbie, isn't it?" he said more as a statement than a question. "Every time you've dated someone before you always told me every details. Now, you won't even tell me the guy's name. Only thing I can think of is it's Robbie. Please tell me that's not true."

He's right. I'm a terrible liar. I laughed nervously, then said, "Why do you think it's Robbie? What . . . What . . ." I stammered. There was no time to even come up with a decent lie to cover my surprise.

"You fucker. It is Robby. How could you do that to me? What kind of friend are you?" He was visibly angry and didn't care that there were other people nearby watching.

I gave up. I knew I might lose my best friend right here, right now, but it was time to tell him. I just had to trust that our friendship was strong enough to survive somehow.

"Yes." I looked down at the ground, standing there waiting for his outburst. "It's Robbie."

That first night with Robbie was a year and a half after he and Tony had broken up. Tony was now on to another man, whom he claimed was his soulmate. I could easily rationalize why it was okay to see Robbie, but deep down I knew despite the time, the distance, and the new guy, Tony was still in love with Robbie, and with me. In my heart of hearts, I knew this new 'Bama guy was just an attempt to find someone to fill the holes left his in his life by the two of us. The fact that Robbie and I had gotten together undoubtedly made Tony feel abandoned by the two people he loved the most.

He stood leaning against the dips bar for a long time before he grabbed his phone and hit the power button, bringing up the picture of his new Alabama man. He stood there staring at that picture until the screen went dark, then pushed it again. Tears welled in his eyes.

"Why didn't you tell me sooner? Why'd you lie to me about it? I knew you were lying," he said angrily.

"Because my first trip out there without you you said if I saw Robbie you'd never talk to me again and I was scared," I responded quietly. "I never meant for anything to happen with him except for dinner. I'm sorry, Tony."

"I don't fucking believe you," he said, turning away and walking off to the water fountain. I stood there watching him to see if he was coming back or if he'd leave. I don't think he knew which he'd do either, but after getting a drink he turned and walked back toward me.

"You slept with my boyfriend, Dave," he said, his face red and angry.

"Robbie's not your boyfriend, Tony. You have a new boyfriend whom you say you're in love with. You're moving down there to be with him," I said. "I'm sorry you're hurt by this, but buddy, you have a whole new life, one you're excited to get start down in Alabama. Do you care that much if Robbie and I find some happiness together?"

"I've never slept with your boyfriends. Anytime you showed interest in someone, I backed away and let you have him."

"Not true. We both know there've been times when people I'm interested in stop being interested in me because of you." Many times over the years after I introduced Tony to a guy I was interested in, all the guy wanted was Tony's phone number. It's part of the reason traveling with Tony is so difficult. Every time there's a nice-looking guy, I'm nothing but a sucker to hold their drinks.

"Yeah, maybe, but I never slept with your boyfriend." I was confused that he kept calling Robbie his boyfriend. It seemed a strange choice of words, given his current relationship.

"Look, man. I'm sorry. I am. I guess I never should've tried to go to dinner with him. I never meant to hurt your feelings." Now it was my turn to tear up. Tony was an important part of my life. I didn't want to lose him.

We stood there quietly for a while as the gym moved around us, oblivious of our conversation now. After a while, Tony looked up and said, "It's gonna take me a long time to get over this, Dave. But it'll be okay."

"I hope so," I whispered. "Our friendship means a lot to me, even if you're about to move away."

We silently went back to finishing the workout and spent maybe another twenty minutes not talking. At the end, after we grabbed our gym bags and headed out, back to our cars, I asked, "Can we do dinner tomorrow night?"

"Yeah," he said and turned to give me our nightly hug. This hug was different; distant, brief, against a hardened body. We said good night and headed home.

Tony and I had spent every day together for the past four years, supporting, helping, encouraging, and fighting with each other. The times weren't always happy, but we were like family and always came back. I knew him better than anyone else, and him me. Tonight, I felt that coming to an end, both because of my involvement with Robbie and his upcoming move to Alabama. My heart was breaking as Adele competed with the sounds of rush hour traffic, singing about broken dreams and a new love taking her place.

Damn you, Adele.

LEVEL 2
THE FUCK BUDDY

Chapter 57
FRIENDS WITH BENEFITS

The friends with benefits, or fuck buddy level of the modern relationship pyramid is distinguished from the pinnacle relationship in many ways. A friends with benefits relationship has the following characteristics:

- Friendship
- Sexual relationship
- No emotional investment
- Non-monogamous
- No fidelity

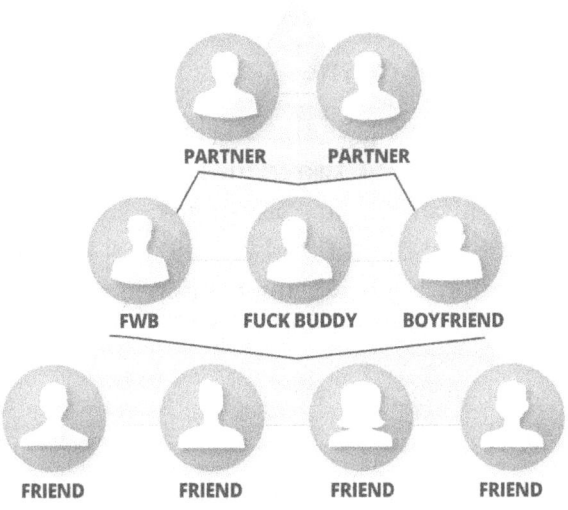

Figure 6 - Friends With Benefits/Fuck Buddies

Friendship

A threshold to a relationship at this level of the pyramid is a friendship. A friendship at this level carries few expectations and therefore few commitments. If expectations or commitments arise, the relationship begins to change from friendship to a partnership.

On the flip-side, though, a friendship has more endurance because it lacks the expectations or commitments of the pinnacle partnership. While a friends with benefits situation may not last long. These relationships can often translate into friendships without sexual relationships.

Sexual Relationship

This level of the pyramid shares with the pinnacle level a sexual relationship. It may be frequent, or not. It may be one-on-one, or you may share the person with your partner or others. It may be sex just like you have with your partner, but usually not. Usually, the friends with benefits relationship addresses some sexual need that's not being met by the primary partnership.

No Emotional Investment

One of the greatest benefits of this level of the pyramid is that the connection between the two friends requires little emotional investment on their parts. Their private lives are pretty much off-limits, and jealousy isn't permitted. If jealousy exists, this friends with benefits relationship is seeking to supplant the pinnacle relationship.

Non-Monogamous

Friends with benefits don't have the right to demand nor expect a monogamous relationship. It goes without saying that the individuals in this relationship can go out and be with other people, including pinnacle partners.

No Fidelity

Since there are no commitments and few expectations in these second tier relationships, there's also no fidelity expected nor required. The only expectation is the friendship continues forward with the parameters set before the sexual relations began. That's the only expectation.

We've discussed before; it's possible to be in adult love with your partner and romantic love with someone else. A problem, though, arises with classifying this second type of relationship. The romantic love we feel for someone else doesn't place them at the pinnacle level, but it's also more than just a friendship with sexual benefits. I place these relationships based in romantic love at this level of the pyramid because it would be my expectation that the relationship based on romantic love doesn't have the depth nor the emotional investment of a pinnacle relationship.

No doubt that a second loving relationship creates potential problems for the entire structure. Most relationships based on romantic love aspire to become more, and last longer, perhaps indefinitely, but since there's no room at the top, so to speak, these relationships are capped by the limits of this mid-level of the pyramid.

It's easy to see how a pinnacle relationship is threatened by any romantic love relationship at this level of the pyramid. I suspect that making this arrangement work takes serious confidence in the strength of the pinnacle relationship, but at the same time, I've seen it work. In these situations, the third-party boyfriend is usually the one to set the limits of expectations for his role. In other words, in the situations where I've observed this dynamic, it's usually the third party boyfriend who wants to keep it romantic, but simple.

A true friends with benefits relationship has many mutually desirable characteristics. The relationship is usually based on sexual needs. Convenience of parties is important. There's no standing expectation of a sexual encounter. A participant in one of these relationships can explore certain aspects of his sexuality that he can't with his primary partner. There is usually no emotional break-up at the end of one of these relationships. A friends with benefits relationship can be a great addition to a person's sex life.

Chapter 58
RUNNING OVER ROBBIE

Two months had passed since, sitting on a runway at SFO, I said goodbye to Robbie forever. My head wedged against the window of 2A during takeoff to hide my tears, I watched the city drift off and felt empty. The "fight," if you can call it that, was brief and confusing, but final. Robbie's push accomplished his objective and I walked away, telling him I wished him nothing but happiness, and I meant it. I knew no one who deserved it more. The city that held my heart had sent it back.

It took two months before I felt like retuning to San Francisco. Appointments got dodged and meetings postponed while I found excuses to avoid the city but I could delay it only so long, and eventually returned determined to focus on work.

I knew I shouldn't have wandered back into the Castro that night. All weekend, there was anxiety I might run into Robbie or somehow invade his space and validate his decision to call things off. I was conscious of the time of day I'd be out and about, knowing that, on the weekends, Robbie worked late and was probably sleeping during daylight hours. Since both of us used Scruff pretty much nonstop, it was impossible not to notice when was online and how far away he was.

I guess I could've just blocked his profile. I lived in fear he'd do the same to me. To be honest, though, I liked looking at his pictures sometimes. It reassured me to know he was still out there, hopefully happy. Robbie never posts naked pictures or anything even remotely compromising, so it wasn't that I wanted a cheap thrill, but there was one picture of him climbing a tree smiling up at the camera, so damn handsome, that always brought a smile to my face.

Over the weekend, while I was finding guys to meet up with, I noticed from Robbie's profile that he didn't go anywhere at night; he was always the same distance away from my apartment. Based on that distance, it looked like he was staying at home. The only thing I could think of was he gave up his night job and was back on a regular nine to five schedule at the porn studio. While I was curious and even a little concerned for him, I began to be less worried about running into him in the Castro.

Saturday night, when the sun was down and I thought his shift at the club would've started already, I saw that Robbie was at home and figured I could wander Castro without too much fear of running into him. Still anxious, there was a lingering hopefulness, too. Fuck. I'm not sure what I wanted.

My original plan was to grab a quick bite and meet Mark and Cade at High Tops to watch the World Series. Watching a major sporting event at a gay bar is a unique experience. Most of the crowd isn't actually into the game. Most are using the excuse of the World Series gives to congregate, drink, and wear clothing that screams "I'm a jock!" Sounded like a good plan to me.

Starving after a long day of meetings, I stopped by Pie Hole. It was packed. There's a TV inside on the wall, and the game was on. Why people hangout at a pizza by the slice joint to watch the World Series, I'll never know. Pie Hole was more crowded than most of the bars.

I ordered two slices of pepperoni, grabbed a tiny sliver of the counter, and pretended to be interested in the game. Okay, I'm actually a sports fan, so even though I don't regularly follow baseball, I felt the energy of the event and was infected by it, but the pizza was better.

Pizza scarfed down, I headed back out onto Castro to meet Mark and Cade, but fate had other plans. Turning left out of Pie

Hole would lead to High Tops. Turning right would take me to Robbie's bar. What the fuck. I turned right.

I knew he wasn't there. I'd been on Scruff at Pie Hole, returning messages, sending new ones, and noticed that his profile was nowhere nearby. Since the bar was almost right next door, I felt okay going in. But why did I even go? I could give you the lawyer answer and say I like the crowd at his bar, and I do, but there was another reason that night. It was just meant to be.

My $1 cover paid, I bellied up to the bar, and got a Stella to watch the game. One of the bar-backs came up and said I was too damn hot, and he was buying me a drink to cool me off. He introduced himself as Max and bragged he had the best ass in San Francisco. Max invited me to grab it and see for myself. Sure enough it was round and rock-hard. Max didn't look too fit and I was surprised at his rock-solid butt. Not sure what he was doing to get an ass like that, but he was putting some definite work into it.

Feeling secure I wouldn't run into Robbie, I started to relax and enjoy the game. Giants were up, and the crowd was happy. I had two beers, which is normally my limit, and just ordered a third, when out of the corner of my eye I saw Robbie. He was just outside the bar, moving to come in. I panicked and dodged my way into a corner. I bet I looked silly, standing perfectly still watching the game one second, then stooping over and bolting for the corner the next.

My fear was Robbie would think I'm some weird stalker and get angry. As much as I deep down wanted to see him, I was doing my best to respect his space and not intrude on it, but here I was, at his job, hanging out at the front door. Fuck. I was caught.

Hiding in the corner, I watched the front to see if he'd walk in so I could sneak out, but he never came in. I checked my phone. It was 8:01 p.m. Maybe his shift had started and I'd missed him coming in. Maybe there was a side entrance or something. Time to bolt! Except it wasn't. As I dodged my way through the crowd, out the front door, I took a deep, relieved breath . . . and ran straight into Robbie, almost knocking him to the concrete.

No fucking joke. I grabbed his arm as our bodies collided and our eyes met. In that split second I saw happy surprise on his face as he recognized me, then a transformation into curiosity, but I chose to ignore it. "Hey!" I said with a smile and squeezed his arm, but kept walking. He said "Hey" back with a smile and kept walking too. I glanced around and saw only his back as he headed into the bar, never turning around.

I kicked my own ass for the next eight blocks as I relived that brief two or three second catastrophe. What the fuck was I thinking? What must he think of me? Why the fuck was he going into work at 8:00 p.m.? Damn it! But it was also so good to see him, and so good to touch him.

Was I hoping for that the whole time? Honestly, I know part of me needed to see him again, but I knew if I forced myself on him at all, it would be the last time I saw him. I was trying my best to avoid him, I suppose, because I knew one day we would see each other again, and I wanted to be able to say, look! I gave you space just like you asked!

Tonight I'd blown my chance, though. My shirt might as well have screamed "Stalker" across the front. I chewed myself out, calling myself every name I could think of. Should have just gone to High Tops; now it was over. Any chance I had with Robbie was trashed.

All the way down 18th Street, I rolled my eyes and kicked the sidewalk, thinking, how stupid; then I heard my phone go off with a sound that, for a second, I didn't recognize, but one I couldn't long forget. It was the xylophone sound I'd assigned to Robbie's number. Robbie sent me a text.

"It was nice seeing you. Hope you're doing well."

Dead stop on the sidewalk. I was just across the street from Dolores Park. A wave of relief and excitement passed over me. Maybe I hadn't fucked up. Maybe . . .

A tentative conversation followed, halting, about how we were both doing and what was new in life. It continued after I reached my place, where I laid on the living room floor rug and cuddled with Stella to ease some anxiety.

"Wish you stayed," he texted.

"Me too. Wish it was a better hello!"

"Bar is gonna die down in a bit if you want to come back."

I was grabbing my shoes. Stella was sitting there with her big green eyes, giving me dirty looks. She must have thought, what a strange creature, indeed, coming in and out all the time, instead of just curling up in a nice warm blanket!

What a different walk back down 18th! Now, I had something to look forward to. Although there was still anxiety about what would happen when I got back to the bar, my heart was beating again. My stomach was turning at the potential for embarrassment, rejection, and the unknown.

No kicking the pavement this time; instead, I just pounded it, methodically moving one block to the next, definite purpose and excitement. Over and over in my head, I saw that first text and smiled.

At the bar, I quickly made my way straight through the crowd toward the back area, vaguely keeping an eye out for Robbie. I moved with purpose to the part of the bar I felt was more private and empty. I didn't make it far.

There he was, right in the middle of the bar as I moved through, no escaping, no hiding, and no privacy. Whatever was going to happen, was going to happen in full-on sight of this entire World Series-watching crowd of bears. My mind shouted fuck! Was he going to give me a nod? A handshake? A drink coupon?

He looked up and saw me, and a sly smile spread across that handsome, dark face and his eyes lit up. I no longer gave a shit about any audience. I walked up to him, slowly wrapped my arms around his body, and he gently did the same. Eyes closed, my head buried in his neck, he felt perfect against my body. After a few seconds of quietly holding each other in that mass of sports fans, shouting and drinking, I moved my hand to the back of his head.

I lifted my face to his and our lips touched. He tasted amazing. I can still taste him even right now.

I stayed at the bar about 45 minutes, catching up, sneaking intimate contact whenever he'd make his way to where I staked out a spot, but it was early, and he wouldn't get off work for another five hours. I asked if he wanted to hang out after the bar closed. He hesitated and looked off.

"Maybe. I'll have to see how I'm feeling. Plus, I'll need a shower and stuff."

"No pressure, Robbie. It'd be nice to see you outside of the bar before I leave tomorrow," I said, hiding the flood of anxiety of rejection. He looked back at me and smiled, tentative, but friendly and warm. Maybe that was all I should expect. Maybe I should be happy with just that.

He walked me through the crowd and we said goodbye on the sidewalk. I did my best to be relaxed, not over-doing it, but also not distant. I wanted him to know I was happy with whatever came next, as long as we were talking.

Is it possible for a street so physically familiar to look so different in the span of just a few hours? 18th Street was getting schizophrenic.

Chapter 59
NYE IN LA

The idea of having someone on the side, either as a couple or a single person not wanting to commit to a relationship, is nothing new. It's been the norm in most cultures throughout the history of men, including France, the Ottoman Empire, Imperial China, and even pockets of our American society.

Today, the friends with benefits relationship is experiencing a renaissance. Over 50% of people in their twenties report being in one of these relationships at some point. With the nearing equilibrium between the sexes, an individual drive for success in the world of technology, and other factors tending to help people be more independent, the convenience of casual, predictable sex is a good solution for more and more people.

There are also fewer expectations in this relationship, as the name implies. There's a formal distance between the participants. They're limited to being friends, and friends don't make rules for each other. Friendship assumes the continuation of the relationship over a period and a degree of depth not associated with acquaintances.

"I don't want to be your friend anymore" may be a phrase you hear on the playground in fifth grade, but isn't generally something you hear in adult relationships. The vision of friendships present in this comment presumes you can switch it on and off, one day you're my friends, but the next you aren't. Practical experience is this doesn't happen often.

Also, the word *benefits* implies "I'm voluntarily giving you something and could chose to take it back at any moment," so don't take me for granted.

The structure appears to play out differently based on gender. Research shows that men appear to focus more on the benefits and women more on the friendship.

The two people entering a friends with benefits relationship have often been friends or lovers first, although that's not necessary all the time. They may have met on Grindr, had a smoking hot hookup and just kept each other's numbers at the top of the iMessage list.

Lines clearly drawn, expectations laid out, friends with benefits can enjoy regular, casual sex without all the messiness of rule-making. Obviously, in this sort of relationship, participants are pretty realistic about each other and see their friend with all the attached flaws of our humanity.

How do these relationships come about? My friends with benefits situations came from tricks where the sex was particularly good, but where neither of us was looking for a relationship. We stayed in touch and talked about meeting again. There was an easy chemistry between us. The steps are:

- Flirting
- Hooking up
- Laying out expectations (or lack thereof)
- Hot sex
- Keep talking to each other afterward

They don't always last long, but can last for years. It may be the couple sees each other every night for a stretch of time, or they may go months and months, but because the expectations are nominal, this is often not a problem.

Jealousy can creep in but, because the relationship is defined as "friends," there's no exclusivity implied, expected, or even tolerated in some cases. When jealousy does come into play it's because one of the friends wants more than the expectations permit. Since there's no rule-making at this level, jealousy is a dead end.

Are these relationships emotionally fulfilling, or are they just physical? By definition, they're not intended to create an emotional connection, so there's no expectation that they will. If one friend begins to crave more emotion, the relationship is deteriorating, or morphing, away from friends with benefits.

Friends with benefits relationships offer the advantages of a caring and supportive friendship, though, coupled with sexual adventures without the emotional commitments. The disadvantages include that they lack the intensity of romantic love, and especially the depth of true love. Also, in the long run, they will always be second best to the partner who wishes to have a committed and intimate relationship.

There are people, however, who shouldn't pursue friends with benefits relationships. These people tend to set expectations as part of their DNA. They tend to get jealous, associate sex with love, engage in patterns of romantic love and fall in love because the sex is good. If this sounds like you, it probably won't work out, and you should examine the expectations you place on your sexual partners. Maybe take a step back and start small.

There are advantages to friends with benefits situations for some people. A single mom, trying to hold down a job and balance life after a divorce, a man who travels all the time, someone just out of college focused on getting his career started; all good candidates where friends with benefits can be comfortable, satisfying, and adventurous.

Friends with benefits can also facilitate exploration of sexual urges or desires that a person isn't comfortable exploring with his partner. Strap on some leather, get out the rope, try some toys. This level of relationship is premised on sexual freedom.

Don't plan on breakfast, though. When the sex is done, the friendship aspect is triggered and should provide the context for whatever happens next; time to hit the gym together, or run the park, or just say "see you next time, bud."

Does this mean the two friends are simply using each other to get off? That dynamic seems abusive and objectifying, but it's misleading since this isn't just sex with a random partner, this is sex with a friend. This is someone with whom you have a relationship, perhaps a deep one. It's something beyond someone you just met off the street.

Some people say that the best candidates for friends with benefits situations are people who are available, and I agree; however, people coming out of relationships are "unavailable" in that they're not interested in starting anything with anyone. Contrary to what some might believe, I think these individuals may benefit the most from a good friends with benefits situation. I know many of my clients sure would.

The primary reasons these relationships come to an end are:

- One friend becomes too attached for the other's comfort
- One finds someone he wants to date
- Bored with each other sexually
- End of a period like a trip, graduation, new job, or moving

When friends with benefits relationships end, it's with a whimper. The texts dry up, responses slow, or they become more perfunctory, "Hey, how's your day" instead of "you free this week?" There's little drama associated with the end of these relationships, too. Since the initial expectations were low, there's just not much to be upset about when it ends. Mostly, these couples stay friends, even when there's no more sex.

Over the past twenty years I've been in many different types of friends with benefits relationships, lasting anywhere from eight years to just a few weeks. Some have been great while others haven't ended so well.

My sexual relationship with Tony started up again after two years of just being friends while we were in LA for NYE. We were traveling with a group, but Tony and I had our own room. At the time, we were both single, hooking up occasionally with other guys, but nothing serious.

Our friendship was pretty intense, like family. We spent pretty much every free minute together, at the gym, hanging out, eating, everything. We reached that stage where we'd finish each other's sentences and could have whole discussions with just a few words. I still had feelings for him, but they were pretty quiet and, for the most part, didn't get in the way of our relationship. I would still get jealous, though, when he would show interest in other guys. I did my best to hide it, but no doubt it creeped out sometimes.

Tony would never admit having any feelings for me. He was adamant that our friendship was just friends and nothing else, but under this facade, there were signs that he wasn't being honest. There's no doubt that when a hot guy found me attractive, but not him, he would get jealous. A pretext for his angry outbursts would be hauled out like, "I never leave you on your own for dinner just for a trick!" or "Are you going to text your surfer boy all day or are we going to work out?"

Not only would Tony get jealous and upset about my interest in other guys, he'd also get physically aroused around me. We'd always hug goodnight, or goodbye, even in the middle of the gym. It was just a thing. If we were fighting and I didn't feel like hugging, he'd be more upset about that than the fight sometimes. Blowing off the hug was an indication that this was a big fight, but sometimes, when we were making up, or something emotional happened to one of us I could feel him getting aroused and start to pull away in an effort to hide it. It was comical, him standing there with a hard on and me trying to ignore it.

Outwardly, though, it was all strictly friends; until LA.

In LA for New Year's Eve, we went to a big venue dance club. Tony had the attention of all the "A"-listers and was his typical social butterfly self. There were some amazingly hot men after him, but he had his eye on this dark-haired, scruffy guy, about thirty years old who was quiet and brooding, and a good dancer.

"Fuck! That guy is so hot!" he said for the tenth time that night.

"Yeah, he's pretty amazing." He was, but not more so than the other five guys around Tony giving him all their attention. The guy was giving a few glances in our direction, too, so there was interest back. "Go talk to him!"

"Naw. I don't do that. I'm too shy. You know I'm never the one who starts the conversation." This was true. I was the ice breaker for most of the people we knew. Tonight wasn't going to be any different.

"You want me to go talk to him?" I said.

"Ugh. If you want. Don't say anything, though!" he said emphatically, grabbing my arm. "I don't want him to think I sent you over." Is this high school?

I started moving in his direction, just kind of going with the music, trying not to be obvious. After a few minutes, I was next to the guy. He noticed me and started dancing with me, moving in closer and closer until we were touching. His hands started moving around my bare waist, then up to my chest. This was unexpected.

It quickly became sexual, and we started making out, slowly at first, tentative lips touching, becoming more passionate. I looked back over at Tony. He'd stopped dancing and was watching with an angry look. He mouthed, *what the fuck?* and turned and started to quickly walk away.

I told the guy I'd come back, but never did. In a hurry, I went after Tony. He was moving so fast, and with such determination, I didn't catch him until we'd left the venue through a side door.

"Hey, wait up!" I said when I finally got close to him.

"What the fuck, dude?" He spun around. "What were you doing?"

"What do you mean? He started kissing me!" I laughed a little. "You've got every guy in there after you! You can't get angry at me because one hot guy shows an interest in me instead of you!"

"You knew I was interested in him and you went over and started making out with him! What kind of best friend is that, man? What the fuck?"

He was right to a certain extent. I did know he was interested in this guy, and while I thought the guy was hot, he wasn't someone I'd picked out as a potential hookup. I probably should have tried to keep it casual and introduce him to Tony, but it's hard to say no when Tony gets all the attention. Suddenly someone he thinks is incredibly sexy picks me instead! That just doesn't happen often. Going out with Tony is usually a pretty certain guarantee that I'm sleeping alone that night.

"Look, I'm sorry. You should have come with me! We can go back in, and you can have him. I'll just introduce you guys and then back off, okay?"

I could see he was too worked up to go back. "No, I'm just going back to the room."

"Seriously?" It was 4:00 a.m., and the party still had a few hours left. "Come on, Tony, this is a little of an overreaction isn't it?"

"I'm done. I'm just gonna catch a cab. You should go back to your new guy." He turned toward the street where a line of cabs waited, his naked back sweaty and his jock strap sticking up out of his jeans.

Fuck it. I was pretty much done anyway, and if I went back without him, there was going to be an even bigger fight tomorrow, so I followed. We rode back together without saying a word all the way to the room.

Once we got into the room he renewed the argument. "I just can't believe you'd do that. We're supposed to be best friends. Best friends don't bird-dog each other like that, man," he said without looking at me, stripping down to his black Calvin Klein underwear, getting ready for bed.

"Look, I said I was sorry, and I am. It ruined my night, too. I don't think I did anything so bad that you gotta act like this," I said in response. I was getting ready to crash, too, and went to brush my teeth. When I came out, Tony was lying face-down on his bed with just his underwear on, face turned away, lights still on.

I walked over and sat on his bed. "Tony, look, I'm sorry okay? You okay?"

"I just don't know why you do that to me," he said quietly.

Maybe it was the drinks, maybe it was the intense make-out session with the dark-haired guy, but I reached over and started massaging his shoulders and back. He didn't move, and he didn't say a word.

I kept at it. After a few minutes of massaging his back, I was aroused. I gently grabbed his underwear and began sliding them off. He lifted his hips to help, but otherwise just laid there. I kept up the massage and started running my hand along the inside of his legs. He spread them wider to give me better access.

I slid my underwear off and brushed against his naked body with mine. When he felt me press against him, he lifted and pushed back into me. That's when I leaned in and kissed his neck, gently lowered myself on top of him.

It was aggressive, vindictive sex. His anger came out as he hit me in the chest a few times while he was on his back and I was on top of him. We fucked pretty hard, without intimacy, but plenty of intensity. At the end, I came inside him, and he flipped me over, pushed my head into the bed, and did the same.

After it was done, we didn't talk. I went back to my bed, and he stayed in his. It took a couple days to talk about it, and another month before we repeated it, but that was the night we restarted our complicated sexual relationship.

For the next six months, we continued to hook up. Sometimes it was his idea and sometimes mine. We went about our friendship normally, with maybe a heightened level of jealousy. I know I felt jealous when he'd go out and find some guy and hook up with him. Yeah, I started getting more and more bothered by that.

Similarly, when I would find someone attractive or get someone's attention, Tony would express his jealousy by finding some reason to get mad at me, usually claiming some kind of double standard. He knew I was upset by him hooking up, and he felt that me doing the same made me a hypocrite. I suppose he was right, but was it the chicken or the egg? In truth, we were both jealous of the other.

You know how it ended, I was never what he wanted in a partner, but he was getting great satisfaction from our relationship and the sex, each time more intense, but still very distant. So he went looking for someone who could give him both and found a nice beach boy to fit the bill.

Our sexual relationship didn't die with a whisper. I tried to accept his new guy, but couldn't bring myself to be happy about the fiction it created. He demanded I support his new relationship, and I refused. The seed was planted for an eventual fallout as friends.

I made many mistakes in my relationship with Tony, but if you asked me if restarting a sexual relationship with him was one of them, I'm not sure I can answer. It set him up to create a fantasy with his new guy because he so desperately wanted a boyfriend with whom he could do the things we were doing. It resulted in the end of our friendship and my replacement by the next "most incredible man," but it was also an amazing time of closeness, connection, and real emotions with him that I enjoyed. I think my life is fuller having gone through that second life of our relationship.

This wasn't a friends with benefits relationship, though. It was emotional, there were expectations, it didn't end well, and we were both jealous. We were friends and we fucked, but that isn't a friends with benefits, or fuck buddy, or relationship. Honestly, I'm not sure what we were. I'll leave that up to someone with some objectivity.

I've had successful friends with benefits relationships, though. For me a successful one starts with no drama and ends with no drama, if it ends at all. Lack of drama is a key characteristic of a successful friends with benefits relationship.

Tyler and I met at Pridefest in Seattle many years ago. He was shorter, maybe 5'7, 22, and built like a football player; so handsome, too. A friend introduced us, and my first thought was, this guy is way out of my league! We talked and drank and walked around, and I only remember two things distinctly about that afternoon. He asked me to guess his age and I said 27. He was devastated. No joke. The other thing I remember is how into me he was. I had his full attention, and he was very attentive.

We didn't hook up that day, but did make out before he went his way with his friends, and I went my way with mine. It was a couple months later that we finally took the step of sleeping together.

The situation with Tyler was different from the expected friends with benefits situation in that our friendship came from mutual physical attraction first. You might think this would put us on course for romantic love, but we were different people and he was seeing someone I knew at the time. There was no possibility of much beyond fantastic, wild sex.

It was, too. He pushed my limits and I let him explore things, and the two of us went to town with some pretty kinky shit. It was awesome. Because he was seeing this guy I knew, we never took any steps to date, but a friendship quickly grew from our secret afternoons that still exists today. While writing this, I stopped and sent him a quick note to let him know I was thinking about him.

Tyler lives in LA now, and I'm not sure what's going on in his life, he was always private. His family lives in the Seattle area and whenever he comes to town I get a text, "Hey. Wanna meet?" Still blows me away that Tyler's interested in me, but fuck yeah I do!

I'd call that a successful friends with benefits relationship that has survived all my other relationships during the last eight years; romantic love, a relationship of true love, and several other less successful friends with benefits relationships. I don't expect much from Tyler, nor he from me, but we remain friends and we have some fucking incredible sex.

LEVEL 3
FRIENDSHIPS

Chapter 60
KEEPING FRIENDS

"In poverty and other misfortunes of life, true friends are a sure refuge. They keep the young out of mischief; they comfort and aid the old in their weakness, and they incite those in the prime of life to noble deeds," said Aristotle. Friendships are vital for our wellbeing, but they take time to develop and can't be artificially created.

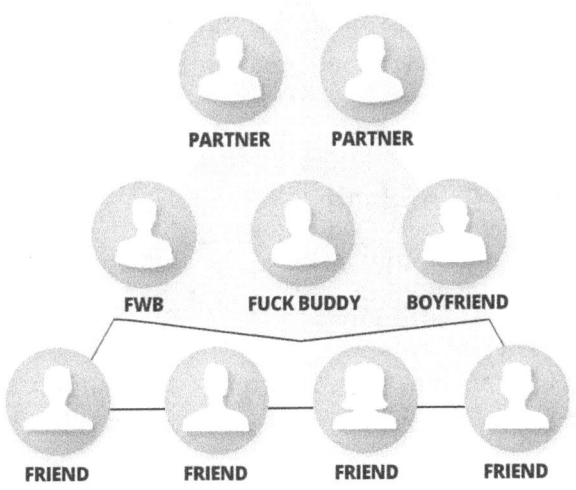

Figure 7 - Friendships

At the foundation of the pyramid structure of modern relationships are the friendships we've made and sustained throughout our lives. The location of friendships at the bottom of the pyramid isn't meant to despair their importance in a modern relationship, rather to reinforce their role as the most stable, consistent, and supportive level of all. These friendships may have arisen from sexual encounters, or may not, but there's no sexual relationship at present.

True friendship is so much more genuine than romantic love. Our model for friendships is more natural and relaxed. Fluid, evolving feelings are mirrored in our true friendships. They change, grow, and wilt, and require effort to maintain. It's a naive man, indeed, who thinks he can neglect his friends and expect their love to pick up right where it left off.

A friend is someone special to you; not just because you've known him for a long time or because you share mutual interests, but because you love each other. This love provides the base and support you need for the levels above it. A pyramid is made stronger by a solid base of true friendships.

The friendship level of the pyramid represents one of the most important, yet least understood areas of psychology--the role of friends in our lives.

Importance of Friendship

When it comes to happiness, all the research agrees, friends are the key. The causes of modern social problems, from divorce to homelessness and obesity, are commonly thought to come from conditions in life such as poverty, stress, or unhappiness, but the research shows that we're missing an important part of this equation—friendship.

In studies, if you ask someone why he became homeless, why his marriage failed or why he overeats, he'll often say it's because of a lack of true friendships. He feels outcast or unloved. The nexus between the strength and support of friendship and a person's happiness is undeniable. Friendships in a modern relationship are a recognized part of the relationship structure exactly because they are so important.

As opposed to the linear traditional relationship model, with two points and a line between them representing a couple, the pyramid includes friendship as the foundation for the other relationships. Segregating friendships out of the traditional linear structure puts responsibility for a partner's happiness all in one place; the other partner. As we know, this is often too much pressure or a partner just isn't up to it and the relationship fails under its own weight.

Under the traditional paradigm, we prioritize the boyfriend and make him somebody to pour all our hopes and fears into. In turn, we neglect our friendships, seeing them as something secondary, a lower order of happiness when compared to our Prince Charming. As Prince Charming and Cinderella shut themselves off from their friends, they slowly slip from their friendship groups into an isolated life of Sunday football and scotch on the rocks.

Conversely, in a modern relationship, the partners in the pinnacle relationship maintain and foster close personal friendships, often even recognizing these friendships as more important than the pinnacle partnership! You may swap out your partner, but why would you change out your friends?

The pyramid structure recognizes the pivotal role of friendship in a modern relationship. In this structure, we realize that the lifetime of our relationships will always include friendships as equal partners in our happiness, not placeholders for our emotional needs until we find the next "most incredible man".

Friendship does so much for our lives, including sharpening our mind, giving us happiness, helping us know ourselves better, inspiring us to reach goals, advancing our careers, even leading us to meet our romantic partners. Finally, friendship is proven to help us live longer and healthier lives.

Health

Research on the direct link between friendship and successful, happy lives is powerful. If your best friend eats healthily, you're five times more likely to have a healthy diet yourself. Married people say friendship is more than five times as important as physical intimacy within their marriage. Those who say they have no real friends at work have only a one in twelve chance of feeling engaged in their job. Conversely, if you have a "best friend at work," you're seven times more likely to feel engaged in your job.

Because friends share in your life, help you celebrate good times, and provide support during bad times, they have a direct impact on your wellbeing. Close friends:

- Increase your sense of belonging and purpose
- Boost your happiness and reduce your stress
- Improve your self-confidence and self-worth
- Help you cope with traumas, such as divorce, serious illness, job loss, or the death of a loved one
- Encourage you to change or avoid unhealthy lifestyle habits, such as excessive drinking or lack of exercise

To take the most advantage of the friendship dynamic, you have to put effort into sustaining your closest friendships. While the emotional investment in a friendship is different than the investment with a pinnacle partner, give and take and balance are essential to feeling supported in a friendship.

Technology and Friendships

Technology is impacting this level of the pyramid in amazing ways more so than the other levels. First, there's the increased volume of friends. You're not sharing the intimate details of your sex life with your 5000 Facebook friends (I hope) but friends who would have drifted away without the social media connection are sustained by simply reading their posts and updates or checking out their pictures from vacation and birthdays or just Sunday Funday. Technology enables us to be part of their lives in a passive, but important way, and allows us to do so for many more people.

Second, the communication between friends is vastly improved, thanks to technology. It's faster, more frequent, and of higher quality. Additionally, while it might not be the most personal, we can "blast" our life events to our closest friends with little effort.

Since communication by text message is so easy, it's also more frequent. It doesn't take much effort to blast a friend and check how his date went this weekend, or send him a "Happy Friday!" note. You do it when you have a free moment, and you check his response when you have another. This way, friends stay relevant and active in our daily lives.

The quality of the communication, at first glance, might draw snickers. "'Sup?" is hardly a deep and meaningful hug, but technology's enhancement of communication goes beyond just truncated and abbreviated "pokes". Technology allows us to have rolling conversations over a period of days, supporting each other, exchanging meaningful pictures, or links, and even FaceTime chats scattered around for good measure.

Studies are showing that the quality of the communication enabled by technology is actually deeper than the concepts covered in Shakespearian text, meaning that even though our text message may be short bursts of poorly written, grammatically incorrect, sentence fragments, the concepts we're tackling are deeper, in balance, than Shakespeare!

Wall posts or group blasts allow us to instantly share something important with a group of friends, instead of how it used to be done with a series of phone calls or letters. Before technology opened up the ability to do "touches" this way, communication was linear, one after the other, consuming precious time and resulting in a smaller group of close friends. Technology is responsible for sustaining friendships that would otherwise have drifted away, perhaps permanently.

One fascinating study, using brain size, predicts that the maximum number of close relationships a human can sustain is 150, called the Dunbar number. The Dunbar number is reached by looking at primate behavior and extrapolating brain size. Amazingly, the number holds up in hunter-gather societies, where village size was capped around 150. Even up to the eighteenth century, 150 people seemed to the most functional size for a village or town.

Today, the Dunbar number is hidden by our worldwide network of friends who may not even know each other, as opposed to the small medieval communities. In that situation, all 150 were the same 150 for the entire village. There was a direct, one-to-one link between every villager. Researchers worry that this diffuse modern network lessens the sense of community and therefore the attachment we have as a species; however, the very same technology that creates the diffuse network enables a bigger, more powerful community by creating and sustaining a web of interconnected personal networks. People joke that the Facebook has reduced the "6 degrees of separation" between any two people anywhere in the world down to two or three, but it's true. That's the ridiculous power of our modern Dunbar network.

Like the neurons in the human brain, the power of technology is enabling a worldwide Dunbar network of friends. The sprawling network of neuron connections, rather than linear connections, results in magnitudes of increase in intelligence in brain function. The same concept holds true with the 150 person, worldwide network of friends. We might only be able to sustain true friendships with 150 of our 5000 Facebook friends, but those 150 true friends are close to 150 others, and so on. In just four steps, the entire world becomes one big, sentient community.

Honesty of Friends

Who but your closest friends will tell you that your attempt at a modern haircut was a catastrophic failure, or tell you to your face that your latest romantic interest is going to end in tragedy?

Because friends know us so well, they can see things that we can't or won't. True friends aren't afraid to share their dose of reality with us.

There's a reason <u>personality</u> researchers ask for "other" reports to compare to the self-ratings that participants themselves provide. These "other" reports can come closer to the mark, especially for individuals whose personalities ironically make it hard for them to see themselves in a realistic light.

The honesty of friends versus the placation of followers is critical to balance and perspective. Knowing the difference between the critical opinions of a friend and the soothing soft peddle of a follower distinguishes someone living in a fantasy from someone who's able to keep his head on straight despite the flattering ego pump.

Individuals at the various levels of the pyramid may move up or down or out of this modern relationship. A friend may become a friend with benefits, and a friend with benefits may become a friend. It's also true that a friend may become a pinnacle partner, and a pinnacle partner may become a friend with benefits for a friend. Nonetheless, all three types of individuals make up the pyramid of the modern relationship.

Movement between these layers of the pyramid is extremely common. In the modern relationship, though, movement out of the pyramid is quite uncommon. Unless the marriage or relationship existed solely on romantic love, friendship endures and the pinnacle partners remain in each other's pyramid structures even after the relationship fails. In a modern relationship, the people in our lives stay in our lives.

Acceptance of this pyramidal relationship structure was widespread among the gay couples I met in San Francisco and Europe, even though they were mostly unaware of it. If people passed judgment on these couples, they didn't express it. In fact, if judgment was passed at all, it was on the monogamous couples where the most common things being said were "they're new" and "it's only a matter of time before they open it up."

Chapter 61

ROBBIE COMES OUT

By the time I got home from saying goodbye to Robbie that night on the sidewalk in front of his bar, I was already anxious about what might happen later and whether I'd hear from him. His hesitant reaction worried and confused me, and my brain wouldn't stop trying to solve the puzzle.

Stella met me at the door of the apartment and we sat on the floor in the hallway for a nice quiet talk about the problem of expectations. Her tail flicked me side to side as she rubbed against my bent leg.

I'll admit it, I set my alarm for 4:00 a.m. to make sure I was awake if Robbie texted. Until then I got restless sleep as the anxiety from our "goodnight" rolled around my head. Uncertainty about what Robbie expected from me and from our relationship moving forward, preoccupied my thoughts to the point of distraction.

My alarm went off and I rolled over, checked my phone, and decided that I was up; there was no point in fighting it. After a few minutes of thumbing through emails, checking Scruff, and saying good morning to a friend in London, another in Malta, Brian in Philly, and Lexi in Seattle, I wandered down the hall in my soft gym shorts to make myself coffee. Making coffee here is a process. They use a kettle and a drip filter to make coffee one cup at a time. This necessitates standing there and waiting for each and every cup.

Stella must've heard me wake up because after just a few minutes of being in the kitchen she rounded the corner and started talking to me. Since I had some time to wait till the coffee brewed, I laid on the kitchen floor, and Stella and I had a nice conversation about my anxiety this morning. She's a great listener and very supportive.

Coffee made, I headed back to my room and laid in bed. Grabbing my computer, I started reading the news. There was no desire to fly back to Seattle that afternoon, so I checked to see if my airfare was one that could be changed, but it wasn't.

Around 4:30 a.m. my phone went off with the xylophone sound; a text from Robbie.

"Hey. You up?"

Not the warmest good morning, but I figured he was just getting off work. "Yeah, just woke up. What are you doing? How was your night?" I replied back.

"Long. I'm tired. :(still not feeling a hundred percent." The reason he stayed at home the last couple days was he'd been fighting a cold.

This felt like he'd decided not to come over. I wanted to give him some assurance that it was okay if he needed to go home and sleep.

"Hey, if you need to go home and crash I totally understand. I'd love to see you and cuddle up for a bit, but I know you had a long night."

"No, Dave. I want to come over for a bit, if that's okay?" he replied back.

":) Definitely," and I gave him my address. He said he'd be over in about ten minutes.

I jumped out of bed, sprinted to the bathroom to brush my teeth, comb my hair, and try to make myself look presentable. Should I put on a shirt? Change my shorts? I decided to go with a comfortable look and just wear my comfy gym shorts.

Sure enough about ten minutes later my phone made the xylophone sound and Robbie said he was out front. I went down the stairs, let him in the front door, walked him into my little Airbnb apartment, then turned and pulled him into my arms.

There's just something magical about hugging Robbie. His body is so responsive to mine, and I feel him merging with me in an embrace. He put his head on my shoulder and turned it outwards. I could tell he was tired and had a long night, so I just held him for a few minutes, quietly standing there rocking back and forth.

After a few minutes, Robbie pulled his head off my shoulders and raised up to my lips, just a gentle, soft touch at first, his mouth matched to mine. Our scruffy faces slowly rubbed against each other. As the kiss became more intense, I could feel myself getting aroused.

The sex that morning was slow, gentle, and more intense than any other time. Once it was over, I nodded in and out of consciousness for a few hours, not moving, holding him in my arms while his chest heaved up and down.

Robbie slept wrapped in my arms under the covers for three or four hours before he slowly rolled over and said, "Good morning" with a groggy smile. I leaned over and gave him a kiss saying good morning back.

It was 9:00 a.m., the sun was up, and it was a beautiful cloudless day in San Francisco. We laid in bed and talked about little things like his work, my work, the weather, and the gym. He teased me about the night before almost knocking him on his butt. I joked about making out in the middle of the World Series at his bar and all the extra tips he must have gotten. It was nice just to lie there with him and enjoy the morning for a little while.

Reality crept back into our day as Robbie said he needed to get home and get more sleep; still no discussion of depth and substance around our relationship, or how it came to an end.

I decided I'd walk up to the coffee shop with him, then walk him home. Dressed and ready for the public, we headed over to the corner coffee shop one block down the street. I grabbed a to-go cup, and we started walking toward his place.

"Hey," I said. "You want to come with me to the top of Dolores Park and hang out for a bit?"

Robbie didn't look like he liked that idea much. I could see a grimace on his face and he didn't look me in the eyes.

"Just for a few minutes," he conceded.

We wandered up to the top of Dolores Park, to the area people call the gay beach. Just a bunch of dog owners down by the children's play area, but otherwise we had the park to ourselves. It was such an incredibly beautiful morning; you could see the downtown area glittering in the distance. I decided to try and have a discussion about something deeper.

"I'm sorry for how things ended with us, Robbie," I said. Turning to him, I put my hand on his bent knee. "I was just hoping we could have something more than hookups. I'm sorry I crowded your space."

Robbie sat quietly for a few seconds, then put his hand over my hand on his knee. He turned to me and said, "Look, Dave, I enjoy our time together, and I do like you. But I don't think I'm ready to date anyone. Well, anyone else."

I sat silently for a moment and contemplated what he just said.

"Anyone else?" I asked hesitantly, squeezing his knee slightly.

He sighed heavily and looked off into the city sitting quietly for a moment. "Yeah," he said. "I've kinda been seeing this couple in Palm Springs, and I didn't know how to tell you about it. It's been going on for about six months, and I like spending time with them. But I like spending time with you, too. I just feel like your expectations of me are things that I can't meet."

What expectations? I'm not sure what Robbie thought I wanted from him, but he seemed to have a totally wrong idea about what I was looking for. This made me sit up.

"Robbie! I didn't have expectations that you and I were going to date exclusively. I was just hoping we could go on a date! All of our time together has been spent in the bedroom or walking between our two places," I said, putting my arm around his waist.

I didn't know what was going to happen after this conversation, whether we would have any kind of relationship or not, but I wanted to be 100% honest so that the air was cleared.

"Really? It seems like you wanted an exclusive relationship. I mean, that's what you've been in before, and it feels like you judge people here in San Francisco for being in open relationships," he said, looking at me with those big brown eyes. I could see a flash of anger.

"No, man," I said, slowly shaking my head and smiling. "I don't judge people for being in a three-way relationship, or any relationship for that matter, unless it's a complete fiction or fraud. Even then, I just try and keep my mouth shut."

We both knew I was talking about Tony. Robbie had the same opinion of Tony's relationship as I did.

"You know I'm on Scruff all the time, and I know you're on Scruff all the time. We both know we're hooking up," I said, "and that's totally okay, Robbie. I don't have any expectations of you. I don't!"

"So you don't care that I'm dating these guys in Palm Springs right now?"

"Nope, I don't. I think it's kinda hot. I want to hear more about it. I can only imagine how sexy these guys are that they convinced you to join their relationship. Fuck! Show me some damn pictures!" I laughed.

"Ha ha! Well, maybe later. I'm not sure I'm comfortable showing them to you right now," he said, looking away. "Maybe now you can understand why I couldn't answer your question about the possibility of dating."

"Yeah. I kind of understand that," I said, leaning into him. "I wish you'd felt comfortable enough to talk to me about it. It's confused me over the last couple months, but, I respected your choice. And I want to keep doing that. I just hope you give me the chance to get to know you better. I don't have any expectations or plans to be boyfriends with you, Robbie."

We both sat quietly for awhile, staring off into the city. I laid back on the grass, one arm over my head, and reached my other to Robbie's back. He looked over, smiled, and laid down, putting his head on my chest. We stayed like that for a few minutes, quiet and not talking.

After awhile, Robbie sat up on one elbow and looked at me with a smile. "I gotta get home, or I'll fall asleep here in the grass."

I laughed, rubbed his back some more, and said, "Okay, let's get you home." We stood, made our way down the hill, and headed toward Robbie's house. When we reached his doorstep we pulled each other close one more time for one last long hug. Stepping back, Robbie said, "Next time you're here, I want to take you to dinner."

My heart leapt in my throat, but I didn't want to let on to how happy that statement made me. I just looked him in the eyes and said. "I'd love that, handsome." He smiled.

I made my way back to my apartment, walking slowly, enjoying my last morning in San Francisco for awhile. Coming to peace with Robbie was an unexpected joy of my weekend. I was confused at his assumption that I disapproved of three-way relationships and sad that he didn't feel comfortable talking about his friends in Palm Springs, but I understood his anxiety over my perceived expectations. Given his relationship, any sign from me that I wanted to date him would put him immediately on the defensive.

I don't know what I said or did or who Robbie talked to to give him the impression I judged three-way relationships, but obviously I don't. At a different point in my life, sure, I passed judgment on open relationships of every type. I was born into a world of exclusivity, monogamy, and marriage, but over time, as I grew into my own skin and explored my own desires for relationships and for sex, my opinions about relationships have changed.

I spent the rest of the morning writing and playing with Stella. When it came time to head to the airport, I sent around goodbyes to the new friends I made this weekend, as well as the old ones, thanking them for the fantastic weekend. I sent Robbie a simple note telling him thank you and that I looked forward to our dinner. I'm not sure how frequently we'll stay in touch between now and then, but now I know that we will, indeed, pick up where we left off. I look forward to that dinner. A lot.

Chapter 62
CLOSING ARGUMENT

Technology is impacting every aspect of our lives. Commerce, work, finance, and travel are forever different. Changes range from the life-saving to the time-wasting. Every day, technology's influence on society expands as clever people find new ways to make our lives safer, more fulfilling, entertaining, and connected. Technology saturates everything we do.

In some ways, though, we remain blissfully ignorant of its influence. How quickly we forget the difficulties of communication just ten years ago, and what life was like before texting and email. We laugh at things like a Walkman, phonebooks, and travel agents. Did we ever need those things? The shifts in the basic functions of living that we've seen in the past ten years are colossal when compared with the fifty years before, and there's no end in sight.

We get up-to-the-minute updates of our kindergartener's progress as a teacher notes "gold stars" on her iPad, instantly notifying the parents. Elementary school kids know more about our iPhones than we do, and middle schoolers are setting up Minecraft servers. The floodgates are open, and we never even noticed the dam.

If you can step outside the trees for a moment and look at the forest, it's an amazing sight. In every aspect of life, technology is exploding and ushering in social change in how we work, learn, play, and yes, love.

Out of the trees and looking at the forest, it's naive to think these radical shifts in everything else in our lives aren't also changing our relationships. Of course they are. Based on just the external changes, we can see a fundamental shift. Technology has changed the way we:

- Find a mate
- Entice them
- Date them
- Stay in touch
- Conduct a relationship

These external changes are easy to see and to quantify with data. Thanks to the explosion of dating sites like Grindr and Tinder and social media sites like Facebook, we know more about behavior than ever before, and the data is undeniable; relationships have changed.

So why stop there? Why assume that the "process" changes listed above, and driven by technology, are the whole story? They're not.

Technology is driving fundamental changes as much as it is these process-type changes. Relationship types are changing, our expectations are changing, our commitments are changing. Is it just a fad? Is technology a fad?

For some reason, we balk at marriage. That, our mind says, can't change. Technology can't be impacting marriage because marriage is immutable and indestructible. It's always been this exact way and it will alway be this exact way, people say.

History says otherwise. Logic says otherwise. Twenty years as a divorce lawyer say otherwise. Marriage is a creature of social invention and will always shift and change with changes in society. That's how social inventions work. Marriage is subject to the same pressures of change as anything else. Today, the pressure to change marriage is coming from a culture created by technology, and marriage is doing a poor job of responding to that pressure. Data doesn't lie. If the institution doesn't fundamentally change quickly, it will dwindle into obscurity and irrelevance, existing only in name. Statistics project a grim future, absent an evolutionary response to the changing needs of modern society.

How does marriage need to change to survive? Should it? Data and observations indicate that the expectations of traditional marriage are out of line with the needs of modern culture. In a culture driven in so many ways by technology, traditional marriage remains static. It's failing to support the types of committed (not necessarily monogamous) relationships people are entering.

People are entering these modern relationships anyway! They're just not choosing to create marriages. Instead, they're choosing to form structures that meet their expectations.

That's how the institution of marriage should respond; adjust the heavy expectations set by the generations before, and modernize the paradigm of what we should expect from each other if we enter into a marriage. Marriage should look more like *Will & Grace*, than *Leave It to Beaver*.

Wait! Will is gay and Grace is straight! They didn't have sex and instead were hooking up with other people! Setting aside the fact that I've seen plenty of marriages with that exact same dynamic, you can't deny that the relationship between Will and Grace was loving, supportive, honest, and equal. Truth is, their paradigm fits modern relationships better than *Leave It to Beaver* ever could.

Regardless of whether the institution of marriage survives, technology has started a sexual revolution. Everywhere you look, people are sharing more, showing more, and doing more. Fetish is cool, kink is hot. Hooking up is open and unashamed, and sex is coming out of the shadows. The revolution is here already, but you just might miss it through all the trees.

THE END

www.ingramcontent.com/pod-product-compliance
Lightning Source LLC
Chambersburg PA
CBHW062014170626
46813CB00001B/153